# THE OSHKOSH CONNECTION

A MAX FEND THRILLER

ANDREW WATTS

POINT WHISKEY PUBLISHING

If you can walk away from a landing, it's a good landing.
If you use the airplane the next day, it's an outstanding
landing.

— CHUCK YEAGER

# CHAPTER 1

HUGO THE ASSASSIN arrived at Baltimore-Washington International Airport on the 4:35 p.m. flight from London. He grabbed his Samsonite carry-on bag from the overhead compartment and walked confidently through the airport.

The stop at immigration was quick. He had nothing to declare. On a personal visit. Staying about a week. Thank you. You have a nice day as well.

Hugo left out the part about being paid to kill people while he was here.

The muggy July air hit him like a wall as he stepped outside to fetch a cab. The drive to Dupont Circle took just over thirty minutes. Hugo had rented a flat online the night before. Just a five-minute walk from James Hoban's Irish Restaurant, where he ate a BBQ burger with bacon and grilled onions at an outdoor table, sweating while watching the streets and waiting for his assignment. He licked BBQ sauce off his fingers. He had to admit, Americans knew how to cook good burgers.

The courier arrived by bicycle. A know-nothing. Just a shaggy-looking man wearing spandex, eyeliner, and a nose ring who delivered envelopes for a living. Sometimes there were special instructions. This was one of those times. The courier placed a manila envelope on the table with the bright red scarf, then departed without saying a word. A block down the street, a man watching from behind a half-closed set of blinds texted confirmation that Hugo had received the envelope. Within seconds, that confirmation message was relayed to the second-highest-ranking intelligence officer stationed in the Pakistani embassy.

Inside the envelope was a hand-written note. A coded meeting location. Hugo took the strip of paper with the writing on it, ripped it up, and dunked it into his ice water. It dissolved instantly. The assassin left the rest of his meal uneaten and hailed a second cab.

"The Smithsonian."

"Which one?" asked the cab driver.

"The Castle."

The driver nodded, and the car began moving. Hugo caught the driver's curious glance at him through the rearview mirror.

"Where are you from?"

Hugo didn't answer, and the cab driver didn't ask a second time, not wanting to affect his tip. The car dropped him off a few minutes later and Hugo paid in cash. He then made his way along a brick walkway that wound between several Smith-sonian museums. The Smithsonian Institution Building—"cas-tle" was probably too generous—stood to his right. The red sandstone, faux-Norman architecture, and four-story towers seemed out of place in this city. But it made a good meeting spot.

A wide-open courtyard before him. Pedestrian tourists strolled and sat along a peaceful garden filled with lavender and goldfish ponds. The smell of honeysuckle hung in the air.

The assassin's eyes darted from person to person, scanning each face, each set of belongings, each person's wardrobe. Checking for inconsistencies—red flags that might give away someone in the American government. It was a crowded summer night, and most of the people he saw were tourists, walking to and from some festival being held on the National Mall one hundred meters away.

A Pakistani man sat on a bench fifty feet ahead of the assassin.

The assassin's client.

* * *

Abdul Syed wiped sweaty palms on the front of his khaki pants. He had taken all the proper precautions. His team of ISI countersurveillance experts had been watching the assassin since he had departed the airport. Still, now was when things got tricky.

If Hugo had a tail, the Pakistani operatives performing countersurveillance would let Syed know, and the meet would be aborted, along with tonight's mission. But this close to the rendezvous, even an aborted mission presented the risk of his man being detained and questioned.

Syed had participated in many operations like this before, but never on US soil. The Pakistani intelligence officer's blood pressure was abnormally high, triggered by the persistent worry that one of the FBI's counterintelligence teams might be watching.

While Syed's official posting at the Pakistani embassy was that of an agricultural counselor, the Americans knew better, and they regularly followed him. Syed had spent every night for the last few weeks in the same fashion. Riding the Metro around D.C., visiting different museums and restaurants, meeting acquaintances in locations far from one another. Innocuous locations using hard-to-follow routes. It took considerable time and effort, but Syed was sure that he had lost his surveillance each and every night for the past week.

Every one of those surveillance detection routes had been

in preparation for this meeting. The assassin could have no connection to Pakistani intelligence. The Inter-Services Intelligence agency, or ISI, had been accused by Western governments of holding double standards in the fight against terrorism. Syed must not give them any more reasons to support that belief. Even more important, he must not allow them to discover his current operational plans.

Despite what both nations proclaimed, the United States was not a friend of Pakistan. And it was up to the ISI and its officers, brave men like Syed, to ensure that American imperialism would falter. American minds were brainwashed with propaganda. In Pakistan, everyone knew that Al Qaeda was not responsible for the attacks of September 11, 2001. Several ISI and Pakistani military officers had known of Osama bin Laden's whereabouts, less than a mile from the prestigious Kakul Military Academy in Abbottabad. Syed himself had known. He had been infuriated on that day when US Special Forces soldiers had illegally flown their stealth helicopters into his country, killing innocents and taking bin Laden. The CIA had not shared that operation with the ISI ahead of time, because they had known what Syed had known.

The US and Pakistan were enemies, playing at a dangerous game. The ISI and American intelligence agencies put on the charade of friendship, as the politicians demanded. But each agency did its best to sabotage the operations of the other. The Americans would love nothing more than to catch him tonight, planning the assassination of American citizens on American soil.

A man sat down next to him on the park bench.

Syed did not make eye contact with the man. Instead he continued to scan the courtyard for American agents who might be posing as casual observers as he removed an envelope from his pocket and placed it between them on the bench. An encrypted thumb drive was inside. One that, unless the correct procedure was used, would delete its contents upon insertion into a device.

The man took the envelope, stuffed it into his pocket, and walked away without saying a word.

Syed couldn't help but cast a sideways glance in his direction as he departed. He snorted air out his nose, shaking his head. The assassin was quite unremarkable. It was hard to believe that he was responsible for so many deaths…and would soon be responsible for so many more.

# CHAPTER 2

*Blue Ridge Mountains*
*4000 Feet Above Ground Level*

"WE'RE GOING TO CRASH."

The plane's nose was angled down, the green Appalachian Mountains now filling most of the cockpit windscreen.

Max Fend said, "You're overstating the problem, Renee. You really need to learn to relax. It's so peaceful up here. Away from the world, away from all of your troubles. Nothing but blue sky...well, as long as you look up. Maybe not straight ahead. Those are mountains."

Renee's voice was an octave higher than normal. "I'm not kidding, Max. Please, just..." She gripped the yoke of Max's Cirrus SR-22 tight enough that her knuckles went white, and she was unable to finish her thought.

Max grinned, scanning the various digital readouts on the instrument panel. "Hmm. Actually, you *are* losing quite a bit of altitude, now that you mention it."

"Max, *please*. Take the aircraft. This is not funny."

He looked over at Renee, who was sweating through her tank top. They sat side by side in the small single-engine aircraft. Renee sat in the left seat, holding the side-mounted yoke with her left hand and the throttle with her right. Ray-Ban aviator-style sunglasses—a gift from Max—hid what was likely the look of genuine fear in her eyes.

Max's voice remained steady, and only slightly condescending, as he spoke through his headset. "Look, this is how you learn. Finding your way out of a sticky situation on your own will make you a better pilot—"

"Take the aircraft right now."

He folded his arms across his chest. "No." He was a teacher, and she his pupil. Sometimes the teacher needed to be stern.

"*Fine.*"

Max began second-guessing his teaching approach as Renee pulled back much too hard on the yoke and the nose pitched way up, filling the windscreen with a hazy white sky and bright yellow sun. Compounding the rather excessive control input was the unfortunate fact that she had forgotten to add power.

"Well, *this* is going to be interesting," Max said as the nose continued to pitch up. Max watched their airspeed bleed off precipitously. And, like a heavy truck trying to get up a hill without adding any gas, their climb slowed, the airspeed continued to decelerate, and the sinking feeling in Max's stomach grew as he knew it would only be a moment until...

A high-pitched warning tone sounded.

"What is that?" asked Renee. Her voice panicked. "Max. I'm not joking..."

The nose of the aircraft plunged downward like the lead car of a roller coaster as it dropped past the peak of a towering hill.

Renee screamed profanity all the way down.

Max grinned as the aircraft dove, his stomach left somewhere five hundred feet above. "You are using your French-Canadian churchy curses again. I must tell you, I really love it when you do that."

The aircraft's dive caused their airspeed to rocket back up.

Max laughed to himself. Renee still had too much back stick. The increase in speed would cause the aircraft to nose back up, and the roller coaster would soon begin again. Yes, they were getting lower—closer to the Appalachian Mountains—but Max was paying close attention to their altitude and would make sure they didn't really get into trouble. This was fun. He was glad that Renee had finally agreed to take lessons.

Max said, "There's nothing you can say that will make me take the aircraft. It's important that you understand aerodynamic principles if you ever want to—"

She looked at him over the top of her sunglasses, her dark eyes menacing. "Take the controls *right now* or I will *never* sleep with you again."

Max immediately placed his grip on his yoke and throttle. He cleared his throat. "*My aircraft.*"

Renee let out a long steady breath, collapsing backward into her seat and letting go of the stick. She closed her eyes for a moment, her chest heaving. Then she opened her eyes, turned, and punched Max in the shoulder. "*Don't* do that again."

Max added more power and climbed back up to altitude. He watched as the altimeter ticked up, saying, "I think you're really getting the hang of it. You showed a lot of grit today."

Renee glared at him.

"Okay, enough fun for now. We'll have to head back if we're going to make the surprise I have in store."

"Which is what, exactly?"

"It's not a surprise if I tell you."

Max banked the aircraft into a wide right arc. Beneath them, a shimmering Shenandoah River wound through the Blue Ridge Mountains like a snake. Renee was looking out the window, admiring the view. Hopefully the scenery would improve her mood by the time they returned.

Max made his approach from the west into Leesburg Executive Airport. Another single-engine aircraft, a Cessna 172, was in the downwind ahead of him. He made all of his traffic calls over the radio, completed the landing checklist, and then maneuvered the plane onto final.

"You sure you don't want to take the landing?"

"No, thanks."

"Landings are the best."

"Not right now, thank you."

Max waxed poetic. "Landings always give me a kick of endorphins. The sound of the wheels touching the pavement. The blur of runway zooming past. The satisfying sense of accomplishment that once again, I have not killed us."

"Can you please not joke like that until we're on the ground?"

A moment later, Max had parked the Cirrus on the flight line and shut down the engine. Together they allowed their cockpit doors to slide open, letting in the summer breeze.

"You have anywhere you want to eat tonight?" Max asked.

She shook her head at him as she took a swig from her water bottle—ice cubes clunking against its plastic walls. "What am I going to do with you?"

Max's phone buzzed in his pocket. He took it out and read the message.

WOLF TRAP IN ONE HOUR

"Who is it?"

"It's our surprise for the evening. I've just gotten us concert tickets. The outdoor amphitheater at Wolf Trap."

Renee's expression finally warmed. "Now that sounds lovely."

Max didn't bother to tell her that it was his CIA handler who had decided on the venue. And he would be working.

\* \* \*

The summer concert series at Wolf Trap was one of the cultural gems of Northern Virginia. Thousands of men and women were sprawled out on blankets on the well-trimmed lawn that surrounded the amphitheater. The grass banked downward toward the concert stage area, which was covered by an architecturally stunning wooden structure. The amphitheater—known as the Filene Center, after the woman who had donated the land now operated by the National Park Authority—was constructed of Douglas fir and southern yellow pine. It could seat seven thousand under the covered section, but on a clear night like this, Max and Renee enjoyed sitting on the lawn.

"They're good," Renee said of the string quartet on stage. Her fingers tickled the hairs on his forearm. She lay on her side, facing him, and leaned over to kiss his cheek. "Thanks for taking me out tonight. I forgive you for almost letting us crash today."

"In reality, we were in very little danger…"

He turned towards her and smooched her on the lips, then turned back towards the stage. Max rested on his back, partially propped up on his elbows.

Renee had a glow in her eye. The glimmer of unrestrained and optimistic love. While the pair had dated once before, when they were both in college, it had been so many years ago that their current reboot felt new and fresh.

The Max and Renee relationship "take two" had been going on for about a year. Since a well-publicized near-death incident on the shores of northeast Florida. Max, an ex-DIA operative, had been accused of hacking into his father's company, Fend Aerospace. Charles Fend's multibillion-dollar firm did a lot of work for the defense department, and the hacking incident had quickly turned into a national manhunt. Renee had helped Max to solve the puzzle and avert disaster. Well, with minor help from the FBI's Hostage Rescue Team. But other than that, Max's only assistance had been from the lovely French-Canadian hacker lying next to him.

Renee wore a low-cut tank top that showed off her sculpted shoulders, and a pair of skimpy shorts that revealed a pair of magnificent runner's legs. A small but elegant flower tattoo ran up her right thigh. She had been a college athlete, and while she was getting close to age forty, she kept in excellent shape by competing in road races and mini-triathlons.

On stage, the young quartet finished playing "Clair de Lune." A scatter of polite applause rose up from the crowd, silenced a moment later by the beginning of the next song.

Max checked the time on his Breitling wristwatch. The watch had been a gift from his father. A way of saying thanks for undergoing such an ordeal last summer. Max's father felt responsible for placing his son in harm's way, since it was his company that had been targeted. Hence the watch. Max thought it was enormous, but it was starting to grow on him.

He turned to Renee. "You want a beer?"

"No, thank you. I'm still nursing my wine cooler."

She really did look beautiful tonight. "You know, I'm a lucky guy."

"Trust me, I completely agree." She winked. He laughed.

He turned and marched up the grassy bowl that surrounded the amphitheater. The deep bass notes of a cello mixed with rich violin filled the air. Max weaved his way in and out of the patchwork of blankets and concert patrons.

All the while keeping an eye on his mark.

\* \* \*

His handler was a man by the name of Caleb Wilkes—a veteran of the CIA who had built a career running agents in various parts of the world. While Max was happy to take Renee out to Wolf Trap on a nice night like this, it was Wilkes who had asked him to be here.

Max had been conflicted about working for the CIA after all that had happened last summer. It wasn't that intelligence fieldwork was an undesirable occupation to him. Quite the contrary. Max had spent over a decade under a nonofficial cover for the Defense Intelligence Agency and hadn't left of his own accord. The higher-ups had forced him to make a career change based on their needs, without asking his opinion, and without being transparent about the circumstances. Because of that, Max would probably always be leery of trusting men like Wilkes, a senior operations officer who pulled the strings from the halls of Langley. But as an experienced operative, Max knew better than to completely trust anyone, including his new handler. The world of international espionage was littered with the graves of the trusting and gullible.

Wilkes understood Max's reservations. With his experience and social stature, Max wasn't a normal asset. He was special, and Wilkes had to treat him that way.

Wilkes had given Max a few months without contact after the Fend Aerospace incident last year. At which point he had begun paying Max regular visits. The two usually met for beer or coffee in the Georgetown district of Washington, D.C. Max was getting his MBA at Georgetown University. Wilkes often worked out of Langley, so at first, he attributed the meetings to the convenience of "being in the neighborhood."

Max knew better—he had recruited and run agents himself while he'd worked for the DIA. He knew that Wilkes wouldn't waste his time paying social calls unless there was something to be gained. By the third "friendly happy hour," Max told Wilkes to cut to the chase.

Max was a valuable agent, and Wilkes wanted him on his team. Max came pretrained and experienced, having honed his skills in Europe and the Middle East. And he certainly had access. Max's family wealth and network allowed him to recruit assets and gather information that other agents just couldn't. He was expected to eventually take a job at his father's aerospace company after he finished his MBA, furthering his stature.

But Max wasn't just skilled and reliable; he also had the most sought-after motivation a handler could ask for. It was Max's sense of national duty and his continued desire to serve and protect that motivated him to participate in the program. Max was serving his country for patriotic reasons. And perhaps for the excitement of the game. Turning foreign assets and uncovering terrorist networks could be an intoxicating thrill, as long as you didn't get burned in the process.

But there was still a level of apprehension—a feeling of slight betrayal after the way Max had been forced out of the DIA and wrongly implicated in a crime last year. The way Wilkes didn't fully divulge all of the details of the operation until it suited him. That pesky trust issue.

So the two men had come to an understanding. Wilkes would reach out to Max when he had work, and Max might sometimes decline, based on the situation.

Tonight, Max had been called up for the first time.

"I need you to keep an eye on someone. It's critical." Wilkes had said.

Abdul Syed, officially a Pakistani diplomat operating out of the embassy in D.C., was actually under the employ of the ISI. Wilkes was working with FBI and CIA counterintelligence to monitor Syed's activities, but that was proving difficult. Abdul Syed was adept at losing surveillance. He'd lost them each night for the past several weeks. But something about tonight would be different, Wilkes had told Max.

"We've received intelligence that Syed is going to make contact with one of his American agents. But he won't do it if he sees his tail. I need you to be there instead. Watch Syed. See who he meets."

Unusual circumstances. An intriguing assignment. FBI counterintelligence was supposed to have several men who would keep an eye on Syed. Wilkes was expecting Syed to give them the shake. This Syed fellow must be quite a talent, to do that. FBI counterintelligence were some of the best in the business. Why did Wilkes want Max doing this, instead of someone else? *Probably because he wants it to be unofficial. But why?*

And how did Wilkes know where Syed was going to be? He wouldn't give Max the answer to that, but somehow, Wilkes knew.

The Pakistani intelligence officer was a mere fifty yards away from Max and Renee's spot on the lawn of Wolf Trap. He was sitting alone, listening to the serene music, looking about as pleasant as someone getting a root canal.

It was crowded, and Syed could be planning to communicate with any of the thousands of spectators now listening to the concert. Maybe he already had, Max thought. After all, he hadn't seen Syed enter. It had taken Max fifteen minutes to spot him. Renee thought he was crazy, moving their sitting spot on the lawn twice. She'd thought it had something to do with his obsessive need for perfection. Like how he kept all his belongings meticulously clean and organized.

But that spot had given Max a perfect view. And the moment he'd seen Syed get up and walk to the top of the half-moon-shaped lawn area, heading towards the row of concession stands, Max followed.

## CHAPTER 3

MAX WALKED towards the concession stand, scanning the crowd, using his peripheral vision to observe anything that might be out of the ordinary. The habits of an intelligence operative who had spent more than a decade hiding in plain sight. Syed was now pretending to talk on his cell phone, but Max could tell he was really just looking for surveillance himself. Walking one direction for a few moments, then circling back, scanning the crowd like a pro. Max needed to be careful not to be spotted.

Syed was brown-skinned, with dark bushy eyebrows. He wore gray slacks and a buttoned short-sleeve shirt, with a bright white Washington Nationals cap on his head, which Max found to be a comical addition.

Max approached the window of the snack bar and ordered a beer, paying in cash and receiving a large plastic cup foaming to the brim. Cold and tasty. Perfect on a warm summer's night. Turning around to face the amphitheater, he observed Syed walk past him and out through the concert exit.

Hmm. No one else was leaving yet, so Max couldn't just follow him without being obvious.

The exit gate was a chokepoint. A great way for Syed to be sure that he was clear of coverage before he tried to communicate with his agent.

Max had a decision to make. Follow him out, or wait? Spook him and any illicit activity could be called off. Maybe it already had been. Maybe he'd spotted Max and that was why he'd departed. The thought bothered Max. But then, through the covered entryway, past the bare metal turnstiles and roundabout blacktop driveway, Max saw the Pakistani man slow his step.

Max stayed put, half-concealed by the entrance structure, sipping his cold amber beer, eyes locked on to his target. Syed loitered across the rounded drive just outside the gate. The Pakistani man came to a stop near a park bench that rested in a mulched garden. A grove of trees swayed overhead.

Then the crowd erupted into loud clapping and whistling, and Max could hear the chatter of people rising from their spots on the lawn to leave. The concert had ended. Shit. Syed was still just standing there. Waiting. Soon throngs of people headed through the exit turnstiles, racing each other to get to their cars in the parking lot.

A flash of panic hit Max as the empty area filled with people and he momentarily lost his quarry. Lines forming at the restrooms and exits all served to block his view. A bottleneck of foot traffic formed at the concert gate. Max maneuvered, poking his head around the crowd and trying to keep eyes on his mark.

A gap in the crowd lined up perfectly. Just for a moment. But that was all it took. A split-second line of sight from Max to the park bench, and that was when it happened.

Syed moved fast.

To the untrained eye, it would have looked like nothing more than bending down to retie his shoe, or perhaps brush a speck of dirt off his pant leg. Max knew better. Syed had been standing near the park bench. When he'd dropped down low, his hand had gripped the front of the bench seat, his knuckles going white as he'd pressed down. Then he'd stood up and begun walking away, towards the parking lot. From this far away, Max could just barely make out a round white object on the wooden bench seat.

A thumbtack? A sticker? Whatever it was, it was a signal.

Max's heart beat faster as he realized that the timing had been precise. The wooden bench was now surrounded by departing concertgoers. The signal could be meant for any one of them. Max would just have to hang out and wait to see who came and sat at the bench. If the agent was really good, Max might not even pick him up.

"*There* you are." Renee interlocked her arm with his. "Were you going to come back to me? I got our blanket. I'm ready if you are…" Looking up into his face, seeing his expression, she whispered, "What's wrong?"

He kept his eyes on the bench, nudged her forward, and began walking. "I need your help. Please follow me. This is important."

Frowning in confusion, she said, "Of course."

He threw his half-drunk beer into the trash—normally an unforgivable sin—and they walked out with the crowd. Max took out his phone and led Renee under the grove of trees on the mulched area behind the park bench. He positioned Renee so that the Wolf Trap sign and entrance were behind her… along with the bench. The crowd would be directly in front of him as they departed the concert area.

"Let me take a few pictures of you. Stand right…here."

"*Really*, Max?" She sighed and forced a smile for the camera.

"Really."

She arched one eyebrow, hands on her hips, but then gave up and smiled for the camera.

One minute of picture taking later, Max caught his fish.

White male, forty to fifty years old, medium height, medium build. Every cop's favorite description. The man's eyes were staring in the direction of the bench. His gaze hovered on the thumbtack for two beats too long. Maybe he was trying to determine the color? Maybe he just wanted to confirm that he really saw his signal. Either way, it was sloppy tradecraft.

And a total break for Max.

Max slid his phone into his pocket and began walking, placing his arm around Renee and bringing her with him. He whispered, "Do me another favor? Get the car and drive around to the exit."

"Max, what's going on?" she whispered back.

"It's okay. I'll find you and meet you there. If I don't get to the car before you leave, just park on the side of the road outside after the traffic cops let you out."

"What? Max, I don't understand. It'll be dark soon. Why are you—"

"I just need to check something. *Please.*"

Renee took the keys and headed towards their car.

Max kept his distance following the man, still keeping a lookout for Syed or anyone else who might be watching. The man who had observed the signal stopped at a silver sedan in the parking lot a few moments later. Max walked by the man as he fumbled for his keys. Max had placed his phone on video mode and was holding it casually by his legs, lens facing outward, positioned to capture the license plate, and then angling it up to record the man's face.

After passing by, Max continued walking towards his own vehicle. When he found Renee a few minutes later, she was waiting in the long line of cars for the exit. Max hopped in the passenger seat and threw on his seatbelt.

"Can you please tell me what we're doing now?"

Technically Max had completed his assignment. But if they

followed the agent, it was possible they might learn more information. Max liked being thorough.

He turned to face Renee. "We're following someone."

"Who?"

He scanned the line of cars and located the target vehicle. About twenty cars in front of them. If Max was lucky, both cars would be let out together before they stopped traffic again.

"Who are we following?"

"Actually, I don't know his name."

The cars began moving towards the T-intersection, a traffic cop standing there with orange-lit cones.

"Go left."

Renee turned. "Which car is it?"

"About five ahead. Silver sedan. See it?"

"Yes."

For the next ten minutes, they traveled through the suburbs of Vienna, Virginia. Lots of colonial homes with finely manicured lawns, barely visible in the summer dusk.

Renee did well. She kept her distance from the silver sedan and drove past without asking when the car stopped abruptly on the gravel shoulder of the Creek Crossing Road.

"What do we do now?"

"Turn into this next neighborhood and park." Max was squinting out the rear window, trying to see in the dark.

After they parked, Max said, "You stay here. I'll only be a second."

\* \* \*

Max crept along the side of the road, walking towards his target's parked car, headlights momentarily blinding him as cars sped by. He could feel the rush of air from the traffic. The gravel of the road shoulder crunched beneath his feet. This was poor surveillance technique, following his quarry into an unknown area by himself like this, but it was the best he could manage right now. He had texted an update to Caleb Wilkes while they were driving but had yet to hear back.

Max crept up to the silver sedan parked on the shoulder and peered inside. Empty. He turned to his left. Ten feet away, a paved path led from the road down into the woods. A buzzing streetlight above was just bright enough that Max could make out the words "Foxstone Park, Fairfax County Park Authority" in yellow lettering on a maroon wooden sign.

Max followed the path, careful to walk slow and quiet, listening for the sounds of footfalls or the snaps of breaking twigs. Instead, he heard only the summertime calls of insects and a bubbling brook somewhere off to his right.

The park wasn't big. The distant yellow windows of surrounding homes rising high all around told him that. Maybe a few football fields in length. One football field across, tops. Lightning bugs glowed every few seconds, giving the woods a magical feel.

A shoe scraped along pavement up ahead. Max's heart raced as he held his breath, straining his ears to listen.

*Bzzzt. Bzzzt.*

In his pocket, his phone began nonstop buzzing. Shit. He reached down and squeezed to silence it. Probably Wilkes, but he couldn't risk a look. The light would give away his position if the buzzing hadn't already. He cursed himself for the rookie move.

A whitish-blue face lit up maybe twenty-five yards ahead, and Max froze. It was the face of the man Max had seen looking at the dead drop signal at Wolf Trap. He had just turned his own phone on and was looking at the screen. For a moment, Max wondered why he would do something like that. He was ruining his night vision, for one. And if he was supposed to be here for a meeting or to pick something up, why would he need to look at his—

A deafening crack echoed through the forest, and the man's head exploded.

\* \* \*

Renee was already nervous, waiting in the car with the engine turned off. She was checking her watch and staring in the rearview mirror, hoping to see Max's reflection as he walked back to her. She knew this had something to do with his past life. His time in Europe as an intelligence operative for the DIA would always be a part of his identity. She had known he was speaking with Caleb Wilkes about doing work for him. But she had secretly hoped that nothing would come of it.

While Renee had once worked for the CSE, Canada's version of the NSA, she did not share the same gung-ho mentality as her beau. She didn't like guns. She preferred nonviolent resolution to conflict. And she didn't concern herself with politics or worry much about international affairs.

That being said, Renee wasn't naïve. She knew how the world worked, and that there was a need for men like Max. She just didn't want him to get hurt trying to be some sort of heroic knight. Or whatever he thought he—

Renee heard what sounded like a gunshot and froze. Then she flung the car door open. Her heart raced as thoughts of the worst flooded into her mind. She stepped out onto the sidewalk and slammed the door shut.

Had Max been shot? What if Max had shot someone? *Don't be stupid.* He didn't have a gun. Did he?

Renee looked both ways on the sidewalk, tapping her foot. She had to do something. She reopened the door, leaned into her car horn and pressed down. The loud noise echoed through the night. Dogs in a nearby home, already agitated by the gunshot, barked louder in response to the horn.

She slammed the door closed behind her again and sprinted towards the parked car.

She stopped in her tracks as a tree branch cracked and someone ran out of the woods ahead of her. The dark silhouette of a man outlined by distant car headlights. The figure stopped at the sidewalk, a good ten or twenty yards away. Renee's stood in place, her heart stuck in her throat.

"Max?"

The figure didn't move.

But it wasn't him.

While Renee couldn't make out his face, this man had a shorter frame, and he carried some sort of long bag—like one of her old field hockey stick bags from college—slung over his shoulder.

The hair on the back of Renee's neck rose as the man stood inspecting her from the shadows, silent and motionless. Perhaps deciding what to do. Renee was about to run when, in an abrupt motion, the man reached down, picked up a mountain bike which had been lying in the grass, and pedaled away.

A million questions collided in Renee's mind, but only one mattered right now.

Was Max hurt?

She hurried down the paved pathway into an unlit park near the side of the road. Into the woods from which the mysterious man had just emerged.

"Max!" she screamed. Breathing fast, she took her cell phone out and turned the flashlight on to see better. Her eyes played tricks on her with every shadow. Lightning bugs blinking in the humid night air. On either side of the woods, outdoor lights were coming on, illuminating the back porches of suburban homes. She called Max's name again. In the distance, a police siren began to wail.

"Psst. Renee, over here, quick."

Max's voice. Thank God.

"Shine the light over here," he said.

Renee headed towards the sound of his voice and the blue-white glow of a cell phone on the ground.

"Max, I saw someone," she whispered. "He was running out of the forest after the gunshot."

Max turned to look up at her. "Did he see you?"

"I think so. Maybe. He got on a bike and rode away from me when he got to the street."

Max turned back to the ground. He was hunched over, working on something.

"I heard him run away," he said. "I think he was hiding in the woods, waiting. I must have walked right past him. Good thinking with the horn. I think that spooked him. He took off after you did that."

"Max, I thought...did he shoot at you? Are you alright?" As Renee got closer, she realized that Max was hunched over a man's body. "Oh my God..." She covered her mouth and fought the urge to retch. Half the man's head was missing—a mass of dark red and gray mush in its place.

"You're moving the light. Keep it over here, please." Max's voice was that of a surgeon at work. His hands glided into the dead man's pockets and shoes, searching for anything he could find. Then he scanned the area surrounding the body. He grabbed the glowing phone off the ground and pocketed it.

The blue light of the first cop car flashed in between the homes up to their right.

"Let's go. If the cops see us, we stay. But I'd like to try and make it to our car before we're seen. If we can do that, we'll leave."

"Leave?" Renee didn't like the sound of that but trusted that Max knew best in this type of situation.

Less than a minute later, they were driving away, Max in

the driver's seat, his eyes scanning the rearview mirror for any sign of trouble. Then they were driving north on the Beltway, crossing the Potomac into Maryland.

"Why didn't you want to stay until the police arrived?"

Max said, "Caleb wouldn't want anyone to know we were there, if we could help it."

"Caleb Wilkes? Who were we following, Max?"

"Wilkes asked me to keep an eye on someone at the concert."

Renee had her arms folded across her chest and was shaking. "Why didn't you tell me?"

"I'm sorry."

She closed her eyes, composing herself. "Who was the man in the park?"

He glanced at her and then back towards the traffic. "The man Wilkes asked me to watch at the concert was a foreign intelligence operative. He placed a signal on the side of a bench outside the concert gate. The second man—the one we followed here in the silver sedan—was the one who picked up the signal."

"How do you know?"

"I could tell."

"And he was the one who was killed?"

"Yes."

"Why?"

"I don't know."

Max's phone began buzzing.

"Fend. Yes, Renee and I are fine. She was there too, yes. We left before they arrived. Yes, I am aware. That's right. You'll take care of it? Thank you. When? Okay, we'll see you then."

Renee folded her arms. "Was that who I think it was?"

"Yes. Caleb's going to stop by and debrief us tomorrow. I assume you're staying with me tonight?"

Renee was a mess of emotions. She took a deep breath and let out a defeated, "Yes."

Max placed his right hand on her neck, massaging it. "Are you alright?"

She took his hand, clasping it in her own. She let out a soft breath. "I will be."

## CHAPTER 4

MAX AWOKE EARLY the next morning to the sound of gulls and a diesel motor. He climbed up the ladder to the aft deck of his forty-foot sailboat, where he had taken to staying during the warmer weather. Sunlight reflected off the still water of Annapolis harbor. A clean white fishing boat motored out of its slip and out towards the bay. Max waved to the captain, who waved back while navigating through the channel markers.

Memories of last night ran though his head. Max had spent almost an hour on the phone with Wilkes once they'd gotten to Annapolis, recounting each detail.

Renee was still in bed. Max wanted to let her sleep in. She was understandably upset. After Wilkes's call, Renee and Max had stayed up talking in bed. The conversation veered from the murder they had just witnessed to a deep discussion around trust and relationships. After not being told the real reason they had gone to Wolf Trap, she was worried that Max was reverting back to keeping secrets like he had as a DIA operative.

Renee argued that things had changed.

"Like what?"

"Us," she had said.

If he was going to be with her, he needed to tell her everything. Max knew she was right. She was always right. It just wasn't easy for him.

Max slipped on his flip-flops and hopped over to the pier. He walked through the nearly empty cobblestone streets of Annapolis until he reached a local bagel shop, ordering a half dozen everything bagels and a tub of cream cheese. Then he walked back to his boat and sat back down at the aft deck table. A canvas tarp provided shade from the rising sun and protection from seagulls engaged in target practice.

Max smeared gobs of cream cheese onto his steaming bagel. In the distance he could hear the echoes of Naval Academy midshipmen jogging to a military cadence. Plebe Summer, the boot camp that indoctrinated Academy freshmen into the school, was in full swing.

He ate his breakfast in peace, gazing out over Annapolis Harbor and towards the distant Chesapeake Bay. A cabin cruiser motored by, its modest waves rippling slowly towards the shore. On each sailboat in the harbor, metal clips swayed on their lines, clanging against the masts in a gentle rhythm. The seafarer's song, the marina's orchestra.

Caleb Wilkes approached Max's boat, the wooden boards creaking beneath his feet.

"Mind if I join you?" Wilkes said.

"Be my guest."

Wilkes gripped the metal rail and stepped over to the sailboat, balancing a cardboard drink holder filled with clear plastic cups. Iced coffees swirling with white milk, dark coffee and caramel browns, beads of condensation on the outside of the cups.

"I come bearing gifts." Wilkes placed the drinks on the table.

Max smiled. "Why, thank you." He heard Renee stirring below.

"You mind?" Wilkes pointed at the bag of bagels.

"Be my guest."

Renee came up the ladder wearing a long tee shirt that stopped midthigh. Her hair was disheveled. But even when she was just rising, she was beautiful to Max. Red lips and alluring eyes. Seeing Wilkes, she glanced at Max, failing to hide her disapproval. Women were excellent visual communicators.

"He's here early."

Wilkes said, "Good morning, Miss LaFrancois. I apologize for my intrusion. Would you care for a drink? I brought iced lattes."

Max gave a sheepish grin. "He brought us iced lattes."

She took one of the drinks and sat down on the bench next to Max, crossing her legs. She plunged a straw into the center of her drink and snatched a bagel from the bag.

She began, "Mr. Wilkes…"

"Please, call me Caleb."

"Caleb, then. I was under the impression, until last night, that is, that Max would only be working for you as an advisor."

"That's right."

"So, you can imagine my surprise when I found him standing over a dead body in the middle of a neighborhood park in Virginia."

"Renee…," Max said, embarrassed.

Wilkes rose from his seat, examining the transparent plastic weather wall that was wrapped into a roll and tied up along the rim of the hard-shell cover overhead. He then looked around at the streets surrounding the harbor.

Max knew what he was thinking. Saturday-morning tourists had begun to walk the brick sidewalks of Old Town Annapolis. Colorful shops, restaurants, and quaint little homes lined the streets. Here in the harbor, the trio was visible from hundreds of windows that overlooked the marina. Anyone with a directional microphone would be able to listen in.

"It unwraps."

"Do you mind?"

Max got up. "Not at all. Let me help."

The men untied the plastic wall and rolled it down so that the three of them were enclosed in a ten-by-ten-foot transparent shell. Max doubted its effectiveness against a professional surveillance team with high-tech equipment, but he was also skeptical that anyone would eavesdrop on them here, unless Wilkes had suddenly become careless and been compromised. The men sat down again.

Renee sipped through her straw, then said, "If Max is going to be working for you and putting his life in danger, I want to know about it. I won't have any more surprises like last night." She turned to Max. "If you want me in your life, you need to be honest with me about these things. You both know that I've worked in the intelligence field before. My IT security contracts require me to hold a current TS/SCI. I'm trustworthy, and I've got the clearances, so stop keeping me out of the loop. Especially if I'm going to end up doing the work anyway." Her chest heaved, and her face was flushed as she eyed both of the men.

Based on Renee's tone and body language, Max didn't think that now was a good time to point out that her work in the CSE, and as a cyber operations contractor in the US, was very different from operational work in the field.

Max looked at Wilkes. "She's right. I should have told her before we went to the concert. And Renee and I have worked well together in the past. Caleb, I would like you to consider us a team from now on." Max hoped he wasn't overplaying his hand...with either of them. How badly did Wilkes want him as a CIA asset? Badly enough to take on the risk of having another set of eyes and ears on Max's work, trustworthy or not? And how willing was Renee to go along with Max's desire to play part-time spy?

Wilkes looked back and forth between them, working

something out behind his unreadable mask. His decision took about three seconds. "Very well."

Max could feel Renee straighten up in her seat a bit. A welcome victory.

Wilkes said, "First things first. I've spoken to my contact at the FBI. He'll be by this morning to ask you both some questions about what you saw last night. Your statement will be kept confidential. Officially, neither of you were at the crime scene. We want to keep both of your names out of the papers."

"Understood."

"The deceased was a man named Joseph Dahlman. He worked as a lobbyist at a boutique shop on K Street that does a lot of work on behalf of Middle Eastern and Central Asian interests."

"What makes a lobbying firm boutique?" Renee asked.

Max whispered, "I think it's a fancy way of saying small." He turned to Wilkes. "What's up with Dahlman?"

Wilkes said, "I've recently begun working on a new project with our counterintelligence division. An investigation that involves one of the Mexican drug cartels."

"Why would you be working on something involving the cartels? Isn't that the DEA's responsibility?" Renee asked.

Max said, "The CIA oftentimes gets involved in counternarcotics operations around the world. Criminal enterprises as big as the Mexican cartels influence national security. They control people, cash, and weapons. The Mexican cartels have their own private armies, often poached from Mexican special forces, some who were trained in the US."

"Why would someone in Mexican special forces go over to the cartels?"

Wilkes said, "It's not like it is here in the US. The cartels control huge swaths of territory in Mexico. Many Mexican institutions, like the police and military, aren't as well respected or well run as their American counterparts. Imagine you're a twenty-something Mexican kid who's been in the military for a few years, getting low pay and being treated like shit, and then you get approached by an old soldier buddy who'll give you a huge salary increase, women, respect. The Zetas, one of Mexico's most notorious cartels, started off as a group of bodyguards for another cartel's leader. Then they were used as a death squad—assassins who killed off rival gang leaders and middlemen, law enforcement or reporters. They began recruiting more and more former military. They had their own training centers and ran the outfit like a professional fighting force. Except for the drugs, booze, and prostitutes, of course."

Renee's eyes widened.

Max looked at Wilkes. "I've heard that some of the cartels are upgrading their intelligence operations as well."

Wilkes nodded. "You heard correctly. About a year ago, we began getting intel reports that the Sinaloa cartel had hired a foreign national to run their security and intelligence operations. That's unheard of among the cartels. Loyalty being at such a premium in that line of business, they like to keep the important jobs to a few key families within each organization."

"Let me guess, they hired someone from Pakistani ISI?"

"Not exactly. But we think the ISI may be in touch with the person they hired."

Wilkes took out his phone and tapped the screen a few times, then held it out. Max could see a tall Caucasian man sitting by a pool. The resolution was poor, and it was hard to make out facial features.

"You're right. He doesn't look Pakistani."

Wilkes said, "The name we've heard the Sinaloa cartel calling him is Juan Blanco."

"Blanco?"

Wilkes nodded. "We assume it's an alias. This is the only photo we have, taken from a satellite while he was at a cartel mansion in Durango. We've been unable to intercept any communications with his voice in them. Although we suspect he's using an echo talker."

"What's that?"

"It's where you have someone else standing next to you by the phone while you write out messages for them to read. As long as you keep changing hardware and locations, it makes it pretty tough for the NSA to find you—no voice ID to run analysis on. An effective technique, if done properly. Some of our analysts peg him as Russian, based on his contacts overseas —the contractors he uses are some of the same ones the Russian mafia uses. But we've yet to have one of our agents see him in person." He shrugged. "It's only a matter of time. We'll get better information eventually, but right now he's a mystery."

"What makes this mystery man so special, aside from being foreign?"

"In short, he's *good*. Hence why we think he's got experience from a top-level intel organization. He travels almost exclusively in the Durango region, where we don't have a big footprint. He only deals with the cartel bosses, a few lieutenants, and his own trusted team of sicarios.

"Señor Blanco has professionalized the Sinaloa cartel's security and countersurveillance operations to a level normally seen only in well-funded national intelligence agencies. The Russians, the Chinese, the Israelis. Within weeks of his arrival, DEA and Mexican counternarcotics programs months in the planning were quickly discovered and rendered useless.

"He's got them outsourcing cyber help now. The cartel's communications procedures and cyber-security became much better, making it brutally difficult for law enforcement to eavesdrop and track them. And he's taken a page out of Los Zetas' playbook—hiring away Mexican special forces soldiers and professionalizing their hit teams."

Max said, "So how does this relate to Syed and the dead man...what's his name?"

"Dahlman."

"Yes, him." Max slurped through his straw as he ran out of iced coffee. Renee shot him a look.

Wilkes said, "The man who placed the signal on the bench at Wolf Trap last night was Abdul Syed, a Pakistani intelligence officer. He works out of the embassy in D.C., and the FBI has been surveilling him as long as he's been in the US."

Renee said, "Well, then, why did we have to—"

"And he's been trying to lose the FBI every night for the past several weeks," Wilkes finished. "Sometimes he succeeded in that endeavor. Other times we only let him think he did. But last night was different. I knew he was going to meet with someone."

"How did you know?" Renee asked.

"Miss LaFrancois, as much as I am grateful for your participation, there are some things that I do not wish to share. That is one of them."

Renee folded her arms.

Max said, "So you called the FBI off because...you didn't want to spook him?"

"Precisely. It was my hope that you, with your exceptional skills, would know what to look for. And unlike the federal agents whose faces Mr. Syed probably knows by heart now, he does not know your handsome mug."

"You really think I'm handsome? Why, thank you, Caleb."

Renee rolled her eyes.

"And the FBI counterintelligence guys were okay with this?"

Wilkes didn't answer the question, which was an answer in itself. Instead, he said, "In using Max, I was able to lull Syed into a false sense of security. I was not aware, however, that Mr. Syed intended to cause harm to his own agent. If I had known that, I would have done things differently. Please accept my sincere apology, both of you, for putting you at risk. I assure you it was not my intention. I only wished to ascertain the identity of Mr. Syed's agent. Your following him and seeing where he went after receiving his signal was an added bonus."

Max said, "So Syed dropped off a message to one of his agents, Dahlman. And then the agent gets shot? Who fired the shot? Syed?"

"I doubt it. He wouldn't pull the trigger. Syed's a pro. He wouldn't take that risk. He would hire out for that."

"That makes sense."

"That reminds me—from our phone conversation last night, I understand that you didn't find anything at the scene other than the phone? I can take that now."

Max slid over the phone he'd picked up.

Wilkes pocketed the phone. "I'll bring this to the lab."

Max knew that Wilkes would take it to Langley, and that he might or might not bring this piece of evidence to the attention of the FBI, depending on what he found.

Renee said, "So the question is, why would Syed want his own agent killed? And I'm sorry—what does this have to do with Mexico?"

Wilkes said, "I have an asset in Mexico. She's close to one of the Sinaloa cartel's higher-ups—a man by the name of Hector Rojas. Rojas handles all financial matters for the cartel. He travels to Mexico City sporadically, for business. My agent spends time with him when he's there. A few days ago, Rojas made one of these trips, and my agent was able to alert us to a meeting between Rojas and a known Pakistani intelligence operative who works in Mexico City. We were able to eavesdrop on parts of that conversation."

Wilkes paused, shaking ice from his cup into his mouth and cracking it in his teeth.

"Rojas implied that our mystery man would be taking part in a meeting later this month. This meeting would include a high-level ISI representative. I assume Syed. The meeting will also include other, unnamed VIPs. They emphasized security measures and some pre-meeting requirements that had to be fulfilled. Hector Rojas indicated that our mystery man approved of an imminent operation that would meet one of these requirements. Then, the next day, an unrelated intelligence source told me that Syed is meeting with one of his American agents. A man we've been trying to identify for months."

"Dahlman."

"Correct."

"So, you think the hit on Dahlman last night was one of these 'pre-meeting' requirements?"

"I do."

"Requirements, plural. So, are we talking about a hit list here?"

Wilkes nodded. "That's my take. But it's something I'd like to confirm."

"So, the Sinaloa cartel is working with Pakistani intelligence." Max shook his head. "Strange bedfellows."

"Agreed. We can trace this new collaboration to the cartel's acquisition of Blanco as its head of security. And now they're orchestrating the assassination of Americans together. And not just any Americans. Pakistani spies."

"I don't understand why this mystery man would care."

Wilkes shook his head. "There's a lot we are yet to understand. But I know this: ordering a hit on American soil is a major risk for both parties. The ISI doesn't normally conduct active measures in the US. And the cartels usually limit their violence to rival gangs or trial witnesses about to snitch. Both organizations know better than to stir the hornet's nest. Yet that's exactly what they are doing."

Max saw now why Wilkes was concerned. "If they're willing to take a risk like this, there must be an important reason."

Wilkes pointed at Max. "Exactly. And I want you to help me find out what it is."

\* \* \*

Wilkes went over his plan for the next hour. Personnel, operational responsibilities, communication methods, timing, equipment, locations, backup options.

When he was done, Max said, "Let me get this straight. You want us to run an operation on the coast of Sinaloa, Mexico, using your pretty female agent to lure in Hector Rojas, kidnap him while he's drunk or sleeping, and get him back to the US for interrogation. Is that it?"

"You'll need to sort out some of the finer details."

"I'll need help."

"I trust that you can put together a team. But keep it very small. One or two people tops. And you'll need to make your visit look legit. Like a vacation. Otherwise their people down there will sniff you out."

"You want me to self-fund?"

Wilkes looked around at the sailing yacht. "Money doesn't look tight."

"Having our bodies dismembered and discarded in the Sierra Madre Mountains is a higher price."

Renee shifted in her seat.

Max saw her discomfort and turned to her. "You still want to be part of this?"

"Yes."

"Fine. But if I let you come with me to Mexico, I don't want you near the actual op when it happens. We'll need to keep you out of harm's way. No offense, but you have no street experience, and just placing you in the same city is about all the risk I'm willing to take."

She started to say something but bit her tongue. "Okay."

Wilkes stood. "I'll contact you again once you're in Mexico. I'm assuming that you'll be able to find a suitable shooter? Someone with experience down there?"

Max nodded. "I have someone in mind."

"Who?"

"A guy named Trent Carpenter."

Max felt Renee's eyes on him at the mention of Trent's name. Wilkes caught the look.

"Who is he?" asked Wilkes.

"A friend. He's former Army Delta. Used to be an advisor to the DEA counternarcotics teams working down in Mexico but got out of the Army over a year ago."

"Sounds like a good pick. Just make sure he keeps this quiet."

"Of course."

"When did you see him last?"

Renee held Max's hand as he replied, "About a week ago. At his brother's funeral."

## CHAPTER 5

THE DAY after speaking with Wilkes, Max flew his Cirrus from Leesburg, Virginia to northeast Pennsylvania. Renee accompanied him, as she had the week earlier for Josh's funeral.

During the flight, he thought about Josh. Until he'd died from a heroin overdose, Josh Carpenter had been one of Max's few life-long friends. They had been roommates all four years of prep school. Entry into the elite New Jersey boarding school had been assured for Max, son of Charles Fend, the aerospace CEO and American business icon.

It had been a different path for the Carpenter boys. Both Josh and his older brother, Trent, had attended on a special scholarship set up for the children and grandchildren of Medal of Honor winners. Trent and Josh's grandfather had been a decorated hero of World War Two.

The school wasn't a perfect fit for the Carpenters. The prestigious high school charged over thirty-five thousand dollars per year for its boarding students. BMWs and Mercedes filled the parking lot, birthday presents for pampered sixteen-year-olds. The Carpenter boys were a different breed. They were proud of their blue-collar roots and traveled back to the family home in rural Pennsylvania on most weekends.

Trent Carpenter had been a senior when Josh and Max had arrived for their freshman year. With his father traveling for business so much, Max had become close with the Carpenter family, often spending weekends at Josh's parents' home. Together the two boys would hike, fish, play football and get into trouble. To Josh, Max wasn't the famous son of a billionaire, he was a loyal friend.

Josh's family treated Max like he was one of their own. The Carpenters had a strong family bond and three rules: work hard, be humble, and don't complain. The ethos rubbed off on Max.

Their senior year, Max was accepted to Princeton, and Josh was denied admission to West Point, his dream school. It had hit Josh hard. But he hadn't complained. Josh had decided that he would still enter the Army immediately upon graduation, just not as an officer. While he had been accepted to several excellent colleges, none of them had offered a scholarship, and money was tight in the Carpenter family. Josh had enlisted in the Army, against the recommendation of his teachers. His parents had been both proud and worried.

Josh's older brother Trent had followed a similar path. To them, heroism and self-sacrifice were a calling. Just because they had gone to one of the top private high schools in the nation didn't mean that they were above being soldiers.

Josh had excelled in the Army, rising up to Sergeant First Class and deploying around the world. After graduating from Princeton, unbeknownst to any of his friends, Max had gone to work as a covert operative for the Defense Intelligence Agency. The two friends had kept in touch over the years, but their contact had naturally grown less frequent over time.

Since he'd left the DIA last year, Max kept telling himself that he needed to reach out and go visit Josh. He had been like a brother during Max's formative years.

And now, flying towards Josh's hometown, Max again felt the pain of knowing his old friend was gone forever.

At one hundred and eighty knots, their flight time was just over an hour. Max had made sure that they departed early enough in the morning to dodge the afternoon thunderstorms of July. They landed on a short two-thousand-foot runway at Skyhaven Airport on the outskirts of Tunkhannock, Pennsylvania. The town and airport were tucked between forest-covered mountains and the Susquehanna River.

Upon arrival, Max signed for their rental car, and they drove towards the Carpenter parents' home, where Trent had agreed to meet them. The narrow roads carved through forest-covered hills. They passed signs for Shadow Brook Golf Course and Lazy Brook Park, and an ice cream shop on the edge of a cow pasture.

"We'll need to stop there later." Renee gave a devilish grin. Max agreed.

At last they arrived at the parents' home, on the outskirts of town. As Max got out of the car, he saw that the home was still busy a week after the funeral. A screen door on the covered porch snapped every few minutes as family and friends came in and out. A smoker grill was lit in the backyard, and a balding man who Max recognized as a neighbor nodded a greeting. Max had met many of the Carpenters' friends and family last week, paying their condolences at the funeral. The support network was still in full swing. One of the town's beloved sons had passed, and they were rallying around the family in mourning.

Max and Renee went inside the home to say hello. The Carpenter parents still looked heartbroken but seemed to be on the mend. They were somewhat confused that Max had returned a week after the funeral. But they accepted that he was here to speak to Trent without asking further questions.

Tina, the new widow, was also present. Her five-year-old son, Josh Junior, sat beside her, watching cartoons on her iPhone.

After Max and Renee made the rounds, they walked out to the backyard. The ranch home sat on a hill, with the rear of the property extending into a pine forest. To the south, they had a magnificent view of the Susquehanna River as it flowed through town. The surrounding mountains were dark shadows, hidden by a thick summer haze. The anvil shape of a giant thunderhead loomed in the distance.

Trent Carpenter was sitting on a lawn chair, whittling a small piece of wood with a bowie knife. He had the knotted calves and muscular arms of a football player, with close-cropped hair and manly facial features straight out of a John Wayne western.

Like his now-deceased brother, Trent was a former soldier. But while Josh had been with conventional Army units, Trent had spent two decades in Special Forces. Max didn't know him as well as he'd known Josh. But he knew enough. Every time Josh or the parents used to speak of Trent, it was with reverence and pride.

Trent stood up when he saw Max and Renee approach, wiping sawdust from his hand and sticking it out in greeting.

Max shook his hand, and Renee went in for the hug.

"Hi, Trent. Good to see you again." Renee's voice had that perfect female touch of empathy and sadness.

Trent had the look of hard-earned life experience and the wisdom that came with it. His were the eyes of a man who knew true loss but had hardened himself against it. His brother, Josh, had died from a heroin overdose, leaving a wife and son behind. Max knew how devastated he had been at the news. But Trent also looked strong. Healthy. Resolute. He would be alright, Max knew.

Renee said, "Your family doing okay? Tina?"

"We're all doing a little better this week, I think."

Max had been shocked to learn the details of Josh's death. Josh had been off active duty for a few years, medically discharged after a bad back injury. The rest was a sad but familiar story. Josh started getting treatment at the VA hospital for chronic back pain. The VA had initially given him a bunch of very strong opioid-type pain meds. Then, as the opioid epidemic had started blowing up, the VA had changed their policies. Tina had told Max that the doctors at the VA wanted him to go cold turkey. To go get acupuncture instead. Josh had tried, but apparently, it hadn't been that easy.

Max looked over at the screen porch. Tina was running her hand through her five-year-old son's hair. A rumble of thunder reverberated in the distance.

Trent said, "Sounds like rain."

"Yup."

"So you said you want to talk. How's about we get out of here? Talk over lunch?"

"Sure thing," Max said.

* * *

Trent drove them about thirty minutes away, past Lake Winola, to another small town on the outskirts of Scranton. There was a quaint little main street that looked like it hadn't changed much since the 1960s. Max had seen many streets like this across the heartland of America. Old-fashioned storefronts with big glass windows. Rounded overhangs covering wide sidewalks. A small movie theater at the center of town, with only a few showings per day. A dilapidated family drugstore. And the insurgent hipster restaurant, with its neon chalk menu out front.

Trent parked his Ford pickup in an angled spot on the main street, and they walked into a busy bar-restaurant.

"You guys like burgers? They make the best ones here."

Trent waved to the bartender, who greeted him by name. Max surveyed the place. It wasn't bad. Hardwood floors and finished oak tables. An empty stage on one end of the diner where a local band was setting up.

Trent scanned the crowd like a pro, his eyes capturing every face, exit, threat, friend, and abnormality in view. Max followed Trent's gaze to see a few rough-looking men playing pool in a back room. A girl that couldn't have been more than twenty watched Trent with interest from a stool in the corner, playing with her tongue ring.

"Well, well...," Trent said.

"What is it?"

"I'll be right back." Trent stood and headed towards the back room.

Renee shot a curious look at Max. "Where's he going?"

Max nodded over to the billiards table. "I don't have a good feeling about this."

He couldn't hear what Trent was saying, but he could read the body language of the others in the room. Trent held the posture of an alpha male. One of the pool players—a big man with a beard, his cheeks flushed from too many pilsners— stood ominously close to Trent. The bearded man held a pool cue with both hands, his jaw clenched. The guy must have been six feet six, and three bills.

"What are they saying?" Renee asked.

Max shook his head and shrugged. "Not sure."

Then Trent walked to an exit door at the far end of the billiards room and gestured for the big man to follow. Trent's face was steady and unafraid.

Renee said, "Is he going to fight that guy?"

The big man yelled something at Trent, spittle flying out of his mouth. Heads in the restaurant part of the establishment shot over in their direction. Trent, the big man, and everyone in the poolroom headed out the door. Max got up, and Renee began to follow.

"You should stay here."

Renee rolled her eyes and kept walking. "Please stop saying that."

Max opened the rear door and saw that a small circle had formed around the two men. Trent stood still in the middle, rotating to keep his body facing the large bearded man, who was now circling him like a boxer in the ring. The big guy was cracking his knuckles and stretching his neck. Trent kept turning, looking loose and ready, his opponent in view.

"Kick his ass, Danny!" said the girl with the tongue ring. "Wasn't your fault his brother couldn't handle—"

The man with the beard took a swing at Trent. Trent sidestepped and brought up his knee into the man's stomach. Then he came down hard with his fist, knocking the large man to the pavement. His face made contact with the ground hard enough that Max winced.

Max felt a tickle on his forehead as rain began to fall. A long rumble of thunder came from the darkening clouds overhead.

Trent stood over the big man on the ground, his large chest heaving, a trickle of blood leaking out one of his nostrils. He didn't look very tough anymore. He looked scared. So did his groupies, who each took a few steps back.

"Did you sell to my brother?"

The bearded man nodded, looking away. Max recognized the type. Max had dealt with scum like this while working for the DIA. The big guy on the ground was a bottom-feeder, a low-level drug dealer. Preying on the weak, because he himself was weak of mind and morality. The big man wasn't averting his gaze because he was ashamed, but because he was afraid to finally face judgment. Life was easier that way, and men like him always took the path of least resistance.

Max glanced at Renee standing next to him. Her hair was

now covered by thick droplets of rainwater. The outer rim of the storm. Renee's arms were crossed, her pretty eyes looking at Max. She was concerned about what Trent might do. Max held out his hand. His instincts told him not to interfere.

The bearded man began to get up, but Trent placed his foot on his chest, pushing him back down. Trent was expressionless, a spartan soldier at work.

"Screw off, man. What do you want me to say? Sorry? I'm fucking sorry, okay? It wasn't my fault. Leave me alone."

Trent just stared at the man. "I don't want an apology."

The girl with the tongue ring hissed.

One of the others watching said, "Then what the hell do you want, asshole?"

"Show me a bag."

The man frowned in disbelief. "What?"

"Just show me a bag."

"What the hell are you talking about?"

"You got a bag on you? Show me one."

"Let me sit up."

Trent took his foot off the man's chest. The bearded man reached into his pocket and took out a small plastic bag. Trent snatched it from the man's grasp and held it up, examining it. Max could just barely make out a gelatinous black substance inside.

The dope dealer said, "Are you...are you looking for some for yourself? I can get you better stuff, but it's not on me."

"Is this what you gave to my brother?"

The man on the ground didn't reply.

Max watched Trent's fist tighten and momentarily worried that he was wrong about the situation. That Trent really was going to kill this guy.

But then Trent calmed himself and simply pointed a finger at the man's face, whispering, "Don't show up here again. I mean that." Then Trent flung the bag back at the ground and turned away.

The bearded man picked up the bag and hustled to his feet. He and his cohort looked at each other, stupefied, then fled down the alley. As the rain began to come down harder, flashes of lightning illuminated the sky, the rumbles of thunder growing louder.

Max placed his hand on Trent's shoulder, his tee shirt getting wet from the rain. "Let's go back inside."

Trent looked up at Max. "It was black tar."

Max looked at Renee, who was biting her lip. She shrugged, not understanding. Another clap of thunder sounded nearby. "We should get out of the rain."

"Black tar?" Max asked.

Trent walked towards the back entrance of the bar. "Black tar heroin. They make that shit in Mexico. During my last assignment with the Army, this is the stuff we were trying to stop from coming into the country. It's nasty stuff. The cheapest type. And it's what my brother was getting high on when he overdosed."

Renee looked at Max again, her eyes watery. Max held open the door to the poolroom, and they were flooded with a soft yellow light as they headed back inside.

Max felt guilty for thinking it, but he realized Trent was going to be the perfect recruit.

# CHAPTER 6

THEY WALKED THROUGH THE POOLROOM, the bar area. The bartender glanced at Trent. "Everything alright?"

Trent nodded back to him. "Yeah. Let me know if I owe you anything for scaring off your customers."

"Not a thing, brother. They weren't good customers."

Trent gave the bartender an appreciative smile and continued to walk with the group.

The band onstage was warming up. Country music.

Max went over to the bartender and asked if they could get the side room that looked like it was available for exclusive parties. The bartender agreed and showed them into the room through saloon doors. The band noise was muted there, and the room was empty of other patrons. A waitress approached and took drink orders.

She said, "Frank told me to make sure that you're left alone in here. Is that right?"

Max said, "That'd be great. Thank you kindly."

They sat down, and the waitress took their orders, then left to fetch drinks.

Max got Trent talking.

Trent said, "Black tar heroin is some ugly stuff. But it's

cheaper and easier to make. After the cartels couldn't make money from weed, they switched their focus to heroin."

Renee said, "Why couldn't they make money off marijuana anymore?"

"Because we legalized it in the US. Criminal organizations couldn't participate in the legal marketplace. And opioid demand was rising fast. So, the cartels shifted to heroin."

The conversation seemed to be therapeutic for Trent. He got going about everything that was eating him up inside. He talked about Josh's fight with opioid addiction, and about how Josh had tried to keep it from everyone. Trent had retired from the Army fourteen months ago so that he would have more freedom to help his brother fight his addiction.

"I never would have left the Army that early. But Josh needed my help. And things went well for a while. But drug addicts get good at hiding stuff," Trent said, sadness in his voice.

Ironically, Trent's last tour with Army special operations was on the front lines of the war on drugs. Trent had been in Mexico, advising the DEA and training Mexican security forces. While he didn't say it outright, Max knew enough to speculate that Trent had also done a few black bag jobs while down there. When the head of the Sinaloa cartel had been captured in early 2016, US military special operators like Trent had reportedly been on hand. One of them might even have been Trent.

Trent said, "Sometimes the dealers lace bags of heroin with the more potent synthetic stuff. It gets 'em hooked on the better stuff so that the next time they can jack up the price. The problem is that the synthetic drugs are often ten times more powerful. Sometimes hundreds of times more powerful. And if you take it in the wrong dosage, it'll kill you. That's what happened to Josh, they said."

"Mind if I ask you something? You could have done a lot of

damage to that guy in the alley back there. But you let him go. Why, if you think he's responsible?" Max needed to push the recruitment now, and to evaluate whether, after losing his brother in this way, Trent was stable enough to handle the job.

Trent sighed, staring down at his calloused hands. "It won't bring my brother back. Beating the hell out of him could put me in jail, though. That would just cause my parents more pain." He met Max's eyes. "Men like him aren't worth it. And they aren't the real problem."

Bingo.

Max said, "What if you could go after a few of the men who *were* part of the real problem?"

\* \* \*

The dinner conversation with Trent lasted another thirty minutes. Renee left to use the bathroom, leaving the two men alone. Max didn't finish with a hard sell. He told Trent that he could have a day to think it over. But Trent didn't need any more time.

"I'm in, Max."

Max nodded. "Good."

Trent took a swig of beer. "You know, I saw you once. When I was deployed."

"Where?"

"Syria."

"You're kidding. Why didn't you say anything?"

"Didn't seem appropriate. You were with a bunch of spooks, and it looked like you didn't want to be seen. My A-team leader was there with you in the building you were in. To be honest, I had forgotten about it until just now, when you mentioned you used to do this type of work."

"Why didn't I notice you?"

"Probably the beard, back then." Trent smiled.

Max snorted and shook his head. "So you already knew about me."

Trent nodded. "Josh had mentioned something, a while back. So you were CIA?"

"DIA, actually."

"But now you are working for the CIA?"

"Yes."

Trent looked confused. "So..."

"It's complicated." Max grinned, and then turned serious. "Hey, Trent, before we get into the details, I just want to make sure that with everything that's happened with Josh and all—"

"I know, Max. I won't lose my cool in Mexico."

"No, that's not what I mean. I mean, you know that this isn't your fault, right? Your brother."

He looked away. "I know."

"Are you going to be alright?"

Trent held up his beer. "Nothing a few of these can't fix."

"Well, make that the last one. I know your parents, and they'll kill me if I bring you back to the house drunk."

"I fear my mother too much to come back drunk." Joking. A good sign. "So what's with Renee? How is she involved in this?"

Max looked at her as she walked back into the room. "She's got a superpower, and it should come in very handy. Also, she told me that I'm not allowed to keep secrets from her anymore, which apparently includes international espionage."

Trent said, "What's the secret power?"

"Superpower," Max corrected.

Renee reddened. Max knew she disliked praise. "I'm good with computers. I believe that's what he was referring to."

The look on Trent's face told Max that this was still insufficient, so Max said, "Renee's background was with the Canadian version of the NSA, the Communications Security Establishment. She's also done cyber security for a variety of firms, including US intelligence agencies. I've worked with her on high-level assignments that were vital to national security, and I vouch for her."

Renee kissed his cheek. "You say the sweetest things."

Max had taken some liberty in his use of the word "assignments," but this information seemed to have the intended effect. Trent looked impressed.

Renee said, "So, Trent, what exactly should we expect down in Mexico?"

"Based on where Max said we're going, we'll need to be very careful. Assume that every set of eyes and ears is working for the narcos, or at least reporting to them. I'd like to check with DEA on—"

Max held up a hand. "Sorry. We're on our own on this. No one but us and my handler at CIA."

"Okay, then. Well, I would say that rule number one is don't trust anyone down there. The Mexican government and their law enforcement agencies are filled with people on the cartel payroll. Those who can't be bought are often killed. Brutally. If there's one thing the narcos understand, it's how to send a message. That's rule number two. Don't get caught."

\* \* \*

The next morning, Max and Renee were once again at the Carpenter parents' home. They had agreed to stop by for breakfast before flying Trent down south.

Max couldn't help but flash back to the funeral he'd attended a week earlier. The town police had led the funeral procession. A column of cars had followed with their headlights on. More than two dozen had shown up from Josh's old Army unit. They'd worn crisp uniforms and drawn proud stares from the locals.

The funeral had been nice, as funerals go. Four of the soldiers had formed an honor guard and performed a flag-folding ceremony. They'd handed the flag to Tina Carpenter, who was a wreck.

The tears had flowed, especially when Mr. Carpenter had given the eulogy. He'd recalled the best of times. He'd highlighted Josh's generous and spirited personality, and the love Josh had held for his wife and son. It had been painful to hear, knowing that he was gone.

Now Max sat at a plastic table on the screened-in porch. Josh's five-year-old son was eating cereal across from him. Puddles of milk surrounded the bowl. There was an iPad on the table. Someone had put on a cartoon. But the boy wasn't watching it. He was looking at Max, chewing his food.

"My mommy said that you were friends with my dad."

"I was. Very good friends."

"Do you like Penn State football?"

Max smiled. "Your dad sure did."

"He used to watch all the games with me."

Max didn't reply.

The boy took another bite of the cereal and began watching his cartoon.

\* \* \*

The weather was already getting hot and humid by midmorning when they had finished breakfast. Cicadas made a racket in the forest behind the home. Max wandered to the backyard, sitting in a lawn chair under the shade of an old oak tree.

Renee was playing with little Josh. They were feeding two rabbits in a homemade wooden cage propped up on cinderblocks. A thousand little pellets of food and droppings lay in the grass nearby. Renee's pretty smile and good nature had coaxed several giggles out of Josh Junior.

Tina approached. Josh's widow had lines of fatigue beneath

her eyes. Her voice was weak, like she didn't have any more energy to be sad.

"Josh would have been glad that you were here."

Max just nodded, feeling numb and guilty. They hadn't spoken much last week at the funeral. He hadn't known what to say.

They both just stood there in the morning heat, watching her son pet the rabbits at the far end of the yard. Finally, Tina said, "I don't think he could bring himself to tell you. About the drugs, I mean. He was ashamed of what he'd become, I think."

"He had no reason to be."

She nodded. "He tried to hide it from everyone. At first, he thought he could keep it from me. He tried to convince me that it was just him adjusting to civilian life. There were a lot of changes. He lost a lot of weight. Slept more. Mood swings—crazy ones. When they took away his prescription, someone in town said they could help him get some black-market stuff. It started off with him getting the same thing he'd gotten at the drugstore, except now he had to pay for it out of pocket. But then he couldn't get the pills anymore, and another guy said he could get Josh some sort of patch. Like a nicotine patch, but with fentanyl. Same thing as the pills, different method. But then that stuff dried up too. And eventually he started using the *really* bad stuff, because that's all he could get. All he could afford. It was awful on our marriage. I didn't know what going on at first. He didn't want to shower when I was around, which I thought was weird. I found out it was because he didn't want me to see the needle marks in his arms. Imagine trying to keep something like that from your wife, who sleeps in your bed. I found his box one day while he was sleeping."

"His box?"

"He had a little tin box that he kept under the seat of his pickup truck. Needles inside, carefully stacked. He was always neat."

"I'm so sorry, Tina."

"It's nobody's fault." Her voice cracked, and she wiped away a tear. "I feel like we all keep saying that to each other. That it's not our fault. I don't know if any of us truly believes it. Things weren't like this when Josh and I grew up in this town. Drugs were an inner-city problem. Not here. I smoked a little weed when I was younger. Josh did too. But never the hard stuff. People like us are from good families, with good parents. Good values. This kind of thing isn't supposed to happen here. Or to men like him. Josh was one of the best men I know. And I'm not just saying that because I'm his wife. Ask any of the men from his old Army units. He was one of the good ones. But those drugs changed him. And they have ruined my life. They've killed my husband. He wanted to quit, Max. He tried. But the pull was too strong. Even for someone like him."

Max didn't know what to say. So they just stood there in silence for a few minutes. Sometimes that was the best thing to do.

Tina was looking at her son. Trent was over there now. He had gotten little Josh away from the rabbits and they were playing Wiffle ball.

Tina said, "I'm not sure what we'll do now. I guess I'll have to go back to work. We were living off his disability pay, for the most part...but now I guess that will stop."

Max said, "Are you sure that they won't keep paying you?"

"I don't know. We have a man from the VA who is helping us, but the life insurance folks already said that his drug overdose meant that they wouldn't pay out."

Max shook his head. "Tina, I can help. Let me look into a few things."

She looked up at him, alarmed. "Oh, Max, listen, I didn't mean—I know you guys are well off and all but...look, we aren't looking for a handout, okay? I just was telling you because—"

Max gestured for her to stop. "Please. I know you didn't mean it like that. But let me see if there isn't something we can do to help you guys out. Do you have any immediate needs? Are you okay on money right now?"

She nodded, her lip quivering. Another tear ran down her cheek. "Thanks," was all she managed to say as she hugged him.

# CHAPTER 7

SENATOR HERBERT J. BECKER of the great state of Wisconsin stared into the center of the camera lens, doing his best to imagine that it was the single representation of each and every one of his most precious voters. He had practiced his "stern-but-approachable" look in front of countless mirrors. It assured his constituents that he was the kind of man who would stick up for them in a fight but at the same time shared their family values.

"And let me just say this. Solving this country's growing heroin epidemic is my *number one* priority. That's why I cosponsored the Opioid Epidemic Act. We'll be bringing it to the floor in a matter of weeks. I believe that will have a tremendous impact on reducing opioid use within the United States."

The reporter—a slick-haired kid who was a little too cavalier for the senator's taste—followed up with, "Well, I'm glad you brought that up, Senator. Many in your party were surprised that you cowrote that bill and helped gather so much support for it. It's a piece of bipartisan legislation that many in your party don't like. Some are calling it antibusiness. Even some on the other side of the aisle are saying it will deny access to medicine to those in need. What do you say to that?"

"I would say that this country has been hurting for a long time, and I'm proud of my efforts to combat the opioid epidemic. Businesses will not be hurt by this bill, as they will end up providing consumers with better health care, without the risks of today's surplus of addictive pain medication."

"What about the people who need that pain medication? Many patients need opioids to perform their day-to-day tasks. You're going to deny them that choice? Deny the doctors the ability to prescribe it and the health care manufacturers the ability to sell it?"

"My bill—excuse me, the Opioid Epidemic Act—doesn't completely eliminate opioids as an option. Yes, it will greatly reduce how many pills are sold and used. But in the long run, it will make our country healthier and more vibrant. Now I thank you for your time, but I'm afraid I have to—"

"Senator Becker, one more thing before you go—some are speculating that you have ambitions for a presidential run in two years. Is that true? Are you going to run for president, Senator?"

The balding politician smiled demurely. "Right now, I'm just focused on doing what's right for the good people of Wisconsin. And as far as elections go, it's this year's midterms that I'm thinking about. I'm up for reelection in my own state. I've honestly given no thought to any political decisions that may lay beyond that point."

*Of course it's true, you little prick, but you know I'm not going to say it here on your low-rated cable news show this far out into the future.*

The kid tried one more time, probably listening to his producer humming in his earpiece. "Is there any chance you would consider a presidential run in two years, sir?"

Becker would have to tell Ron not to book him with this guy anymore. "Well, I never like to close a door fully—but I mean what I said. My focus is on the people I represent in the great state of Wisconsin and making sure that we combat the horrific threat of illegal drugs poisoning our nation."

"Thank you for your time, Senator Becker."

"Thank you."

A group of reporters stood waiting for him to finish the interview. One of them stuck a recording device up as Senator Becker walked away from the camera.

"Senator, a few questions please."

Ron Dicks, his chief of staff, said, "The senator won't be taking any more questions right now, thanks."

The senator walked away from the scrum of reporters, his entourage of aids in tow. "What's next, Ron?"

Ron scanned his notepad as they walked, their footsteps echoing in the capital building hallway.

"Sir, you have a hard stop this morning for the Senate Judiciary Committee hearing at ten thirty. Prior to that, you've got a strategy session in your office with Sarah." His chief of staff rattled off several other appointments throughout the day, finishing with, "Oh, and your daughter called, sir."

"Karen called?"

"Yes, sir."

"What about?"

"She didn't say."

They took the underground subway from the Capitol Building to the Hart Senate Office Building and then made their way to his office. His secretary, a matronly no-nonsense woman of about fifty, handed him a list of calls as he walked in.

The senator sat down behind his desk. "Give me five minutes," he announced to his staff.

"Of course, Senator." Ron stayed in the room, knowing that the senator needed time, not privacy, which he'd given up decades earlier.

Senator Becker held the landline phone to his ear, dialing the number from memory. When he was president, he wouldn't dial anymore, he thought. Only a few years away, if he played his cards right.

Aides floated in and out of the office, placing folders in the senator's inbox and removing them from his outbox. Some whispered into Ron's ear as the chief of staff waited for the senator to finish his personal call. The secretary came in and placed a china set on the senator's desk—coffee and tea biscuits with raisins.

Karen answered on the second ring. "Hello, Dad."

"Karen. To what do I owe the pleasure?"

"I got it, Dad. I wanted you to be the first to know."

Senator Becker frowned, sitting down in the chair at his desk. "What did you get, dear?"

"The Oshkosh spot. They had a dropout and chose me at the last minute. I'll have two performances. You'll be there, right?"

"You're performing at Oshkosh? Why, that's wonderful news. When is your show?"

"Two performances. One earlier in the week, and one at the end."

"And you'll dress...conservatively?"

She let out a sigh of exasperation. "Dad...relax."

Senator Becker flushed, thinking of the outfits his daughter wore when she performed. He was proud that she had reached such a high level in the aerobatics community, being invited to the top air shows in the world. But my God, did she have to flaunt her buxom figure on all those advertisements?

"Let's just make sure that any publicity you get paints you in a good light. I would hate to think that—"

"Don't worry, *Senator*. I understand. I won't do or say anything crazy. Well, not too crazy." She laughed, and Becker saw his eavesdropping chief of staff close his eyes, a pained expression on his face. A few years ago, Ron had had to pay a private investigator twenty-five hundred dollars to destroy a set of files from one of Karen's old boyfriends. The ex-boyfriend had thought he was selling compromising pictures to a tabloid. He was made to turn over all of the files and sign a nondisclosure agreement. Then the PI had scared the hell out of him with what would happen if he violated the agreement. The files had been deleted, but it would have horrified Karen had they gotten out. More importantly, it would have embarrassed the good senator, and probably cost him ten points with suburban moms ages thirty-five through fifty-four.

Karen had been a hellion ever since she was a teen. Her looks had ensured that she never suffered any lack of attention from the opposite sex, and her behavior suggested that she didn't mind.

"Well, I'm thrilled that you'll be performing there, Karen."

"You're coming?"

"Of course, you know I never miss it."

"Great. I'll see you there next week."

As soon as he hung up the phone, it chimed. Senator Becker hit the blinking light. The voice of his secretary said, "Senator, your next appointment is here."

Senator Becker looked at his chief of staff.

Ron said, "Sarah."

"Ah. Yes, please send her in. Clear the room, please. Except for you, Ron."

The aides shuffled out.

A petite woman in a suit marched in and nodded respectfully. "Good morning, Senator. How are you today?"

"Excellent, thank you."

She set up her computer on the coffee table, connecting it by wire to the monitor mounted on the wall.

"What have you got for us, Sarah? Any serious challengers pop up while I wasn't looking?"

While there was a state primary vote in a few weeks that would decide Becker's opponent for reelection in November, none of the candidates were considered a serious threat. The senator had won each of his last three elections by a minimum of eight points. And the trend was improving.

She lowered her voice. "You asked me to put some polls into the field. Widening the pool of voters past Wisconsin…"

Ron glanced at the senator. The lightbulb went off in his head. This meeting wasn't about this year's election. It was about the future.

"Ah. That time already, is it?"

Becker could see the pleased expression in his chief of staff's eyes. A kid about to peek behind the wrapping paper on the night before Christmas. Which was good, because Ron had been nothing but a worrywart since the news about Joseph Dahlman.

The monitor showed a red, white, and blue elephant on the screen. There were few things more exciting to a political junkie than new polling data. Ron and Senator Becker were about to see, for the first time, what national polls said about his prospects for the next presidential race.

"Well, don't keep us waiting."

Sarah tapped a key on her computer and began showing them a series of charts.

"Overall, the news is good. Among likely voters, your name is within the top three potential presidential contenders in your party."

They went over top-line results for the next ten minutes.

"Nationally, the antidrug message is playing very well," said Ron.

Sarah said, "Absolutely. That's what voters know him for. Taking a tough stance on the war on drugs, and helping to fight the opioid epidemic. He's going to need a message that will resonate with the base if he's going to make it past a primary. This could be it."

"Ron here thinks that's a problem," the Senator said.

Ron looked uncomfortable. "I've made my views clear, sir. I think you risk alienating the people who got you here if you appear antibusiness."

"The Opioid Epidemic Act is going to be my signature achievement. You know it's a winner nationally."

"It won't matter if we can't even get past a national primary…"

"You see what I'm dealing with, Sarah? My own chief of staff thinks my biggest legislative achievement is going to hurt me. Well, fine. Let's see if I can't come up with something a little tougher. Something that adds more meat on the bone for the people Ron is worried about losing," said the senator.

Senator Becker looked at his computer screen on his desk. His Internet browser was on a news website, showing soldiers riding in Humvees in Afghanistan. "What was that the DEA was saying last week when we went to visit them?"

"The director?"

"No. When they took us on the tour? Do you remember, we spoke to an agent that had been down in El Paso about what he needed?" They had been looking for quotes that might help them support point papers.

"He was talking about the US Special Forces down there in Mexico," said Ron.

"That's right," said Senator Becker. "He was complaining about how Mexico wouldn't let the US get their hands dirty. We send our DEA agents, military personnel, and all those other agencies down to Mexico, not to mention the billions of dollars in foreign aid…but we're still at the mercy of the Mexican law enforcement agencies. The DEA has to rely on Mexican authorities to make real progress."

Sarah said, "I'm not sure that I follow, sir. What are you suggesting?"

The senator said, "What if we were able to use American troops to really go after the cartels in Mexico? To take the gloves off. Just like that DEA agent was saying. Now, policy like that, that's got some machismo, does it not?"

"It does."

Becker said, "I like this. Let's spitball it a bit."

Ron held up his hands, as if painting it on a billboard. "Stopping the opioid epidemic in the United States means taking the fight to Mexico."

Senator Becker pointed. "And *I'm* the only one tough enough to send our military down there to do it."

"Exactly. Brilliant, Mr. Senator." Ron held up his hands like he was reading a billboard. "If America is fighting a war on drugs, then it's time we use our warriors," said Ron, tagline-testing.

"Very nice." It needed a little work, but Becker liked it.

Sarah said, "Senator, with all due respect, we would need the permission of the Mexican government. They would never go for it."

Ron and the senator shared a glance.

Ron said, "That's irrelevant. We're just discussing campaign communication strategy. It doesn't matter whether we actually *do* it or not."

Senator Becker sighed. Sarah was good at polling, but he would need to replace her once the midterms were over. If she couldn't grasp the difference between a campaign message and an actual policy proposal...

"Sarah, we'll need you to market-test it. But my gut tells me that it's going to be a winner."

He looked out the window at his office. The worker bees buzzing around the streets of D.C. outside. It was remarkable to think how far he'd come over the years. His meteoric rise since 9/11.

It hadn't been that difficult, really. Senator Becker knew he had a way with people. Politics was all about winning hearts and minds. Helping all those unsophisticated voters understand what was really good for them, so that more than half of them approved of how he spent their money. It took oratorical skill. Becker was a masterful speaker. It took intellectual flexibility. Becker was a political yoga master. He had switched parties more than a decade earlier, when he'd seen the tides changing. Becker knew that if you wanted to govern, you couldn't worry so much about ideology, but you sure as hell better care about polls. And right now, the polls told him that he needed to crack down on drugs. It was a winning bipartisan issue. The kind of platform cornerstone that could propel someone into the oval office.

Sarah was nodding. "Alright, I'll conduct some more focus groups. And perhaps run another poll. I'll send you a cost estimate, Ron."

The senator nodded. "Excellent. Thank you, Sarah. That'll be all for now." The messaging might need some work, but they could try a few things. It was still early, but the time to get his ducks in a row was now.

A minute later, Sarah was out the door and Becker was alone with his chief of staff. The chime on his phone and a blinking light told him that his next appointment was ready. He pressed the button and said, "Give us a moment, please."

Ron was taking notes in his leather binder, muttering something to himself. He repositioned his glasses and wrote some more. Becker had worked with him long enough to know to leave him alone when he was like this. This was what Becker referred to as one of his genius moments. It was the way he made his calculations. At last he looked up and took his glasses off.

"I like it. I think it will play well. The libertarians will like the fact that we're not putting our troops overseas and instead focusing on something closer to home. The base will like it because it uses our troops to damage a clear villain. And everyone will like it because it takes a strong stance in the war on drugs."

"Now I know you're lying. There's never a time when everyone likes it."

"Everyone that matters," Ron said.

Senator Becker said, "It'll be a gamble. I'll be like a peacock with my feathers out during the primary, which I know worries you."

"Maybe, sir, but—"

"I know what you're going to say. We'll need to consider the increased scrutiny we'll be under." Becker gave Ron a knowing look.

"I am sorry for any problems I've caused us, sir. I should have been more careful."

The senator ignored him. "Even the hint of impropriety can get blown out of proportion. The opposition research we've faced thus far will be nothing compared to a presidential campaign."

"The contributions were from a 501c. The FEC has no ability to link it back to—"

"You received death threats."

"Sir, they were trying to play hardball."

"Your lobbyist friend is dead."

Ron paused, choosing his words, then said, "Sir, if you want me to go to the police—let them know that you had no knowledge of any of it...I'll fall on my sword, sir."

Becker slammed his hand down on the desk and pointed at Ron. "Don't be naïve. Saying that won't make a difference in the papers."

Ron looked like a beaten dog. "Sir, you could always call off the vote. Or amend the bill to be friendlier to the...investors."

"I'm not going to be bullied. People buy into my agenda. Not the other way around."

"Sir, I never meant to suggest that your strategy wasn't the right choice."

"You leaned on me, Ron."

"Sir, I gave you sound counsel."

"Which happened to align with the direction Dahlman and his backers were pushing you."

"Sir, this bill is counter to many of your own previous stances. My advice lined up with your own—"

Becker cut him off. "Things change. Now I need to know you're loyal to me."

"Of course, sir."

"If people start poking around, this could get ugly."

"I understand."

"Your professional relationship with Dahlman can't become an issue for me."

Ron reddened. "Yes, sir."

Becker said, "You know as well as I do that those clients of his play by a different set of rules. Well, now we're not in their favor anymore. We obviously can't go to the authorities because we don't want them digging around and finding out who you've been drinking beers with at Bullfeathers." He leaned forward and whispered, "But for God's sake, they just shot someone dead. Now I need you to clean up this mess. Figure it the hell out."

## CHAPTER 8

RENEE, Trent, and Max said their goodbyes to the Carpenter family and flew to Virginia. From there they were picked up by a sleek private jet.

"Courtesy of Charles Fend," said Max with a wink.

Trent whistled. "The royal treatment. Please give my thanks to your dad."

Max said, "It'll help us fit with our cover. The wealthy playboy that I play so well, my trophy girlfriend, and our private security man slash luggage boy."

"Trophy girlfriend?" Renee asked.

"Well, I didn't want to say eye candy. I thought you might be offended."

Trent said, "I'm fine with you calling me a luggage boy as long as there's some free booze on board. Hell, usually when they have me fly, the rear ramp gets opened and they ask me to leave halfway through the flight. This should be much better."

Max turned to Renee. "It's important, in the world of spy tradecraft, that you fully embrace the transformation into your cover assignment. You'll need to act like a devoted, fawning girlfriend who completely worships and adores her man."

Renee blinked. "That sounds awful. Why can't I just be myself?"

Two hours later, the jet was headed southwest. Trent slept in the rear of the cabin, aided by two glasses of bourbon on the rocks.

Renee sat in a cream leather chair opposite Max, chewing gum, her thin MacBook Pro on her lap, white earbuds in her ears. Max recognized the pattern. She was in work research mode. Hyperfocused learning, she called it. Conducting her due diligence at the beginning of a new project.

"Look at this."

She turned her computer so that he could see the screen. "Do you know that since 1999, over half a million people in the United States have died from drug overdoses?"

"Half a million?"

"Yes. And the overdose deaths are rapidly increasing— mainly due to the rise in opioid addiction."

Max had been reading up on the cartels on his tablet. Encrypted intel documents sent by Wilkes.

"You know we won't be able to solve the opioid crisis, right? That's not what this is about, Renee."

She ignored him and began typing, her fingers racing over the black keys.

"Hello?"

"Wait," was all she said.

Max did as commanded. A terrier, waiting for his master's command. He took a deep breath. Being in a relationship with a woman who was smart, opinionated, and sexy really hurt a man's ability to pretend he was in charge.

She stopped typing and looked at him. "Okay, I found what I was looking for. I'm ready to debate."

Max held his hands up in surrender. "I've learned that debating you is never in my best interests. How about you just arm me with your newly acquired knowledge?"

Renee began. "The US uses more opioids than anywhere else."

"Okay. So what? Isn't that just because of population?"

"No. This is per capita. The US leads the way, by far. Canada is number two, by the way. So I would be helping your country and mine."

Max cocked his head. "You keep telling me that you're an American now."

"I have dual citizenship. But I still like Canada better."

"Why?"

"Better beer and prettier lakes."

"We're getting better at beer, you know…"

Renee tapped on her trackpad and opened up a window. "This is the DEA's National Drug Threat Assessment. It's one of the most comprehensive annual reports on the illegal drug trade and how it affects the United States. It says that Mexico is the biggest source of heroin for the US market."

"I thought most heroin was grown in Afghanistan."

Renee said, "You're right. Most of it is. But there's a global demand for opium. And most Afghan poppy production ends up sold to European or Asian markets. Cheap Mexican heroin is flooding into the US. And look." She brought up a color-coded map of the United States. "Do you remember the name of the cartel that Wilkes mentioned?"

"The Sinaloa cartel, I believe."

"Right. They—according to this document—are the number one producer of heroin sold in North America. They control the region where it grows. Something about the climate in the warm, mountainous regions is conducive to growing poppies. And they have ultra-cheap labor. Women. Kids. Often working under slave-like conditions, growing the crops. Armed men standing watch over them. And you know how Trent was so broken up about the black tar heroin he found in the dealer's possession? He was right. His brother Josh probably overdosed on Mexican heroin—produced by the same cartels that Trent once went after. I don't know that you could ever point the finger at one person. But I certainly think that if you wanted to hold someone accountable at a high level, the higher-ups in the Sinaloa cartel would be a great pick."

Max said, "Point made."

"There's something else I found that I wanted to run by you."

"Hit me."

"I was trying to find a link between the ISI and the Mexican drug cartels. Specifically, the Sinaloa cartel, where this Blanco is."

"And?"

"I found this one journalist's blog—someone who'd been embedded with US troops in Afghanistan. One of his posts mentioned a rumor he overheard—that the Pakistani ISI are covertly running the Afghan opium trade."

Max narrowed his eyes. "It wouldn't be the first time an intelligence agency got involved in something like that. The Afghan heroin trade is a multibillion-dollar market. That amount of money would attract all the sharks in the region. And the ISI has a lot of sharks. If you've got that much cash, you can fund a whole lot of covert operations to support your cause."

"But even if the ISI is involved in the Afghan heroin trade, what's the connection to the Sinaloa cartel?"

Max looked out the window, thinking, then turned back to face her. "Heroin, obviously. You just talked about the rise in heroin use across the world since 2001. And you also said that North America has overindexed. So growth in heroin use here is higher than anywhere else, but Afghanistan still produces ninety percent of the world's heroin."

Renee said, "The Mexican cartels can't keep up. Is that it?"

"Possibly. Maybe the North American demand is outstripping the cartel's supply. So where can they go to get more heroin to sell in the US?"

"Afghan suppliers."

"And the ISI is brokering the deal."

\* \* \*

Their jet stopped at a small executive airport on the outskirts of Dallas. They taxied next to a hangar where a small moving truck was waiting. Next to the truck stood a tall, thick man with dark curly hair and a beard. Max shook hands with the man and introduced him to Trent and Renee.

Renee said, "I'm sorry, did you say your name was…?"

"That's right, Sasquatch."

The large man's arms were folded across his chest, a wide smile on his face.

Renee looked at Max with bewilderment, not sure if this was a joke. "Why do you go by Sasquatch?"

The man lifted open the truck trailer door to reveal shelves filled with weapons and gear. "I think they call me that because of my good looks."

Max whispered, "Men in his line of work usually prefer that we not use their real name."

Renee nodded.

Trent picked up a large weapon with two hands. It was drab green and had a cylinder-style magazine. "This is nice."

"What is it?" asked Renee.

Sasquatch answered, "It's a multi-use weapon. We've got several different options for ammunition there, sir. Just take a look at the shelf above it."

"Excellent. Very nice selection," said Trent. "These rounds here—any chance you could customize them for close quarters?"

Sasquatch handed him a specially marked crate. "These here

don't have the twenty-five-meter minimum engagement range. They'll arm after about seven meters. Will that do?"

"Yup."

Trent and Max inspected their gear options, made their choices, and then loaded everything onto the jet while it refueled.

"Your payment is already in your account," said Max. "And I gave you a little tip."

"Always appreciated, Mr. Fend. Just let me know whenever I can be of service."

The trio got back into the jet as Sasquatch drove away. A few hours later, they landed at an airport on the coast of Sinaloa, Mexico.

Cartel territory.

\* \* \*

They arrived at a five-star resort on the beaches of Mazatlán. The resort had high cement walls surrounding the property. Men armed with shotguns walked the perimeter, guarding the wealthy patrons. Max wondered how many of those men also worked for the cartels part-time.

"May we take your bags, sir?"

"No, thank you, my assistant will manage fine." Max looked at Trent, who nodded and carried their luggage up to the rooms. The bags would be moved to a safe house later that night. Until then, Trent wouldn't let them leave his sight.

Their hotel room was simple, but gorgeous. Clean floors of reddish Saltillo tile, arched ceilings, and an open-air balcony with a view of the turquoise Pacific and towering palm trees.

But beautiful as it was, the hotel would have been one of Max's last choices if he were vacationing in Mexico. Outside the walls of the resort, the city streets were teeming with prying eyes on the payroll of the cartel, each of them eager to get a bonus for providing a good tip on American law enforcement—or perhaps a prime target for kidnapping.

Their cover story was simple. Max and Renee were on vacation. As many ultra-wealthy travelers do, Mr. Fend had brought along his personal security guard. While Max was well known in the US, due to his father's fame and his own misadventures, here he was just some rich gringo. This partial anonymity allowed him to assist in reconnaissance without drawing extraordinary notice.

The three travelers spent their evenings together in Max's room, with the windows closed and electronic countersurveillance equipment humming on the coffee table. Renee had carefully set up their IT network, an encrypted system that made sure no one could tap in to their phones or computers. She also scanned the room for bugs twice per day.

Still, they knew they were probably being watched. The hotel concierge. The cab driver. The airport security officials. Local police. Even some teenage kids Max had caught tailing him during his first morning stroll. One kid watching him and immediately making a call on a cheap cell phone, probably reporting Max's position to his boss. Max lost the kids during his three-hour surveillance detection route, but the fact that there were so many potential eyeballs on him was a bit unnerving.

Mexico would be harder than he thought.

The group spent the next two days making observations and adjusting plans. Max and Trent took turns walking the streets in and around the operational area. Going over potential getaway routes and choke points, and gaining knowledge of the local pattern of life. Wilkes sent gigabytes of CIA and DEA data to Renee, which the trio studied each night.

Wilkes arrived on the third night to go over the plan.

They ordered room service. Steak and grilled vegetables. Bottled waters. Max wasn't drinking a drop out of the tap. He'd heard too many stories of Montezuma's revenge.

After dinner, Wilkes pointed at the map displayed on Renee's computer screen. On it was a neighborhood block about five miles away.

"So, our break here is that we've been able to establish a new routine between Rojas and my agent. About once per month, he makes the three-hour drive from cartel leadership's headquarters in Durango to the coast here in Mazatlán. Unless something drastically changes, there is a very high probability that Hector Rojas will be in this townhome tomorrow evening, enjoying a night of drinks and carnal familiarity with my agent."

Renee frowned.

Max nodded. "Based on the pattern-of-life reports Wilkes provided us, Rojas rarely stays in the same place more than a few nights in a row. And this special meeting that Blanco and the Pakistanis are prepping for is supposed to be held within the next few weeks. So, we'll need tomorrow night to go smoothly, or—"

"Or we're fucked," Trent finished.

"Or we'll lose our opportunity to discover the location, participants, and purpose of a meeting so important that the ISI is killing American citizens on American soil before it occurs."

Renee said, "Why is the cartel headquarters in the mountains? Why don't they live here? It's beautiful."

Trent said, "It's safer for them in the villages of the Sierra Madres. The cartels live in fear of each other. If they operated here on the coast, there would be a higher chance that one of the competing cartels might try and assassinate the head family, and then steal their share of the market. There's enough going on in beach towns like this that the other cartels might be able to send in a few cars full of their sicarios without getting noticed. But not in Durango. That's flyover country, and everyone knows each other. A single stranger shows up, and they get questioned by the local hired guns."

Max said, "Doesn't sound much like a cartel. Cartels are supposed to work together, colluding on price and distribution. Not kill each other off at the first sign of weakness."

Trent said, "The drug cartels are not real cartels in the literal sense of the word. The Colombians tried to operate that way for a while, but war erupted between them. It's more like the mafia. Competing factions of organized crime families, each following a common code. They have an understanding, and each cartel's territory has been carved out through violent battles over the years. But it's a tumultuous climate. I wouldn't call it a peaceful partnership. They kill each other as much as they kill anyone else, if not more. It would be great if they really operated as a cartel. I suspect there would be much less violence. Much less chaos."

Wilkes said, "Let's talk the schedule of events. My agent will try to slip an incapacitating chemical into his drink. I've trained her on technique and risk assessment. If she can do it safely, Rojas should be passed out pretty hard by midnight. You'll just have his two security guards to handle. Will that be a problem?"

Trent shook his head. "That should be no problem."

"Are we sure it's just two men?" Max said.

Wilkes said, "He's had the same two bodyguards with him every trip he's taken for the past three months."

Trent and Max exchanged glances. Both of them knew how often mission expectations differed from the actual circumstances operators faced.

"We've been scouting the city," Max said. "I'll be parked down the street. When your agent gives her signal that tells us Rojas is passed out, Trent will take out the guards and I'll move my vehicle to the curb. Both your agent and Trent will carry Rojas down to my vehicle and we'll head towards the airport. Caleb, like we discussed, I can't use my father's jet for the extraction, so I'll be relying on one of your air assets. I need you to guarantee me that you'll have someone at the airport at the appropriate time."

Wilkes nodded. "I'll have someone there ready to fly you all back to the States."

"Where in the States? Fort Bliss?"

"No. This is completely off the books. I can't have you guys fly in to a military base. I'll give the pilot a private field to fly into, and the interrogation team will meet you there. You don't need to know the location yet. What's your backup?"

Trent said, "If things get hairy, there's a connection to the townhome next door. Max and I have set up a secondary extraction route through there."

Max said, "When are you going back to El Paso?"

"My jet's waiting at the field," said Wilkes. "I'll be watching the op from EPIC, and I'll send you updates if I spot any problems."

"Won't the people at EPIC wonder why you're having them concentrate their aerial surveillance on Mazatlán? You can't keep this thing from the DEA if they're—"

Wilkes held up a hand to stop him. "Relax. The DEA is doing recon on Rojas, and they know I have an agent involved. My presence at the EPIC tactical operations center won't be unusual, although I imagine they'll begin wetting themselves when they see Trent take out Rojas's bodyguards and your car roll up. But even if the EPIC folks track you to the airport via satellite, they won't see where it lands. I've made sure all of our airborne tracking tools will lose the evac aircraft."

Max said, "That sounds complex."

"It will be. But really, I think hiding this operation from the

DEA should be much easier than hiding it from the cartels tomorrow night."

Max winced.

Renee looked pale.

Trent shrugged. "Easy day."

\* \* \*

Caleb and Trent left, and Max and Renee were alone in their room. He could tell that she was nervous, but also a little excited. He knew this because soon after they were alone, she finished her glass of wine in one gulp, turned out the lights, opened the balcony doors to allow the sea breeze and moon-light in, removed her dress to reveal a sexy black lace number, and began nibbling on his ear.

Latin America was known for being a land of passion. When in Rome...

Afterwards, the two lovers collapsed on top of the sheets, exhausted and covered in sweat.

"Thanks. I think I needed that," said Renee, kissing him lightly on the shoulder and nuzzling into his chest. Skin on skin, he could feel her heartbeat and heavy breathing as she recovered from exertion. Outside, the waves crashed on the beach, and a pale moon rose over the horizon.

She said, "Do you think tomorrow will go okay?"

"We've done our homework and taken precautions. We'll be alright."

"Then what's bothering you?"

Max looked at her.

"Nothing."

"Are you sure?"

"No."

"What, then?"

"I can't put my finger on it." He sighed. "It's probably just nerves. We'll be fine."

They fell asleep to the sound of the waves.

\* \* \*

The next night, Renee sat at the suite's only desk. A "do not disturb" sign hung on the outer doorknob. Max had placed it there when he'd left hours earlier. Her laptop was in front of her, connected only through its satellite antenna. A headset hung over her ears.

She spoke into the headset's boom microphone. "Check in, please."

"In position." Trent's voice.

"Present." Max sounded like a kindergartener speaking to his teacher.

Renee, Max, and Trent were the only people who would be speaking on the encrypted frequency. If Wilkes needed to contact them, Renee would see his message on her computer. She would then notify the team over their earpieces or via a burner phone that each of them carried.

Renee had contacted one of her trusted former CSE partners—a hacker, like her. Approved by Max, this person would help her to monitor the throngs of data she was being fed and ping her with only the most crucial elements. That would free her up to communicate with Max and Trent, giving them the vital real-time information that could make or break the mission. She was also getting the same overhead satellite and drone feed that EPIC was seeing, courtesy of Caleb Wilkes and his connections at the National Reconnaissance Office.

Trent said, "All parties have arrived. With a few extras."

"Extras?"

"Yup."

Renee saw what Trent and Max were talking about. There

were four guards outside the townhome, not the expected two. And instead of one woman and one man in the home—Rojas and Wilkes's agent—the rooftop patio was populated by two men and three women.

Max was right. Things hadn't even started yet, and they were already off script.

# CHAPTER 9

HUGO STOOD on the top floor of the seven-story parking garage at Reston Town Center in Northern Virginia. He watched as the BMW sedan crept to a halt just in front of him.

The man shut off his engine and exited the car. Ronald Dicks. The most senior aide to Senator Herbert Becker.

From the streets below came the sound of an urban outdoor luxury shopping center. The bustle of the crowd headed to chic restaurants and clothing stores. The happy hour crowd departing the bars. Young teens heading to the movies.

Up here it was quiet. Empty. Just two cars and two men. Neither man wanted to be seen with the other, although not for the same reasons.

"You're with the firm?" Dicks asked, referring to Joseph Dahlman's lobbying agency. Ron Dicks had used a back channel to contact them a day earlier. Dicks was trying to figure out a way to smooth things over.

So was Syed.

Unbeknownst to either party on the line, the ISI had listened to the phone call, provided courtesy of a Chinese communications security firm Syed had hired. Their capabilities were excellent.

Within an hour, the lobbying firm had received another phone call rescheduling the meeting for a later date. The voice on the phone was computer-generated, and a perfect match for Ron Dicks.

The ISI had then reached out to Dicks via text message and orchestrated a new meeting time and place. At a discreet location, just like the Senator's chief of staff had requested.

"I am with the firm, correct. Good evening, Mr. Dicks," Hugo replied, reaching out his hand.

Dicks walked towards Hugo, his own arm outstretched. They shook hands and then Hugo motioned for him to get in the passenger seat of Hugo's own vehicle. They both got in and shut the doors.

Dicks was jittery. "We need to find a solution here. Some common ground. I assume your firm is still in touch with the Pakistanis? This wasn't what I signed us up for. There's got to be some middle ground that we can—"

Hugo's movement was swift. He swung his arm across to the passenger side, landing a strong open-handed strike to the trachea.

Dicks' mouth let out an involuntary burst of spittle and air, and then he doubled over, making a choking noise and holding his throat. Hugo leaned back in his seat and looked around the still-empty parking lot. All clear. He opened up the center console of the sedan and removed a prepared syringe. He jabbed it into Dicks' neck and depressed the plunger until it met the stop.

Dicks' eyes went wide at the sting. His body was now flooded with a neuromuscular paralytic. The same type of drug anesthesiologists used, only in much smaller doses.

With Dicks still holding his throat, Hugo started the engine and drove his vehicle so that the passenger side was right next to the trunk of Dicks' BMW. Ron Dicks was now losing control of his faculties. Hugo put on a pair of thin flesh-colored latex gloves and cleaned up his car, careful to wipe off the parts that he'd touched.

He checked his victim by pulling back on his shoulder. A wheezing noise and a twitch of his eye told Hugo that the drug was still in effect. But things were far enough along now.

Hugo grabbed the keys from Dicks' pocket and popped his trunk by pressing the button on the key fob. He shut off his own engine, got out, walked around and quickly but casually transferred the still-alive body into the trunk. From his spot on the parking garage and the time of night, there was about a one percent chance that someone could have seen this activity, and a zero percent chance that someone would see his face.

He shut the trunk and then re-parked his car so that it was in a spot, not wanting to attract attention. Then he wiped it down once more.

Minutes later, he was driving Ron's BMW north towards the Potomac. It was dark by the time he reached Riverbend Park on the south side of the Potomac. He shut his lights off, broke the gate lock, and opened it, driving through towards the water. He arrived at a small boat landing a moment later. Here he was just to the west of Great Falls, where the river turned into a roaring grinder of white water and sharp rocks.

Hugo popped the trunk and removed the body, carrying it into the water and giving it a push into the current.

Ron Dicks' body was discovered the next day, bloated and battered and miles downstream.

# CHAPTER 10

*El Paso Intelligence Center*
*El Paso, Texas*

WILKES FOLLOWED the DEA assistant special agent in charge (ASAC) into the break room of the Task Force Echo ops center. The two men got a quick coffee fill-up before the long night, then walked down the hall towards the secure facility in the central part of the building.

"So your agent is on scene tonight?"

"That's right," said Wilkes.

"Hope she's careful. Sinaloa is rough."

Caleb Wilkes was nervous for his agent, Ines Sanchez. He wasn't sure she was ready for this kind of exposure, but in the field, one had to make do with the materials on hand. Wilkes had done his best to steer her away from kinetic operations involving the violent and unpredictable gangsters of her country.

Until tonight.

Ines Sanchez had grown up in Mexico City, where she had been a part-time model, part-time call girl. Her modeling career had led to a job as an actress for a syndicated soap opera

shot in Mexico City, and she'd stopped taking clients for her
secondary occupation.

Ines had had dreams of getting picked up by a Hollywood
agent and leaving Mexico for the US to become an actress
there. Wilkes had fanned those flames and offered to introduce
her to a few contacts he had in the City of Stars. The promise
of a better future was a case officer's best carrot.

She was young compared to most agents he ran—only
twenty-six. But she was effective, relatively reliable, and brave.
She seemed to get a kick out of working for Wilkes, and was
quite happy with the monthly "consulting fees" that were wired
to her numbered bank account on the island of Curaçao.

"Are you turning me into a spy?" she had asked him one
night, early after her recruitment.

"No, Ines. You're an actress. Think of me as your director.
On my stage, there aren't lights or cameras. There will be no
clapping audience or adoring fans waiting for you after the
show. But you'll have great rewards, if you want them. You'll
help to make the world a better place. And eventually, I'll help
you to become the star I know you can be."

She had liked that. The thought of doing good, and the
twinkle of future fame. Sanchez, like nearly everyone else on
the planet, just wanted a better life. When Wilkes had discovered her six months ago, she had been trying to sleep her way
to the leading role in her soap opera. Determined and shame-
less, but cleverer than most girls her age. Wilkes had seen
potential.

Three weeks after her recruitment, she had begun having
social visits with a Russian diplomat in Mexico City, one that
Wilkes had suggested could be a good person to know, if she
was looking for someone to buy her drinks for an evening.
From the Russian's careless pillow talk, Ines had been able to
provide Wilkes with the names of three SVR officers operating
out of the local Russian embassy. Two had been known opera-

tives, confirming the accuracy of the information. But the third name was new. Not bad work for the new girl.

With a little discipline and training on her part, and some Hollywood arm-twisting on his, Wilkes truly intended to make her into a full-fledged movie star. Then he could really put her to work. Wilkes's team of spies, which included Max Fend, were among the world's most rich and famous. They had exclusive access to elite clubs and social castes. Whether they achieved that status on their own or Wilkes grew them into it mattered little to him. He was about results.

But for Ines Sanchez to blossom into the productive Hollywood star and agent of the CIA, she needed to be alive and unscarred.

Tonight, that could prove to be a challenge.

Wilkes knew that his agent would likely end up in bed with Rojas this evening, and a part of him felt bad about that. But it came with the job. If a few moments of undesirable disgust for the girl meant bringing down one of the world's most powerful drug kingpins, and uncovering a highly placed American traitor, so be it. His occupation involved deception and moral ambiguities, and he had learned to live with that a long time ago.

"You been down here before?" asked the DEA escort as they walked down the hallway.

"First time," replied Wilkes.

The El Paso Intelligence Center (EPIC) was jointly run by the DEA and US Customs and Border Protection (CBP). More than a dozen other agencies were represented there as well. FBI, CIA, NSA, ATF—you name it. There were over three hundred employees in El Paso, all working diligently to counter the Mexican cartels. It was hard work. The drug war against Mexican cartels was a furnace, and each agent stationed here was another coal in the fire.

The DEA man slid his card through the door's electronic

reader, and they both entered the operations center, receiving a few hardened looks from the night crew. The mood inside the room was tense, but Wilkes got the impression that it was routine.

The DEA agent walked to his cluttered desk and sat on the front edge of his black adjustable chair. He scrolled through his messages, then brought up the surveillance schedule to show his CIA guest what was on tap for the night.

A drone flew over the Sierra Madre Mountains. A satellite pass was set up to provide live feed to this center via satellite. Several teams of human surveillance reported in throughout the region. The aerial surveillance video feeds were displayed on screens in the front of the room.

The DEA supervisor introduced Wilkes to his duty section crew. Wilkes asked which screens would show the townhome in Mazatlán where his agent was going to be. One of the DEA men pointed to the right monitor. The imagery was pretty clear but a little jumpy. One of the agents coordinating with the drone operator showed Wilkes how the high-resolution feed was able to toggle between full-color video, infrared, and night vision. The view now showed the front and rooftop patio of an upscale townhouse. A trio of petite, scantily clad women were drinking and dancing under an arbor on the roof. Two men sat at a table, beer bottles in front of them. The narcos.

"This is the drone?"

"Correct. That screen over there is the satellite. We'll have it for another hour. The NSA folks also have access to their signals intelligence during that timeframe."

"Got it."

In Wilkes's experience, the link was only so good whenever satellite comms were involved. But the sophisticated suite of sensors on board the bird would extract extremely valuable electronic data from the area, and that could drastically improve their situational awareness. The whole trade was going increasingly to cyber. Wilkes, like most from his generation, longed for the good old days of the Cold War. Give him a handheld radio and a 9mm Beretta any day.

Wilkes watched his girl on the monitor. One of the three dancing Latinas, gyrating with each other on the rooftop. The unfortunate object of one Hector Rojas's affection.

Rojas was a one-time big shot Mexico City accountant—if accountants can be called big shots. He had been scooped up by the Sinaloa cartel and promoted through the ranks when the previous head of cartel finance had been found missing his lower torso after a run-in with a competing enterprise.

Wilkes had arranged for Ines Sanchez to be introduced to Hector Rojas several months ago, at a party in Playa del Carmen. They had hit it off, but Wilkes had made sure that Ines left for the evening without giving him what he was looking for. She had flirted with Rojas over social media for the next few weeks, sending him revealing photographs and hinting that she would like to see him again.

The messages were carefully curated by a team at the CIA that specialized in psychological manipulation. Rojas could have his choice of beautiful local women. But Wilkes and the analysts calculated that the allure of bedding a semi-famous TV star would reel him in.

EPIC intelligence reports on Rojas indicated that he had several mistresses. But he dropped everything whenever Ines sent Rojas a message that she would be coming to town.

The trap was set.

Wilkes watched the girls dancing and felt internal pinpricks of stress increased in magnitude. He told himself to relax. Trent and Max were both in position. Wilkes had gotten the message from Renee. There were more people at the townhome than expected, but Max and Trent could overcome that. Everything would be fine.

A DEA agent at one of the computer terminals across the

room snapped his fingers to get his boss's attention, concentrating on something he was listening to on his headset.

"What is it?" the DEA supervisor asked.

"Boss, something's up. The NSA folks are picking up some unusual chatter from the narcos."

"About?"

"Several truckloads of foot soldiers, all moving fast."

"What the hell are you talking about? Where are they going?"

The DEA man pointed at the video display. "There. The narcos are sending a shitload of guys to that townhouse."

Wilkes face went white.

\* \* \*

Trent Carpenter sat alone in the darkness, looking through the blinds to the cartel townhouse across the street. Performing clandestine street-level surveillance was painstaking, tiresome work. He was perched like an eagle, eyeing its prey from high up, observing everything in silence.

He'd been here for over ten hours. Three plastic one-gallon water jugs lay on the floor next to him. Two were still for drinking. One was now for peeing. As the only surveillance operator with a clear view across the street, he couldn't risk leaving his post.

A high-res camera stood on a tripod next to him, its imagery uplinked to a satellite one hundred miles above the surface of the earth and then relayed down to Renee's computers. Max had helped him set it up earlier, along with a few other cool devices that could pick up nearby cell phones and activate their receivers, but Trent wouldn't touch those toys unless he had to. Renee was doing all that.

On the floor at his feet was his own set of tools. A large black canvas bag filled with weapons and gear. Trent watched the narco security guards on the street, standing outside their pickup trucks, smoking and shooting the shit. Their bosses on the outdoor patio on the roof, dancing with the full-breasted beauties—imports from Mexico City, one of whom was a CIA informant. He fought the urge to lift up his suppressed rifle from the floor and begin picking them off right now.

These were the men that had made money off the death of his brother. Josh, a father, husband, brother, son, and decorated veteran. Now a dead heroin junkie—a statistic in the war on drugs. A deep rage swelled up inside him whenever Trent thought about it. Which was often.

Trent wasn't completely sure that he trusted this CIA guy, Wilkes. But he trusted Max Fend. Fend was a good dude, and Trent had the feeling that they were both here for the same reason.

Guilt. Or justice. Or some combination of the two. Trent kept thinking that maybe if he had killed or captured enough narcos, or stopped enough drug shipments back when he was here with his special operations team, Josh would still be alive. He knew it was a stupid thought, but that didn't stop it from popping into his mind.

During Trent's time as a special operations advisor to the DEA in Mexico, he'd learned the truth about counternarcotics. The big arrests were only temporary wins. And even those were rare occurrences. Normally law enforcement didn't catch anyone of consequence. Even when they did catch one of the kingpins, if the guy was locked up in Mexico, half the time he still ran his operation from the joint. Those prisons were often nothing more than posh luxury hotels set up as narco penalty boxes. Sometimes the wardens and guards were on the cartel payroll. The guards that didn't go along with it either quit or were found dead. Suicide, with three bullets in their head. Shit.

Tonight would be satisfying. There were several more narcos than expected, but eventually the party would die down and people would go to sleep. If not, Trent and Max had talked about waiting until two or three in the morning and taking them when they were most vulnerable. There were four security guards, and two more narcos inside. Trent was pretty sure he'd have no problem with those odds, especially since he had the first-mover advantage. With Max's help, they were sure to succeed.

"Trent, come in," came Renee's voice through his headset, breaking his train of thought.

Max and Trent had told her to check on them every fifteen minutes. Trent looked at his watch. She was very precise.

"Gentlemen, Wilkes just sent me a warning. Something is wrong. The cartel is sending multiple vehicles towards your position."

Max said over the radio, "ETA?"

"A few minutes, tops."

* * *

Max was in a beat-up-looking sedan about one hundred yards down the street from Trent's position, parked in a lot that gave him a view of the townhome and surroundings.

"Renee, give us more info. What do you have?" said Max.

Renee said, "A few minutes ago, the drone picked up a spike in electronic emissions from the narcos' cellular devices. The NSA techs matched the movements to multiple vehicles moving in the area. The conversations say they're showing up at Rojas's pad. What do we do, Max?"

*Dammit.*

"Hold tight. Trent, be ready to evac through the rear of your building and I'll pick you up."

"Copy."

Max knew that the imagery and electronic sensors were

provided by American drones based out of an Air Force base in Texas. With the quiet approval of the Mexican government, the drones flew almost nightly reconnaissance missions over areas where the cartels ran their operations. But analysis from a drone usually wasn't that accurate in such a short timeframe. Was it possible this was a false alarm? Maybe the cartel trucks weren't really headed there. Maybe they were just going nearby.

Trent's voice. "Vehicles spotted. There they are."

Damn.

Max could see them too. A convoy of dark pickup trucks and SUVs came to a halt on the steep curb just outside Rojas's townhome.

A twinge of fear crept up Max's spine as he watched at least a dozen armed men exit the vehicles.

*Shit. Shit. Shit.*

Renee's voice was in his ear, saying what he was thinking. "Do they know we're here?"

* * *

Trent slowed his breathing and held still. Even though he was behind closed shades in an unlit room, his instincts warned him of the increased danger. It seemed like half the Sinaloa cartel was forming up on the streets just outside his window. Through the cracks in the window shades, he saw the lights of other homes on the street flicker on. The residents were probably nervous about the sudden influx of cartel muscle, maybe sensing that these men weren't the usual type.

"Trent, what are you seeing?"

He answered Max on the radio. "I count twelve additional narcos. They look well armed and are securing the perimeter like pros. Hold up."

Some tall white dude got out of the back of one of the vehicles. He yelled something in Spanish and pointed down the street, with men scurrying about as he did.

"There's a Caucasian male. Tall guy. Probably six five. Looks like he's in charge by the way they're taking orders from him. He's entering the house now, with several of his men."

\* \* \*

Max's head was spinning. This was like watching a nightmare play out in real time.

One of the newly arrived trucks suddenly moved down the block towards Max. He gripped his keys and the wheel, bracing himself.

Then the truck made a hard left turn and positioned itself perpendicular to the empty traffic lanes, cutting off the town-home's street entrance. Two men stood in the bed of the truck, small machine guns slung across their chests. Another narco got out of the passenger seat and stood on the street corner. Each of the men held his weapon in a way that told Max they'd had military training. Their eyes searched the streets, alert and professional.

Max whispered, "We may need to call this off. I've got three of them about twenty yards away from me. They get any closer, and I'm made."

"You wanna abort?"

"Stand by. Not yet."

A tall white guy in charge of a bunch of armed narcos, arriving unexpectedly. Max had a good idea of who it was.

Blanco.

Their mystery man had arrived.

\* \* \*

Renee's knee bounced under the table as her eyes flipped through the multiple windows she had open on her laptop.

On one hand, this was good news. They were finally getting eyes on Blanco, head of security for the Sinaloa cartel. But sitting here in this luxury hotel, miles from the action, she became deeply worried about the safety of Trent, Max, and Wilkes's agent inside the building.

On her computer, Renee monitored the video feed being broadcast from Trent's tripod camera. El Blanco was almost a foot taller than the others and had a long, confident stride. He barked something to one of Rojas's security men and then walked up the front steps. One of them held the door as El Blanco entered the townhome, several of his own men in tow. She could see them through the lit windows as they headed up the stairs.

"Lot of dudes," said Trent in a somber voice. "They don't look like they're here to party."

"Do we have audio?" asked Max. "Can we listen in to what they're saying?"

Renee said, "Stand by."

She typed a message to her hacker colleague who was assisting her from several thousand miles away. A few clicks and a moment later, one of her computer windows showed the audio signature of muffled Spanish-speaking voices. Renee was now using any phones that they thought were in the cartel's building as eavesdropping devices. The audio was then run through a translation program, and text was populating on another window on her computer.

Renee said, "We've narrowed it down to a few mobile devices. There are a few others that we think might be located in the home, but I don't want to clutter it up as we aren't sure. I'll tell you what they say."

On the monitor, Renee watched as Blanco appeared on the rooftop lounge area, pointing at the girls and issuing orders.

"Rojas looks pissed," said Trent.

Renee clicked on the audio options to listen to the raw data. The music on the rooftop stopped as Blanco had it turned off. Two of the girls were made to sit down at the center table.

Blanco pointed at the third girl.

Ines Sanchez. Wilkes's agent.

Renee's heart pounded in her chest.

One of the narcos walked up to Sanchez and placed a canvas bag over her head. Another man zip-tied her hands behind her back.

"Max, they're taking her. They just put a bag over her head."

Trent said, "What do you want me to do?"

Max's voice. "Continue to monitor and report. Do not move from your position."

"Roger."

"Renee, what are they saying?"

Renee was reading the translated text. "Looks like Blanco is breaking up the party. He's taking the girl and telling them to leave the building."

"Which girl?"

"Ours."

Trent's voice was intense. Begging to be set loose. "You want me to intervene?"

"Negative. There are over a dozen of them, and they appear to be the varsity team," replied Max.

On the monitor, Renee observed an intense argument between a surprised-looking Rojas and El Blanco. Clearly Rojas was not happy about losing his prize for the evening.

Renee heard Blanco say in English, "Take one of these bitches instead."

"Sounds like a British accent," Renee said.

"Who?"

"I just heard him say something to Rojas. Blanco sounds like he's from the UK."

Renee dug her fingernails into her palms, feeling horrified and helpless. She watched the Mexican men carry Ines Sanchez down the stairs, kicking and struggling with the bag still covering her head. Max had told Renee what the cartels did to people who cooperated with law enforcement. Their mutilations were usually made public—a message that ensured loyalty from the others.

Ines was pushed into the backseat of the rear SUV. Blanco and his vehicles, including the one parked near Max, peeled out and sped off.

The radios were quiet.

# CHAPTER 11

MAX WATCHED as the narco pickup truck that had been parked close to him departed with its men.

"Is Hector Rojas still in the building?"

"Affirm. He looks like he's gotten over his lost love and is now on to one of the other girls there."

Max was appalled that this Blanco character had just bagged Wilkes's agent and was now driving her away. He realized what had been bothering him the night before, when Renee had asked.

The DEA and others at EPIC knew about Wilkes's agent.

Wilkes had said he was working with the CIA's counterintelligence division. At first, Max had assumed that was just because a foreign intelligence service—the ISI—was involved. But what if there was more to it than that? What if Wilkes was hunting a mole? Blanco had to have found out about Ines Sanchez somehow.

Max couldn't do anything about a leak right now. On the other hand, he *could* do something about Hector Rojas. The senior finance executive of the Sinaloa cartel was still in the townhome, having a good time. As far as Max was concerned, the mission was still on.

Rojas was still on the roof with one of the girls. And there were the remaining four guards on street level, each one carrying an AR-style rifle.

Trent had what he needed. He'd briefed the mission. Knew all the possible options for entry and evacuation.

A buzzing in Max's pocket. He looked at his phone. It was Wilkes, sending a message to the team. Apparently he had the same idea as Max.

*TAKE HIM.*

Max said, "Listen up. We'll need to improvise."

\* \* \*

Wilkes stood on the operations floor of EPIC, feeling pissed and guilty at the loss of his agent.

Unlike Max and team, he hadn't had the street-level view of the Caucasian man and still had no knowledge of Blanco's involvement. But he'd seen the beacon in his agent's phone from the bird's-eye view of the drone as she was stuffed into the backseat of the narcos' SUV.

And that definitely wasn't in the plan.

The tracking beacon was tossed out the window while they were driving on the highway. The drone had kept tracking the SUV into the brightly lit city center. The drone operators did their best to follow the girl as they brought her into a large apartment building. There were so many people and vehicles in the area that it would be almost impossible to monitor all the exits.

Which was why they had taken her there, Caleb knew.

She was blown, and they were escaping into obscurity.

Wilkes's worst fears were realized. The leak the CIA had suspected was now confirmed. He hadn't told Max or team about that aspect of the mission, because they'd needed to keep the information as tight as possible in order to catch their mole. But the fact that they'd known about Ines Sanchez drastically narrowed their list of suspects. Someone with access to a high level of intel was responsible for tonight's epic screwup. Without his agent, Max's team would have a harder time taking Rojas.

But it could still be done, which was why he'd sent his message. Sanchez was as good as gone, he knew. But right now, they needed to salvage what they could.

Wilkes waited for word of Max's movement while also thinking about what he would report to his superiors, mourning the loss of his agent, and sifting through possible leakers all at once.

"Oh shit, did you guys just see that?" A DEA agent on the watch floor had stood up, pointing at the front monitor.

The DEA supervisor said, "See what?"

"Quick, look—one of the security guards just went down."

Wilkes saw what he was talking about. The two security guards who had been standing on the front stairs of the home were now on the ground. The drone feed was back over the townhome, zoomed in and using color video thanks to the bright streetlights. A dark blur was visible on the pavement, expanding away from the head of a dead narco. The doors of the second truck swung open and two more men ran out, holding rifles.

"Those are more security men? Or did they just shoot the first two?"

"I don't know."

"They came from the second truck. I think they're just responding. Doesn't look like they know where the shots came from." The men were turning frantically, holding their weapons out, but not firing.

The two men flailed backwards and fell to the ground. The DEA agent placed her headset on and spoke to the drone operator.

"Somebody's taking them all out. They're moving on Rojas."

Wilkes leaned forward, placing his hands on the desk as he stared at the drone feed. A lone figure ran across the screen, past the four bodies of the narco security detail that now lay dead and motionless in the street.

* * *

From his second-floor window, Trent had a clear shot of all four men. Less than twenty-five yards. Child's play for someone with his experience. He fired four shots from his suppressed rifle within a six-second window. The shell casings landed silently on the soft rug at his feet. He scooped them up and placed them in a zippered pocket while he scanned the streets for movement. Nothing. He was satisfied to see that each bullet had been lethal.

"I'm on the move."

"Copy. I'll bring my car in front of the house on your word," replied Max. Trent was glad to see that he was done arguing that point. At first, Max had insisted on entering the home with him. But Trent was worried about the response time of narco reinforcements.

He grabbed the black bag filled with gear and hurried down the stairs, holding his rifle in front of him, finger pointed forward on the trigger guard. Crossing the dark street, he heard the deep bass notes of the beach resort dance clubs a few blocks away, and the distant rumble of summer storms out over the Pacific. Voices echoed from several floors above.

The sounds of drunken laughter and music. A good sign. It was the sound of targets unaware of his imminent approach.

As he moved, he calculated risk and felt the quick ticking of his internal stopwatch. It was only a matter of time before someone saw the dead men on the street. With half the city on the cartel's payroll, other narcos were sure to come. Trent didn't want to be here when they did.

He crept past the corpses still bleeding and spasming on the sidewalk, scanning the area for threats. The front door was unlocked, as he had expected. In Sinaloa cartel territory, with sicarios guarding outside, why would they lock it?

A moment later, Trent was up one flight of stairs. He could hear one of the narcos in the bedroom. Trent laid down his bag of gear, placed one hand on the doorknob, and readied his rifle with the other.

With one lightning-fast movement, he opened the door, sent a single suppressed shot through the head of the man, and ran forward to cover the mouth of the shocked half-naked woman on the bed, just as she began to scream. Trent tore off a strip of duct tape hanging from his belt and covered her mouth. Then he hog-tied her and left her on the bed.

Trent reshouldered his bag of gear and vaulted up the final flight of stairs. It had been approximately forty-five seconds since he had entered the home. Two minutes since he had killed the men outside on the street. His internal clock continued to tick.

Trent placed the rifle on the floor and removed the large weapon that had been fastened to his back, a rushing sound in his ears as adrenaline pumped through his veins. From the doorway, he couldn't see his targets, but he could still hear them, unaware. Trent stepped out onto the rooftop patio, weapon trained forward.

Incandescent bulbs hung along the outer perimeter of the rooftop, illuminating the area with a dim yellow light. Two couches and several potted plants lined the walls, and a long wooden table rested in the center of the space. An open bottle of wine with two glasses sat on the table. His target was sitting on a chair at the head of the table, with his newly appointed mistress for the evening straddling him, facing away from Trent.

Trent whistled loud.

Both of their faces snapped toward him, and Rojas threw the half-dressed Latina off his lap. The woman instinctively covered herself. Rojas reached for the pistol on the table.

Trent held an M32A1 multishot grenade launcher with two hands, the stock pressed to his shoulder and the wide barrel pointed at Rojas. It was a bulky weapon, painted a drab green, with a round ammunition cylinder similar to a tommy gun. It was designed to hold 40mm grenades, but that wasn't what Trent had loaded into the weapon just now.

As Rojas reached for his pistol on the table, Trent took aim through a holographic sight, its infrared laser designator targeting the man's hairy chest.

THUNK.

A single 40mm blunt-impact projectile round shot into the right side of the man's chest at a speed of 290 feet per second. The round mushroomed on impact, transferring all of its kinetic energy into Rojas's body. This resulted in Rojas departing his feet and flying backward into the air, his arms and legs in trail. He landed hard on his back about five feet away, a motionless heap, breathless on the tiled floor.

The woman screamed.

Trent held a lone finger up to his lips, pointing the weapon at her and advancing in her direction. Trent thought about shooting her too, but these "less-lethal" rounds had once been called "nonlethal." The company's lawyers had insisted upon the change in marketing terminology for a reason—they were known to be unintentionally fatal to a certain percentage of people they hit. Especially at this range.

Trent placed the grenade launcher on the table, walked over to his second nude and screaming woman in the past minute, removed another strip of duct tape, and went to work. He wrapped her mouth until no sound came out. She could still breathe through her nose. He tied her hands and feet together as well.

Trent could now hear Rojas wheezing from a few feet away. Thank God. He would have been pissed if this had all been for nothing.

Leaving the girl tied up, he went to work on Rojas next, quickly using the same duct tape technique to immobilize, blind, and gag him.

Trent unzipped his large black duffle bag and opened it on the floor. He fought his own disgust as he threw the mostly naked man into the bag and zipped it back up.

He brought his boom mike down to his lips. "Max, I'm going to be ready for you at the front entrance in thirty seconds."

Max didn't sound happy. "Uh, that's going to be a problem."

It was at this point that Trent heard the sound of multiple vehicles skidding to a stop on the streets below.

* * *

Max, still in the lot down the street from Trent, counted the vehicles now parking outside the townhome. Five...six...seven if you counted the police car with lights flashing.

Renee was in his ear. "SIGINT is showing massive cartel movements into the area. There are also police coming. But they're on the same radio frequency as the narcos, so I don't think that's good for us."

Max said, "Trent, can you get to the pre-positioned vehicle using your alternate exit?"

"I think so, yes."

"Do it, and let me know when you're safe in the car. If you can get clear, I'll pick up Renee and we'll meet you at the airport. If not, let me know and I'll pick you up at the check-point bravo."

"Wilco."

Max said, "Renee, is Wilkes's CIA plane at the airport yet?"

"He just sent me a message about that. He said that there was a problem with the plane. Something about the size. But it's there."

"What's wrong with the plane size?"

"He didn't elaborate."

Max turned on his car and slowly left his lot, turning away from the townhome. In his rearview mirror, he could see the streets rapidly filling up with vehicles.

\* \* \*

Trent could hear the sound of car doors slamming below. Curses echoing through the street. He risked a peek over the stucco wall.

*Sonofabitch.*

There were too many of them to fight his way back across the street, where his primary egress path lay. Trent counted five trucks. Dozens of heavily armed men, inspecting the dead bodies and looking around.

Trent forced himself to remain calm and think through the problem. The narcos had arrived several minutes quicker than he had anticipated. An unusually fast response. They hadn't yet entered the house. Instead they seemed to be massing outside, preparing to swarm his position with overwhelming force. Wonderful.

Trent pressed the ammo quick-release lever on the grenade launcher and grabbed the other cartridge of ammunition from his bag. This ammunition had the letters "HE" on the sides. High-explosive. He twisted the new ammo cartridge slowly over the cartridge cylinder, like a giant six-shooter from an old western. It fit into place and Trent pressed it in, locking it and snapping it shut.

Trent crept atop the wall again and aimed the bulky grenade launcher at the mass of narco foot soldiers below. He pulled the trigger in rapid succession.

THUNK. THUNK. THUNK.

Ricochets of high-explosive rounds ripped through the streets as Trent unloaded his magazine. Metal fragments shot through vehicles and flesh. After the burst of chaos, the only remaining sounds were the faint moans of the injured. A putrid smell hung in the air.

Trent didn't wait to evaluate the damage. He dropped the grenade launcher where he stood, then squatted down and heaved the zippered body bag containing his prisoner over his right shoulder. Gritting his teeth under the strain, he grabbed his rifle with his free hand and jogged down the stairs and towards the second-floor bedroom.

From the pattern-of-life intel reports they had studied, he knew this was where he would find a custom-built passageway connecting to the adjacent townhome.

Trent found a door behind a standing mattress, which he nudged over with the tip of his rifle. The mattress fell to the floor, and Trent unbolted the door.

He entered the passageway and closed the door behind him just as he heard the first shouts of men entering the narco home.

Now in the adjacent townhome, Trent raced down the stairs, still performing a fireman's carry of his now-squirming prisoner. He ran past a scared-looking family huddled in the kitchen. Two kids behind their mom. A grandma next to them. Trent ignored the family, continuing down to their basement.

Towards the tunnel.

The tunnel was one of many that the cartel had created for quick escapes at several safe houses throughout the city.

Human intelligence had revealed the existence of this particular tunnel to Trent's team, and it had been listed in the mission brief as an "alternate extraction route."

He flipped the lights of the basement on and looked around. Cobwebs and a leaking pipe in the far corner. And a large piece of plywood that was nailed to the wall. Trent walked up to the plywood, pounding. A dull, hollow sound.

The tunnel entrance. He pushed it forward and it gave a bit, rotating upward on a ceiling-mounted hinge.

Shouts and screams from above. The sicarios had entered the home. His shoulder-mounted passenger was now doing his best to give muffled shouts through his well-taped gag.

Trent kept his rifle slung over his shoulder and repositioned the body bag so that he was holding it in front of him with both hands. He used the man's squirming, wrapped body as a battering ram as he forced his way into the wooden tunnel entrance, lifting it and moving forward. The wood slammed down once they were through. Rojas would have a few more bruises. Screw him.

But while the tunnel allowed for a quick escape, he expected the narcos to continue pursuit. Trent grabbed a small device from his waist pack and placed it on the floor, careful to position the shaped charge so that it faced the entrance. He set the motion detector and backed away slowly. Then he once again heaved the body bag over his shoulder and ran down the dark tunnel, carrying Rojas toward a faint bluish light that he prayed was the exit.

Seconds later he was stepping through a concrete cylinder eight feet in diameter—the kind used in constructing an underground sewer—with the tunnel exit in view. He forced his way through the thin metal screen at the opening and stepped out into the night.

Trent found himself underneath the highway overpass, a scant few hundred yards from the narco home.

A detonation behind him shattered the still night.

The mine had exploded on the other side of the tunnel. Adrenaline still racing through his veins, he ran to the nondescript sedan that had been pre-positioned under the highway overpass earlier that day by Max. Trent removed the key fob from his pocket and clicked the button, hearing the unlocking sound and seeing the lights flash. Trent opened the trunk and stuffed the man inside, then slammed the lid back down.

He removed his black tactical vest with its heavy SAPI plate and left it on the ground. Then he placed a ball cap on, started the vehicle, and drove. With his spare hand, he reached to his microphone and pulled it to his lips. "I'm moving."

## CHAPTER 12

MAX AND RENEE arrived at the airport just as Trent pulled in. They were on the opposite side of the main terminal, where only a few business jets were on the unlit tarmac, along with a tiny light-sport aircraft.

"Where's the plane?" asked Max.

Renee said, "Wilkes assured me it would be here."

Trent got out of his car, the sound of a million police sirens in the distance. They each knew that the cartel would be looking for those who had caused all that carnage and kidnapped their man.

"What the hell? What are we doing sitting around with our thumbs up our assess? Where's the CIA plane?"

Max saw a dim green flash from the cockpit of the light-sport aircraft.

"Oh crap."

Max walked over to the tiny plane and sure enough, the door opened, and a man got out.

"You Max?" the man said in Mexican-accented English.

"Yeah."

"Wilkes sent me. Said you need transportation."

The silence of the still night air was interrupted by acceler-

ANDREW WATTS

ating vehicles. Max turned to see two black pickup trucks racing along the perimeter of the road.

Trent said, "Looks like they're heading towards the main terminal. We need to get out of here. They'll check here next."

Max nodded, turning back to the pilot. "How many can you carry?"

The short Hispanic aviator looked between the group. "I only have room for one."

Trent, hearing this, carried the squirming body bag with Rojas over to the pilot and dropped it at his feet.

"What...the hell...is *that*?"

"Cargo."

"Hey, man, I'm not taking it by myself. It's going to be a seven-hour flight, with a fuel stop in the middle."

Trent removed a nonaerosol tranquilizer gun from his bag, unzipped the body bag to reveal a blindfolded and gagged Rojas, stuck him in the shoulder, and then zipped him back up.

"That should last him a few hours. He might need another shot before you guys reach your landing spot."

Max looked at Trent. "What do you mean 'you guys'? We won't be able to fit. Listen, Renee and I have a cover here. And I'm...connected. We'll go back to the hotel and make a call to Wilkes and get them to get us out of here."

Trent frowned. "This is not going to be a good place for you to be. If anyone sees you come back right now—"

"We'll be alright. You need to get in and go now, before we get spotted. If Rojas starts squirming, stick him again, but be careful not to give him too big a dose."

"I'm familiar."

Max turned to Renee. "We need to get out of here and back to the hotel immediately."

She looked scared but nodded and got back into the car.

A moment later, Trent was stuffed into one side of the

light-sport aircraft with his sedated prisoner sitting on his lap. The aircraft buzzed away to the north.

Max and Renee went to a restaurant near their hotel, grabbed a drink, and then came back to the hotel, laughing and hoping that the concierge got a whiff of alcohol as they made their way up to the suite.

* * *

In the room, Max whispered to Wilkes on the secure phone. Their doors and windows were locked, and Renee sat next to Max on the bed, listening in.

"What the hell happened?"

Wilkes said, "I was going to ask you the same thing. What did you see?"

Max went over the events of the evening from their point of view. Every few moments, a police siren sounded outside, and flashing lights shone through the cracks in the shutters as vehicles sped down the road.

Max said, "You've got a mole, Caleb."

He didn't reply.

"We need protection and evac as soon as possible. Do you have any teams here?"

Wilkes said, "I'm working on it. But you'll need to stay the night."

Max closed his eyes. It wasn't the news he had wanted to hear. Every moment they remained was another inch closer to someone connecting them to a street filled with dead narcos.

"Can't we just use our car and drive to—"

"No." Wilkes cut him off. "They've got road blocks set up everywhere. No one's getting out of Mazatlán tonight."

Renee cursed under her breath.

"Did you get the images Renee sent you of Blanco?"

"I did. We're running them through facial recognition software now. Good work. Just sit tight, guys. We'll have a safe transport for you in the morning."

* * *

After a sleepless night, Max and Renee walked through the hotel lobby. A car was waiting to take them to the airport. While Wilkes was supposedly working on arranging for someone to come pick them up, Max wasn't taking any chances. He'd contacted his father's assistant. A Fend corporate jet, designated for his father's personal use, was due to arrive in Mazatlán any moment.

"Hold up." Max grabbed Renee's arm as a convoy of SUVs, looking very much like the ones from the night before, pulled up outside the hotel.

"Oh shit."

A group of armed men emerged, holding AR-style rifles. Max and Renee turned around, hoping to find another exit. As Max was about to tell Renee to run, a second team of gunmen came in the back of the lobby.

"Cell phones and computers, please," one of them said, holding out an open backpack. Another had his weapon trained on them.

Max and Renee froze.

The man repeated the command, louder, and stepped towards them. Max and Renee gave them their cell phones and Renee removed her computer from her bag, handing it over.

One of the gunmen frisked them both.

At least a dozen narcos entered the lobby and walked towards the ocean view restaurant in the back of the hotel. Max noticed that the concierge didn't seem surprised or worried. Probably the one who had contacted the narcos. Everyone was on the payroll.

A British-accented voice said, "I hope you would consider having breakfast with me. I hear the menu here is excellent."

Max turned to see a very tall white man walk in.

The mystery man. Blanco.

He wore a tailored two-button blue suit, sans tie. A bright white well-starched collar. Polished brown wingtips. Sunken cheeks and piercing gray eyes.

He held out his hand. "Ian Williams. I suppose you can provide that to everyone who must be trying to find out my name right now. And you are Max Fend. Maxwell? Maximus?"

Max shook his hand, keeping his face impassive. "Just Max."

"And you must be Renee LaFrancois? Your beauty precedes you."

The cartel gunmen spread out around the restaurant, collecting cell phones from startled patrons who were eating their breakfast. Two of the narcos headed back into the kitchen. Max recognized what was going on. Their protectee was a high-value target. They only intended to stay here for a moment and didn't want anyone giving away the location of Ian Williams.

"We were actually just leaving," said Max.

"No, you weren't." Williams's reply was thick with authority. "You were about to have breakfast with me."

His eyes darted between Max and the rest of the room. He licked his lips and scrunched his face when he talked. Some sort of nervous tic. *Something's wrong with this guy's circuit board. Beware.* Max cursed himself for bringing Renee to Mexico.

Ian Williams led them over to a spot in the covered open-air hotel restaurant with a view of the ocean. The waiter appeared at once, looking jumpy. Williams ordered in Spanish, and the waiter left with an expression of relief.

Max and Renee sat completely still. Max re-counted the number of sicarios in the room—twelve. They each carried black semiautomatic rifles and watched the crowd for any sign of a problem, with special attention given to Max. The frightened-looking patrons kept their eyes on their plates. Max could hear the distant sound of the waves crashing against the shore, tropical birds chirping outside, and light music playing over the restaurant speakers.

But no conversation. Everyone was probably too scared they might be slaughtered by whoever this cartel madman was. They knew what happened to those who showed anything but the utmost deference to the cartel kings and knights who traveled the countryside in their armed convoys.

Williams began, "You know I was made aware of your arrival a few days ago. One of my many reports—notables traveling through our territory." He smiled, his gaze darting again with the wild eyes, and a pop came from his lips.

"We've been on vacation."

Williams began shaking his head with short bursts of motion, his pointer finger slicing Max's proclamation into shreds. "People don't vacation here. Not people like you. But I said to myself, Max Fend is a fellow traveler. Let him enjoy the sweet offerings of the Sinaloa beaches. Sip a few piña coladas. Dip his feet in the water. But then *last night* happens…"

He paused, peering into both Max and Renee's eyes, waiting for a reaction. A deafening, uncomfortable silence. But no reaction. Williams said, "It *stank* of American haughtiness. So, I did what any good investigator does. I thoroughly evaluated all of the information available to me, paying close attention to the details. The devil is in the details, you know, Mr. Fend. We've had very little unusual activity in this area, but for your arrival. That, as I said before, was notable. Not exactly what you and I, being from civilized countries, would say meets the burden of proof, if I were to accuse you of a crime. But, Max… *Max*…I hesitate to inform you and your lovely companion, lest I scare the royal shit out of you both, but my business associates here cut off limbs for much less than the coincidence of timing."

Ian Williams paused again, cocking his head. Getting no response, he continued, "So then, the proximity of your arrival to last night's horrific violence—what am I to make of it?"

The restaurant was deathly quiet. Ian Williams was the Cheshire cat, licking his lips and in need of a psychological evaluation.

"Mr. Williams, I'm sorry, but we're only here on vaca—"

Williams slammed his fists down on the table, the silverware rattling. Then he whispered, "Where were you last night?"

"We went for dinner and drinks," Max answered calmly. He turned to Renee. "What was the name of the—"

Williams clicked his tongue, his head moving side to side again in rapid tiny shakes, an ugly frown forming on his face. "No. Please. Just stop."

Max kept still as an uncomfortable silence resumed. Ian Williams's gray eyes studying his prey. He took a deep breath. "This would go much better for you if you don't play dumb. Do you know who I am?"

Max answered truthfully, "No. Should I?"

"I know who you are. I know all about you, Max Fend. And you, Miss LaFrancois. Not a 'Mrs.' yet? Tsk tsk, Max. Where's the ring?"

Max had to admit that while he was prepared for just about anything Williams might say to throw him off balance, he wasn't expecting *that* to be a topic of conversation.

Williams smiled for the first time, revealing a crooked and discolored set of teeth. "Never mind. Excuse the poor manners. But, Renee, should you grow tired of his antics, feel free to come visit. I'll show you some proper appreciation."

Renee's face went crimson.

Max shook his head. "Sorry, buddy, but she'd eat you alive. Trust me."

Williams laughed, an awkward-sounding guffaw that revealed more bad teeth. "Let's cut to the chase. An interesting night it was, eh? I must admit that I don't quite yet know what to make of it. I show up and pay a visit to a colleague, Mr. Rojas..."

He paused to gauge the facial reactions of Max and Renee at the mention of Rojas.

"And I happen to find a woman with him who I now know was working as an informant against my employer."

He paused again, watching their expressions. Max was confident in his own poker face. He wasn't so sure about Renee's.

"Now, several events occurred after I removed Miss Sanchez from the premises, resulting in death, dismemberment, and what I suspect to be Hector Rojas's kidnapping by you Americans. Perhaps the DEA, but I doubt it. The CIA? Now why would they be involved? And how warm might I be, *Max*?"

Max shrugged. "I wouldn't know."

Ian Williams said, "But now you tell me that you were out eating and drinking and enjoying this shithole of a country. Okay. Okay. Ah. Here we are. Let us pause..."

Williams's eyes lit up as their food came. Hot plates of tortillas, beans, a red ranchero sauce, limes, and two fried eggs, sunny-side up.

Renee was silent, but Max could feel her unease. She stared at her plate, not wanting to look up.

Max couldn't help himself. "I presume that if you plan to kill me, you'll shoot me, not poison me, right?"

Renee slowly turned to him, horrified.

Williams lifted a glass of juice in a toast and winked in response. "Right you are, Max. Right you are. Eat up."

Max nodded. Then he took one of the tortillas and made it into a sandwich.

Renee looked back down to her plate and closed her eyes.

"Can I also presume that since we're still here, eating in this restaurant and not at some exclusive private residence of yours, you intend to let us go after this conversation?"

Williams nodded. "I can see that you're a man of unmatched deductive reasoning." He swallowed a forkful of food. "Max, we both understand that it is the nature of my business that there will be the occasional unpleasantries such as what occurred last night."

Max could see the two narco gunmen glaring at him, holding their weapons. They were probably friends with the dead.

"But there is a more important matter I need to resolve. I want only to find my associate. It is *imperative* that I find him. Now, my belief is that your arrival here in Mazatlán, and your past employment history, are much too coincidental. But...by the same token, I will grant you that any man of your experience, Mr. Fend, would be a complete fool to stick around after last night's fiasco occurred, if they were indeed a part of it. So, maybe you really were here for innocent reasons? Let me ask you." He looked at Renee. "Both of you. Do you know where my associate, Hector Rojas, is located?"

"I'm afraid we don't," Max answered.

Renee shook her head, "No." Her voice was soft.

Williams just nodded. "I thought so."

Williams turned to one of his gunmen and nodded towards the beach. The gunman headed through the lobby, towards the hotel's street entrance.

Max watched Williams's expression grow dark. He recognized this look. Men like him felt the need to demonstrate power. Whatever was about to happen was a warning.

Heads turned at the sound of a woman's scream. The double doors to the hotel's front entrance flung open as two of the sicarios walked back in, rifles slung over their backs. In their arms, the men carried a bloodied woman. She had deep lacerations along her back and breasts, and her dark hair was matted with dried blood. She swayed and whimpered as they carried her through the hotel lobby and restaurant area, then out towards the beach.

Renee's hand went up over her mouth, and Max noticed her eyes watering. As the men hauled the woman through the restaurant area, some of the patrons let out gasps. But many just looked away, not wanting to be a witness to whatever the narcos might do. Max moved to stand up, but the sicario behind him forced him back into his seat and pointed his weapon at Max's head.

They dumped the woman on the beach, just twenty yards in front of the restaurant, a disturbed flock of seagulls clearing the area as they did. One of the gunmen propped her up on her knees.

Williams said, "Now, I think there's a good way to determine if you are or are not working with the American intelligence or drug enforcement agencies. This woman here, Miss Sanchez. Is she a spy?"

Max didn't answer. Neither did Renee.

Williams nodded, his tone sterner. "Do you know where Rojas was taken?"

No answer.

Renee was beginning to breathe heavy as she watched the woman on the beach kneeling down like she was about to be executed. Williams saw Renee's reaction and leaned towards her. "Miss LaFrancois, I put this girl's life in your hands. Tell me where Rojas is, right now, and you can save her."

Max said, "We don't know. Is this really necessary?"

Williams nodded to one of his men, who came up behind Max fast and placed him in a headlock, pulling him away from the table.

Max knew better than to fight too hard.

Renee was crying. "I don't know. I don't know where…"

Williams used his thumb and forefinger to make a gun shape and then pointed to the girl on the beach.

Several loud shots rang out. There was a collective shudder from everyone in the restaurant, and then quiet. Anonymous weeping and cursing in the restaurant. Angry squirming from Max. But mostly just quiet. The narcos had all the power here.

Max could see Ines Sanchez's lifeless body, now filled with bullet holes. Dark crimson blood painted over white sand.

Williams stood.

"This is the way business is done in this place. There is a code which must be followed. A balance to be kept. Eye for an eye. That sort of thing. If you break the rules…if someone betrays us, this is what happens."

Max glared at Williams. "She was a girl."

Williams shrugged. "The rules apply to everyone. Otherwise we are just a pack of wild dogs." He walked over to Renee and caressed her neck, allowing his eyes to wander. He clicked his tongue. "Still, dogs need to be fed. Fed in all sorts of ways." Williams backed away from her and motioned to his men.

Max was released. The gunman trained his rifle on Max and forced him to sit back down.

Renee, her eyes red and watery, gritted her teeth, saying, "Everyone here saw…"

Williams laughed. "You think that matters here?" He leaned forward. "Now, I don't know with total confidence that you were involved last night. And…let's face it. Max, your father is famous. You can thank him for your safety. It would cause me headaches if you were to go missing. But don't think that because I show you leniency today, this can't happen to you, Max. Or her." He looked towards Renee.

Max clenched his jaw and forced himself to slow his breathing. Control his anger, before it endangered them all. He decided right then and there that someday soon, he would kill this Ian Williams fellow.

One of the guards approached and whispered something in Williams's ear. He looked up and smiled. "It appears that our breakfast has come to an end."

Max could hear a distant rumble of helicopters. Big ones, by the sound of it. Someone whistled, and the Mexican gang emptied the bag of cell phones onto one of the central tables in the hotel restaurant. Then they left the hotel, getting back into their trucks.

Williams pointed to Max and Renee. "For these two, make sure you take their phones and electronic devices with us. Don't give them back."

The man nodded. "*En el auto.*"

Williams rose and said to Max, "If you're working for him, tell Caleb Wilkes I said hello. And tell him that his agent was a delicious lay for my men."

He strode towards the door. Before walking out, Williams turned and yelled, "Max, you have two hours to leave this city. If I see you again, I'll come for Renee and feed her to my men as their next meal."

With that, Williams turned and left.

* * *

Three army-green Chinook helicopters landed on the beach. Dozens of Mexican military troops poured out, marching up to the hotel and securing the perimeter. A man wearing sunglasses, a blue polo, and khakis walked up to Max and Renee.

"You Max Fend?" he asked in American-accented English.

"Yeah."

"Phone call."

He handed Max a cell phone, which he held up to his ear.

"My God, are you two alright?" Wilkes's voice.

"Hello, Caleb. How are you?"

"I got notified you were in cartel custody there and moved as fast as I could. I had to call in a lot of favors to get the Mexicans to send in the cavalry. You're both lucky you weren't chopped to pieces. You have any idea what they do to their enemies down there?"

Max knew he was right, and he was furious at himself for letting it happen. It was reckless of him to bring Renee to Mexico, and even more stupid to come back to the hotel. Not that he'd had a choice. He looked at Renee standing on the pool patio, the wind from the helicopter rotors blowing her dark hair into streamers.

Max noticed that Renee didn't look scared.

She looked *pissed*.

And not at him, for once, which was nice. Max's intuition told him that their little meeting with Ian Williams had cemented Renee's resolve.

Max said into the phone, "We found out Blanco's name. Or at least an alias that you can look up. Ian Williams. We actually just sat down with him. I watched him execute Ines Sanchez, Caleb."

Wilkes swore on the other end of the line. Then he said, "Okay, thank you for letting me know."

"Where's Rojas? When can we get there?"

"Not over the phone."

He was right. Max was stupid to have said that. If the cartels or the ISI were able to hack into this phone call, Max would have just confirmed that Rojas was in US custody. There was no excuse for the error. Max was rattled after witnessing that poor woman's death, and seeing Renee so close to a murderer.

He tried to keep his conversation more vague. "Caleb, I want to see this through."

Wilkes ignored him. "The guy that handed you the phone is DEA. He'll see that you get out of the country safely. And soon. I've assured State Department that you had nothing to do with last night, and that my request to protect an agent in Mazatlán this morning is purely coincidental timing. Keep out of trouble. I'll talk to you when you reach the States. Goodbye, Max."

Max handed the phone back to the DEA man, who said, "I have orders to get you back to the United States. Do you have transportation?"

Max nodded. "It's at the local airport."

Thirty minutes later, Max and Renee were once again flying in his father's private jet, this time north, towards the US. The aircraft cabin was long, thin, luxurious, and empty. Two pilots up front, with the cockpit door closed. Max knew both of them by name. They had been on his father's personal staff for decades. A single steward sat just aft of the cockpit, blending in with the wall, his senses attuned to the tiniest glance from one of his passengers.

Renee and Max sat facing each other near the back of the cabin, out of earshot of the steward. Max said, "I've asked the pilots to fly us to Texas. I'm hoping to get in touch with Trent. Or see if Wilkes will let me join Rojas's interrogation." He paused. "Are you alright? Look, I understand if you want to head home. We did what was asked."

She had been looking out the window, but now she turned to face him. "I'm with you now more than ever."

Max knew that she was thinking of the female agent executed on the beach, perhaps holding herself responsible. Or maybe she was thinking of Josh Carpenter's little boy. Josh had been killed, in a way, by the same men.

Max said, "I want to find out more about Ian Williams."

"No problem. Give me a few hours once we touch down."

"I just wish we still had our phones," said Max.

"Why?"

"Because I'm getting the feeling that Wilkes is putting us on ice. He used us for what he needed and will use other assets now that he thinks we're a known quantity to Williams."

Renee shook her head. "What's that got to do with our phones?"

"We no longer have the encrypted phones. And you don't have your computer. We needed them so that we could contact Trent and meet up with him. Otherwise we'll just have to wait for Wilkes to decide whether he wants to keep using us."

Renee gave him a funny look.

"What?"

"Max, I made a clone of each phone and uploaded it to my secure cloud storage. I always do that. Same with all of the data on my computer. Come on. What year are you living in?"

"So, we'll be able to contact Trent?"

"Yes. What do you think I'm here for, eye candy?"

* * *

J. Edgar Hoover Building
Washington, D.C.

Caleb Wilkes sat in the corner of the room, his legs crossed, and mouth shut. He was still a bit groggy from the red-eye to DC, but thankfully he wouldn't need to do much talking. This was the FBI's show. Wilkes was here as a courtesy. He was, however, very interested in the discussion.

Senator Herbert Becker, a member of the Select Intelligence Committee and the Judiciary Committee, was now being interviewed after the mysterious death of his chief of staff. In his preliminary statement to the FBI, Becker had told investigators that he had information related to his chief of staff and Joseph Dahlman, the dead lobbyist.

Senator Becker sat next to his lawyer. His lawyer opened up a leather-bound case and took out a stapled document, which he slid forward on the table.

The FBI agent leading the interview said, "What's this?"

"Please read it."

Three copies were circulated, and Wilkes's eyebrows shot up when he began reading his.

Senator Becker,

If you are reading this, then the worst has happened. I can't tell you how sorry I am.

A few years ago, I became aware that Joseph Dahlman's clients were not simply businessmen representing multinational corporations, as they were initially advertised to you. Dahlman had connections to Pakistan's intelligence agency, the ISI. I should have told you, and I should have informed the FBI. I didn't, because I knew that it could ruin everything we have worked for.

Whoever reads this should know that Senator Becker is innocent of any wrongdoing. He knew nothing of Dahlman's relationship with the ISI. I was overzealous and cowardly. I take full responsibility for any improper actions.

This document serves as my insurance policy against personal harm. If I am killed, it will be sent to Senator Becker. He may do with it what he likes.

The following is a list of names, dates, activities, and bank accounts which implicate me and the ISI in illegal activity.

Ronald Dicks

Wilkes read through the document. He recognized a few of the names. No one stuck out, but they would cross-reference everything against the intelligence files of the CIA and other agencies. The FBI agent handed the document to one of his colleagues, who left the room looking grim. This would reach the director's desk within minutes.

One of the agents in the room muttered, "Seems like the insurance policy didn't work."

The lead FBI agent sat back in his chair and took a deep breath. The whole room sat on pins and needles.

"Let's start with the relationship between your former chief of staff and the lobbyist, Dahlman. Why did they meet?"

"Mr. Dahlman's firm represented business interests that were important to my constituents."

"Important to your constituents?"

"That's correct. They represented companies that did business in Wisconsin."

"What kind of companies?"

"Several types. Health care-focused, mainly. Medical device manufacturers. Pharmaceutical manufacturers. However, I fear that Mr. Dahlman's clients' interests diverged from my own policy stance in recent months."

"How so?"

"I am the coauthor of the Opioid Epidemic Act. It's the most aggressive legislation Congress has ever put forth to fight the opioid crisis in our country. But some pharmaceutical companies fear that the bill will hurt their bottom line. These drugs are very profitable. Naturally, some are upset. But it appears that I was ill-informed on just who these people were, and how upset they had become."

"You thought Dahlman's lobbying firm represented Big Pharma?"

The senator shifted in his seat, looking around the room. "Until I received this letter, this insurance policy from my chief of staff, I believed Dahlman's agency represented multinational corporations that benefited from legal narcotic production, among other things."

"Multinational?"

The senator's lawyer spoke up. "Mr. Dahlman's firm was in full compliance with the Foreign Agents Registration Act, and the senator's campaign contributions were in accordance with campaign finance law. This conversation is about the senator's recently deceased chief of staff. I would ask that we narrow the questions to that subject."

"But while you thought the clients of this lobbyist were—to use your term, multinational—you also knew they were upset with you. What made you think that Mr. Dahlman's clients were upset with your legislation?"

"Ron told me as much." The senator cleared his throat and looked at his lawyer, who nodded. "Approximately three weeks ago, Mr. Dicks received a phone call that threatened the both of us if I didn't change my vote."

Caleb Wilkes leaned forward in his chair, waiting for the FBI agent to dig.

"Threatened you? How so?"

"The man on the phone said that Mr. Dicks and I were likely to be physically harmed. I don't remember the exact wording, but it was vulgar."

The FBI agent looked incredulous. "Did you report this to anyone?"

"No."

"Why not?"

"We didn't take it seriously at first. At the time, I didn't know what was in the contents of this note. I didn't know that these people represented a foreign intelligence service. When we read that Dahlman was shot, Ron and I both were of course alarmed. Ron especially so. But I didn't imagine in a hundred years that..." His voice trailed off. Wilkes could tell the senator was upset.

"Take your time, Senator. Would you like some water?"

"No, I'm fine. You have to understand my position. If the papers get a hold of this, I'll be part of a scandal. And regardless of the fact that I have done nothing wrong, it will hurt me."

Wilkes wrote down a question and handed it to the special agent conducting the interview. The special agent looked at Wilkes and nodded.

Wilkes addressed the senator. "Senator Becker, did Ron Dicks have access to classified intelligence?" Wilkes knew the answer, of course, but he wanted to hear Becker's response.

"Of course he did."

"How often did he access the CIA's high security research room in Northern Virginia?"

"I'm on the Select Intelligence Committee. Ron was crucial in making sure that I was informed on all matters pertaining to my work on the committee. He went to that site regularly to get information and would share the top-level findings with me prior to committee meetings and hearings."

"Do you have any reason to believe he would have shared that information with a foreign national? Or with anyone who wasn't cleared and appropriately read in?"

"If you'd asked me that question a few days ago, I would have said of course not. Now, I'm not sure what to say."

"Thank you, Senator."

Wilkes stayed for a few more moments and then politely excused himself from the interview. The senator seemed truthful. He was a politician, motivated by fear and ambition. But it was Ron Dicks, his senior aide, who had been regularly accessing the classified intelligence that Wilkes now knew contained Ines Sanchez's name.

Ron Dicks had likely passed that information on to Dahlman, who had in turn passed it on to his ISI handler, Abdul Syed. Syed had gone missing two days ago, just before Sanchez was rolled up. Just before Ron Dicks was killed.

Had Ian Williams given the order to Syed to burn down that part of his network? The value of that intelligence stream to the ISI would be incredibly high. Why would Syed agree to snuff out such a valuable asset? What was worth that price?

* * *

Karen landed her aircraft on the runway and taxied up to her hangar. She shut off her engine and finished the checklist as the propeller spooled down. Then she slid open the canopy and removed her headset, long tousles of blond hair falling down over her flight suit.

A black sedan waited in the parking lot behind the chain-link fence. Her father stood next to it, waving. She waved back to him, smiling, and headed his way.

She was glad for the surprise visit. He rarely came out to see her anymore, even when he was home. Especially during a midterm election year like this, his time in Wisconsin was usually packed with town halls and visits to various groups of his constituents.

Karen's coach and agent both walked with her as she made her way from the plane towards the hangar area.

"That's your last run until we perform next week. How did it feel?" asked her coach.

"Good. How'd the spin look from where you were?"

"I think you entered it a bit aggressive."

"It was under control…"

"Karen."

"I'll ease up next time."

Her coach kept talking while she tried to signal her father through the fence. She yelled to her dad, "Give me five minutes!" The senator, who was on the phone now, nodded and gave her a thumbs-up.

Karen's agent, a woman in her late twenties who repre-sented several singers, a touring magician, and two actors, said,

"Your conference call with the reporters is tomorrow. I was going to prep you with the publicist."

"Let's do it tomorrow. I'm tired."

The agent pursed her lips. "Fine. I'll call you later."

Aerobatics pilots didn't normally have agents. Karen was the exception. Her looks and family name had gotten her a book deal, and now she was in talks for a possible documentary series. The agent always seemed put off at Karen's lack of interest in publicity. Karen saw it as a necessary evil. But it wasn't rocket science. For the crowds and cameras, she just had to smile and wink and shake what god gave her a little. Her real work was in the cockpit. The agent wouldn't understand.

In the locker room, Karen changed into tight designer jeans with a few tears in them—to make them more stylish. Karen couldn't understand why the three-hundred-and-fifty-dollar jeans had holes in them, but it gave everyone a little more glimpse of her tanned thigh. Not exactly something she wanted to show off in front of her father, but a lot of her fellow aerobatic pilots on the circuit were training here this week too, and maybe she'd join them for beers later.

Seeing her come out to the parking lot, Senator Becker said into the phone, "Gotta go, I'll call you later."

She hugged her father. "What brings the good senator to town? You weren't supposed to be here until next week, when I perform. I just spoke to you on the phone a few days ago. What gives?"

"We need to speak about something."

"About what?"

"Ron Dicks is dead."

"What?" Her mouth gaped open. "Dad, I'm so sorry. How?" Karen saw the look on her father's face. "What's wrong?"

"It's happening, Karen. Just like you said it would."

\* \* \*

"You think it was them?"

Her father nodded somberly. "I do."

He forked a piece of rare steak into his mouth and chewed. The two were alone, other than the two local police officers who were roaming the perimeter of the two-acre property. The senator's two-story home rested on the shores of Lake Winnebago. The police security detail had been arranged after his conversation with the FBI. The authorities were taking the Senator's death threats seriously, while keeping them confidential at the senator's behest.

Senator Becker had cooked a dinner of steak, asparagus, and corn on the cob on his Big Green Egg smoker grill. Cooking was one of his hobbies from a life of calm long ago. The red juices of his steak now covered his plate. He broke off a piece of hard roll to sop them up, then stuffed it into his mouth.

Karen looked out over the lake. A summer storm brewed in the distance, brilliant flashes of lightning branching up through the clouds on the horizon.

"I'm trying not to say I told you so."

"Say it."

She shook her head, fuming. "I'm very sorry about Ron. But he made poor choices by introducing you to these men. So did that wretched woman you had with you."

"Don't bring Jennifer into this. That's not helpful."

Karen turned away. Years ago, she and her mother had come home from a shopping trip to then-Congressman Becker and one of his female staffers in a compromising situation, in this very house. That had led to a quick but painful divorce from Karen's mother.

Karen had forced herself to blame the staffer, a woman by the name of Jennifer Upton. It was easier than blaming her dad. Upton had been toxic. An easy scapegoat in Karen's mind. And while Karen knew her father had his flaws, he also had a great many gifts. He was a master politician. One of the few left who could garner support on both sides of the aisle. A true statesman with a powerful intellect. She knew in her heart that he would be president someday. And she believed he would make a great one.

But while Karen was able to forgive her father and to look past his shortcomings, the ugliness of politics had changed her. Karen had been just out of college back then. Interning on her father's congressional staff, intent on beginning a career in D.C. Then her eyes had been opened to how none of it worked the way it was supposed to. She'd found out what really motivated the people who worked in Washington. Ambition. Power. Truth and principle be damned. Her idealism was soon shattered.

Jennifer Upton and Ron Dicks were perfect examples of this. They were always conspiring together. Bending and breaking every rule. They just wanted to win, no matter the cost.

One day her father, Jennifer Upton, and Ron Dicks had arrived back from an overseas trip. Upton and Dicks acted like they'd won the lottery. Decided right there on the spot that Becker could run for Senate the next cycle. Some new source of funding that they wouldn't talk about. But it was a game changer.

When she'd confronted him, her father had told her what was going on. He'd always been honest with her. Ron and he had made a deal. Landed a big fish. Some powerful men were going to bankroll him. She had asked if it was illegal. He'd told her no, but she'd known better. He was blinded by his own ambition, and his future was brighter than ever. The group just wanted a little help on some Afghanistan policy proposal, Ron had said.

But it was never that easy. Not with men like these. Before long, Karen had overheard signs of trouble. The mysterious power brokers turned out to have dark connections.

Karen had asked her father to break off all ties with the foreign group. Told him he should go to the authorities and tell them who they were. Jennifer Upton had argued the opposite. The funders' policies were identical to their own. What would it hurt if they were to continue to accept untraceable money?

Ron Dicks was neutral.

That was when Karen had caught her father having the affair with Jennifer Upton. She'd used it as leverage. A moment of rock bottom to snap her father out of his death spiral. She'd given him an ultimatum, demanding that Upton leave, in return for Karen's own silence to the press about the affair. She also demanded that he break off communication with the international group that had been funneling money to his campaign. Her father had probably doubted that she would ever go through with it. And he was right. But the senator was a transactional man, and he knew that he had to give something to his daughter. So, he'd cut Upton loose and promised that he would break off contact with the group.

In truth, it wasn't the affair Karen was trying to stop. She wanted Jennifer Upton's negative influence on her father gone. The next year he had become a senator, and Karen convinced herself that the dark financiers were a thing of the past.

While she'd chosen a career that had nothing to do with politics, Karen remained politically astute. A savvy strategist, her father had for years tried to convince her to come to D.C. and rejoin his staff, or perhaps go to get a master's in public policy at the Kennedy School. He could easily get her in. But Karen had found flying, and now she wanted little to do with any of that.

"Why are they acting this way now? After all this time..."

"I've turned my back on them."

"You were supposed to have done that long ago."

"I've done it for good this time."

"And they killed Ron for it?"

"And a lobbyist that served as their intermediary."

Karen covered her mouth. "Have you told the authorities?"

"Not everything. But enough. I met with the FBI today. I've told them what they need to know, and that we received death threats. That's why I have a police escort now."

"You received death threats?"

"Ron did. He claimed the threats extended to me. He also left a note. He implicated himself and proclaimed me innocent of any wrongdoing."

Karen studied her father. "Are you?"

He looked hurt. "Of course. I didn't know the details of who these men were."

"That was intentional. Plausible deniability."

"It matters little now."

"I don't understand. Why would they kill Ron? And the lobbyist? What did they have to gain from that?"

"At first I thought they were trying to scare me. To change my vote on a key piece of legislation they didn't like."

"That's behavior I would expect from the mafia."

"You may not be far off."

Karen finished her glass and sighed. "Dad…"

"I know."

"Do you think they're going to come after you?"

"I don't know. I'm still trying to understand their motivations. I fear we aren't dealing with rational actors."

"They know you're done with them because you have no more use for them. Or no more need. Because you're running for president next year, right?"

"There's my smart girl."

"And when that happens, people will start digging into your past like never before. They'll find all the skeletons. So they're getting rid of them. That means eventually they will…"

She looked up at her father, too disturbed to finish her sentence.

But her father's look told her that he'd understood. "You're reaching the same conclusion that I did."

Karen sighed, shaking her head. "I warned you that they were bad news."

"I'm sorry. I should have listened."

She shrugged.

"Have you ever spoken to your mother about any of this? Or anyone else, for that matter?"

"Never. You told me not to."

"I've asked you not to do a lot of things, and that never stopped you." Her father smiled.

She laughed. "Well, I listened this time."

"Good. We will be able to get out of this. But no one can know the truth about who these men are."

"What are you going to do?"

"I'm coming up with a plan. It's still a work in progress."

"Be careful."

## CHAPTER 13

IAN WILLIAMS SAT on a stone patio, looking out over one of his boss's sprawling family ranches, ten miles from Durango. To the east, steep green slopes formed the backbone of Mexico, the Sierra Madre Occidental. A fiery sunset painted the sky a brilliant red. Williams liked this time of night in Mexico. It was muggy, but peaceful.

The Martinez family was inside, the cartel boss's wife reading to his young children. Armed men in cargo pants and tactical boots roamed the premises, carrying machine guns. Even here, on the home turf of the Sinaloa cartel, they could never let their guard down.

Especially now, when they were so close to the meeting.

As the relatively new leader of the Sinaloa cartel, Ian Williams's boss, Juan Martinez, was already a target to many. The city of Durango, along with Sinaloa and Chihuahua, formed one of the corners of the Golden Triangle, the infamous section of Mexico whose unique climate, elevation, and terrain made it the ideal place to grow most of the poppies that fed America's insatiable appetite for heroin.

Williams would have laughed if someone had told him two

years ago that he would end up as head of security in one of Mexico's drug cartels.

After his forced departure from MI6, he had gone to work for a commercial research and strategic intelligence firm based out of London. He spent six months there, doing opposition research on political candidates and potential corporate board members. But apparently it wasn't enough that MI6 had fired him from that job. The spiteful bastards had gone on to ruin his reputation outside of the agency as well. Word was out. If you hired Ian Williams, you were on their blacklist. And no one in Williams's line of work wanted to anger one of the chaps at the Secret Intelligence Service.

The official break from MI6 had been years in the making. Too many pissed-off members of Her Majesty's Diplomatic Service, and too many unexplained dead civilians.

After his firing, Williams had quickly reached out to his connections in Pakistan's intelligence service. His close collaboration with the ISI had been one of the reasons MI6 had cast him away. He was now ready to cash in on that relationship.

Abdul Syed had arranged for Williams to take a job as a security consultant in Mexico City. But that was just a seed investment. A starting point for Williams to learn the country, grow his network, and infiltrate the organizations that ran Mexico: the cartels.

A glass sliding door opened and Juan Martinez, head of the Sinaloa cartel, walked towards him, whiskey glass in hand.

A national bank vice president at age forty, with family connections to Mexico's upper crust, Juan Martinez would've had no problem continuing his successful and legitimate business career on his own. But Ian Williams had made a livelihood out of luring talented and ambitious men into his web. Martinez was the piece that was missing from the ISI's new operation in Mexico.

Together, Williams and Syed had orchestrated a remarkable

coup. It was one of the most swift and complete takeovers of a multibillion-dollar company in modern history. And it was almost completely bloodless. An amazing feat, given the industry norms.

But like many achievements in the world of espionage, it wasn't something that Williams could publicize. Only ten people around the world knew anything about it.

Nine, he reminded himself. One of them had been killed last week, at a park in Virginia.

"Good evening, my friend."

"Good evening, Mr. Martinez." Martinez had told Williams several times to call him Juan in private, but he never did.

The Martinez family had been the aristocratic land owners in Durango for generations. Juan's parents had moved north, to a wealthy housing district near Mexico City, when the cartels had moved into the area. It was ironic that he would end up moving back to the area to run the cartels.

Williams, having quickly grown his book of business in Mexico City, had done work for the cartels and Martinez's bank. Williams had earned the young businessman's trust as an advisor and problem-solver in the areas in which legitimate businesses couldn't easily participate. Money laundering. Bribery. Extortion. A man like Ian Williams had no scruples about being the go-between. And Williams was happy to see that Martinez had the stomach to allow such flexibility.

With his business acumen, his Durango family roots, and his strong personal relationship with Williams, it was time for a promotion.

The Sinaloa cartel had, through a shell company, used Martinez's bank for several large real estate deals in Panama. Syed had helped to influence the bank choice through one of his ISI agents in Mexico. They'd ensured that Martinez's division would be assigned the account.

At first Martinez had wanted nothing to do with the

project. He had seen enough of the cartels during his childhood in Durango. With his education and upbringing, why did he need to succumb to a life of crime? It was beneath him. Or so he thought.

But Williams had been hired by the cartel as an external auditor. Behind closed doors, he'd convinced Martinez of the benefits of taking on the job. When he'd seen some of the numbers, Martinez had realized just how obscene the profits were.

Williams had convinced Martinez that he could do better still. *Let us meet with a few of the cartel men, and see if we can't get a bigger piece of the action?* Williams was already connected with one of them.

His name was Hector Rojas.

Soon Juan Martinez, with his advanced degrees and years of experience in banking, saw what Williams had been telling him. The cartel's finances, as big as their revenues and profit margins were, were being run by amateurs. After all the articles that Martinez had read claiming that they were being run like Fortune 500 companies, he now saw what was beneath the hood and knew that he could do better.

Much better.

He was in.

Martinez and Williams soon had their hands in all of the Sinaloa cartel's financial dealings. And the higher-ups in the cartel saw their collective worth. Martinez had made recommendations for improvement that increased the cartel's profitability by billions of dollars without breaking a sweat.

Soon Martinez and Williams were taking personal meetings with the head of the cartel himself, a man named Vasquez. Vasquez liked Martinez immensely, seeing him as reliable, professional, and clean. He didn't use any of the product, he didn't drink, and he valued family. Family, and in particular the loyalty one had to family, was very important to Vasquez.

"Would you like to be part of our family?" The former leader of the Sinaloa had posed the question to Juan Martinez, with Williams standing in the background, almost two years ago.

Martinez, while disciplined and professional, was also ambitious. When he had worked as an executive in a company, he'd had the potential to rise up the food chain and one day lead that company. As a member of one of the cartels, he had now increased his risk due to the nature of the work and stepped off the golden path towards being a chief executive. He related this concern to Vasquez. Vasquez smiled.

"You know men have been killed on the suspicion that they wanted to become what I am. Yet here you are, saying it to my face."

The men had come to an agreement. Martinez would take ownership of and operate the newly formed Durango cartel, a tiny offshoot of the Sinaloa cartel. In return, he would pay a cut to Sinaloa and continue to oversee the operations and finances of both cartels. To the chagrin of Vasquez's family members and longtime partners, Martinez was effectively made second-in-command.

Heir to the throne.

Syed had arranged for Vasquez to be killed during an attempted arrest by the federales one month later.

Williams had been ready for it.

Martinez had been like a favored archbishop finding out that the pope had just died. A scramble. Posturing. Gossip and whispers. Uncertainty. Alliances and plans were made.

Martinez had been panicked. "We must flee. These people don't accept me. My family…"

Williams had forced him to hold his ground. Williams had spent months gathering loyal gunmen from the ranks of Mexican special operations, similar to the way the Zetas had formed their cadre of elite warriors. His first order of business now was to invite the upper echelon of the Sinaloa cartel—mostly members of the Vasquez family—to a meeting at the Martinez family ranch in Durango. He'd summoned them—both as an initial gesture of authority and as a way to get the upper hand.

The Sinaloa cartel was Martinez's now.

Williams had done the talking while Martinez had sat at the head of the table, trying to look unafraid.

"I understand that we are outsiders to many of you," Williams had said, "and I understand that many of you harbor hostility and mistrust towards me. So, I will tell you this: I don't care. Pledge loyalty to Juan Martinez now. Maintain that loyalty. Because I will always be watching you. And you have seen what I do to those who are disloyal. There is only one cartel now. And Señor Martinez owns it."

The meeting had broken up with glares and angry muffled voices. But Williams had been telling the truth when he'd said he would be watching. A few days later, Martinez and Williams had been given audio evidence that the eldest Vasquez brother was plotting against them. Williams had known that they could not have anyone in the family killed.

But to members of the cartels, there was a fate worse than death.

The treacherous Vasquez brother had been found hog-tied on the DEA's El Paso office doorstep. The other family members had quickly gotten the message. They might have harbored an inner hatred for Martinez, but they understood the omniscient and omnipotent presence of Williams. No one wanted to be extradited to America.

That wasn't to say that Martinez wasn't capable of extreme violence, just like his predecessor. But he was smart about when and how he used violence as a tool. When members of the Tijuana cartel had refused to pledge allegiance to Martinez as the new head of the Sinaloa cartel, he had rightly begun a war. Three hundred Tijuana foot soldiers were dead within the first two weeks. The leader of the Tijuana cartel was found hanging from a streetlight, his eyes gouged out, a fireman's axe lodged in his chest.

Like a publicly traded company wanting to appear financially healthy to its shareholders, Martinez needed to appear strong to the masses who propped up his empire. The cartels who would join him, and the thousands of employees beneath him. Each of them feared and respected strength. It was that healthy fear that maintained order in a business enforced by violence.

Williams now sat on Martinez's patio. As the alcohol relaxed his mind, he reveled in his achievements. He was the puppet master, and his puppet was the head of the largest drug cartel in the world.

The world was his oyster.

As Williams waited for Martinez to join him, he considered his empire. It was quiet here on Martinez's ranch. Meanwhile, the violent machine that Williams had conquered continued to thrum along. Growing. Producing. Transporting. Selling. Killing. Repeat.

Men and women sweating in the fields and jungles, growing the plants. Just miles away from where he now sat, Williams had observed one of the cartel's many production fields that afternoon. He had watched as peasant farmers slowly drifted through an endless field of poppies, slicing multiple incisions into each one. From these incisions, a liquid would drip down, to be painstakingly collected by the farmers over the next few days. That was the nectar that would be transformed into heroin.

Creating and selling heroin, meth, and cannabis was a business. Williams and Martinez treated it as such. Their bustling transportation network shipped tons of product into the US each day. Williams had taken from his experience in Afghanistan to help the cartel succeed. Working with the suppliers to the south and in Asia. Managing the sales and distribution network in North America. Paying off the police and politicians. And then there was his security and intelligence apparatus. Williams had insisted on improving the latter. Muscle was nothing without knowledge. Williams had hired experts from around the world to improve his security, and to make sure that nothing that could affect his business happened without him knowing about it.

Martinez sat across from him. Williams presented Martinez with a manila envelope. Inside was a news clipping—an article from the *Wall Street Journal*.

"Two dead?"

Williams nodded.

"Was that really necessary? It seems risky."

Williams shrugged. "A message needed to be sent."

Martinez frowned. "What of Rojas?"

"My sources tell me he is in Texas. I should have a location soon."

"Rojas's kidnapping wasn't approved by the Mexican government. I assume our politicians are raising the appropriate objections over this breach of sovereignty?"

"They are."

"Why would the Americans want Rojas this badly? Is he worth such a breach of protocol? Is this all just to get to me?"

Williams smiled inwardly. While Martinez was a very bright businessman, he was not immune to the paranoia that came from being at the top of a criminal enterprise. "Perhaps. With your permission, I would like to see if we can't retrieve him."

"On American soil?"

"It will be carefully planned. Only my best men."

Martinez frowned but nodded his approval.

Williams took another sip of whiskey, looking off into the now-darkening night sky.

## CHAPTER 14

MAX AND RENEE had landed in Austin, Texas earlier in the day. Max got them a room at the Westin while Renee went to the store to buy phones and gear.

Max had sent a message to his virtual assistant, a high-end private service he used to keep his black book contact list updated and handle anything from transportation to confidential communications. The service had promised to have Max's beloved Cirrus SR-22 flown to Texas within the next twenty-four hours. The pilot was instructed to land it at the Austin Executive Airport, pay for parking, fill it up with gas, and find his own transportation home.

Renee had come back to the hotel with boxes of Apple products—a MacBook Pro and two iPhones. She had set up Max's phone, making sure that it had her security software installed, and then they promptly called Trent.

It went to voicemail. They tried several more times throughout the day before he finally called back in the evening.

Trent said, "Where are you guys? Wilkes told me it got a little rough."

"It did, but we're good now. Where are you at?"

"Can I talk on this line?"

Hearing this, Renee gave Max a thumbs-up.

"Renee says we're good."

"Roger. As soon as we landed, they brought in one of those HIG teams to work the guy over. The interrogation team is doing their thing now."

The High-Value Detainee Interrogation Group (HIG), formed in 2009 as a way to combat terrorism, was filled with the nation's most elite interrogators. Members were pooled from the CIA, FBI, and other governmental organizations.

Max found it interesting that Wilkes was able to get permission to use a HIG team in this situation. Was that because of the counterintelligence angle, with the ISI being involved? Or was there something Wilkes wasn't telling them?

Trent continued, "The dude seems scared shitless. Says his boss will have him and his family killed if he talks. But one of the interrogators made a bet with me after the first session that he'd crack within the first day. So it looks good. Are you guys coming down? Wilkes told me I can get out of here...but we're in the middle of nowhere and I don't exactly have a ride. One of the feds is making arrangements for us to stay at a local hotel. They've got a mobile unit set up for the interrogations but that's it. I slept in the hangar last night."

"What's your location? I'll come get you."

"We're on the coast, in between Houston and Corpus Christi. Someplace called Calhoun County Airport."

"We'll fly in tomorrow morning."

"Sounds good. This thing should still be going on. You'll see the eighteen-wheeler with the black SUVs surrounding it. Can't miss us."

\* \* \*

Max and Renee flew to Calhoun County Airport on the coast of Texas the next morning. Trent was right. The airfield was small and desolate. Just a sheet-metal hangar, a handful of general aviation planes, and farmland in all directions. The Gulf of Mexico was a few miles to the southeast. Greenish-blue waves, the beaches filled with tourists.

They touched down and Max taxied the Cirrus to the flight line. Max threw the chocks under the wheels and walked towards the cordoned-off section at the far end of the airport. Men in black, with sunglasses and semiautomatic rifles. A miniature Area 51, right here in Texas.

"Can we help you, sir?" one of the government men asked. The other studied Max and Renee, his hand held loose outside his holster.

Max explained who he was and tried to convince them to let him pass.

The two men looked at each other in confusion. One said, "Sir, this is a restricted area. Please move along."

Max understood. To them, he was just some random stranger with a story. Their job wasn't to let people in, it was to keep people out. He thanked the guards and walked away, taking out his phone while he dialed Trent. "They won't let me in."

A moment later, one of the doors on the mobile interrogation unit swung open and Trent exited. "Gents, they're with us."

The guard swore, looking like he was debating it, but said, "I'd need to hear it from my superiors."

It took about ten minutes of phone calls and arguing. Wilkes was pissed that Max had flown out there. "Next time you better tell me what you're up to," he said. But he made arrangements for Max to enter the interrogation unit.

Walking up the ladder into the large trailer, Max asked, "Where's Wilkes, anyway? Why isn't he here himself?"

"I don't know. He said he had to take care of something else in D.C. But he's monitoring all the reports out of here."

They stepped into a dark, quiet room. Swivel chairs screwed into deck plates on the ground. Two men with clipboards and pens sat in the chairs, listening to the prisoner's interview. They glanced back at Max and Renee, shrugged, and turned back towards the show. A single two-way mirror showed the interrogation room. Sound was being pumped into this section of the trailer via overhead speakers. Rojas sat at a table across from a black man of about fifty—the interrogator.

"What else did you find out?" Max whispered.

"Shh." One of the men with a clipboard placed his finger over his mouth.

Max, Trent, and Renee scooted to the far end of the small space and watched some of the interrogation.

Rojas and the interrogator were conversing in Spanish. Max caught a few words, including Ian Williams's name, but that was about it.

Max and Trent whispered as quietly as they could manage.

Trent said, "He says Ian Williams, the tall white dude that snatched Wilkes's agent in Mexico, has his own agenda. Rojas here claims that Williams influences Martinez, the head of the Sinaloa cartel, to the point of controlling him. He lets Martinez make the legitimate business decisions on production schedules and pricing and all that...but the Brit is the one who handles the darker side of the business. I was surprised to hear he was from the UK."

Max said, "Yeah. Renee dug up some info on him. Ian Williams is former MI6."

Another shush from one of the clipboard men and Trent took the hint. "Let's talk outside for a bit. I'll get you caught up and then we can come back in." The three of them went back into the warm Texas sun, walked past the guards, and towards the flight line where Max's aircraft was parked. They walked about two hundred yards and sat near an empty picnic table on the far side of the airport's only hangar, the only place with shade. The hangar and flight line were empty. An orange-and-white barricade blocked the street entrance that led to the airport, with a state trooper's car parked next to it.

"So Ian Williams was MI6?"

"Yeah. Crazy, right?"

"And he's worked for the cartels for what, a year?"

"Something like that."

"He used to work in Afghanistan and Pakistan for MI6, but got removed for some type of scandal."

"What happened?"

Renee said, "The details weren't available. But the little I could find implied that it involved being too cozy with Pakistani intelligence."

"Very interesting," said Trent.

Max looked back at Trent. "Did Rojas know anything about the man that was killed in Virginia?"

Trent said, "To be honest, I had a hard time following that one. As you saw, the interrogator was speaking in Spanish, and mine is only passable. You might want to ask the interrogation team or see if Wilkes will show you the transcripts. What I think I heard was that Rojas confirmed Williams has a hit list that he's working his way through before this big VIP meeting they've got coming up. Rojas thinks that this guy who was assassinated in Virginia was on the hit list."

"Why does he think that?"

"Because Rojas overheard a conversation between Williams and someone else, talking about the first name in the list being in D.C."

"A phone conversation or in person?"

"I assume phone, but I didn't catch that. Sorry, man, I'm operating on fumes here."

"I thought you were special operations," said Renee, smiling.

"I retired. Now I take naps," Trent said.

Max noticed that the silhouette of the driver in the state

police vehicle was no longer visible. Odd. He had been there a moment ago, and Max hadn't seen him exit the vehicle. He made a mental note of it and pressed Trent further.

"Who else is on the list?"

"Rojas says he has another name but was negotiating for something in return. The interrogators are doing their thing, trying to get everything they can before they start promising him stuff. Rojas is trying to see what leverage he has. A few hours ago, he said he didn't have any names, and that he didn't know anything about the Pakistanis."

"So what's with the meeting? When is it, what is it?"

Trent held up his hand, his eyes squinting back towards the end of the airfield. Max heard the sound of shouting coming from the interrogation unit's trailer.

Max turned to look, saying, "What is it?"

A sudden metallic boom thundered through the air.

\* \* \*

Trent was peering around the corner of the hangar in seconds, his pistol drawn. Max and Renee were slower, deafened and stunned from the explosion. Trent turned back towards them and mouthed something, but Max couldn't make out what he was saying, his ears ringing.

Then he saw Trent pointing towards Max's plane.

"What's going on?" he heard Renee ask, the sounds of the world returning.

Max crept to the corner of the hangar and looked in the direction Trent was pointing. The mobile interrogation unit was a burning heap. Its roof was completely missing, and most of its trailer wall was torn away. Ripped, singed metal, dust, and at least one hunk of flesh on the ground nearby.

Trent said, "One o'clock. See 'em?"

About one hundred yards beyond the blast site, three oversized pickup trucks had veered off the highway and were now bouncing over the grass field surrounding the airport. The trucks were heading towards the burning wreckage of the interrogation trailer.

Trent said, "How quick can you get us out of here in that thing?" He was again pointing to Max's Cirrus, which was only fifty feet away.

"What about the people in the trailer? Is there anyone still alive?" Renee asked. She winced as the loud, rapid rattle of heavy machine-gun fire echoed over the airfield. Men in the pickup trucks fired at the two government SUVs parked near the interrogation trailer. Pops in the metal and shattered glass as bullets riddled the vehicles. Max didn't see any return fire. At least two bodies on the pavement near the vehicles. Neither moving.

Max looked around the airfield, trying to identify all their options.

Max turned to the airport entrance and saw the state police vehicle still sitting there, its blue lights off, with no sign of a driver. Max could just barely make out a spiderweb crack in the rear window.

If anyone was left alive in the police vehicles, they were going to be killed soon. The same was true for anyone left alive in what remained of the smoking trailer. Trent had a single handgun, as did Max, but his was still in the plane. Their enemy had them outnumbered and outgunned, and they had too great of a head start.

If they were going to live through the next few minutes, they had two options. Hide and hope the attackers didn't make their way over to them, or run to the Cirrus and get airborne before the gunmen saw them.

Performing calculations and risk assessments in his head, he made a call. "You're right. Let's head to the plane."

The trio sprinted to the Cirrus. Max grabbed the chock off

the pavement, opened his door and let Renee throw herself into the rear seat. Trent hopped next to Max in front. Max started it up as fast as he could.

"They see us yet?"

"Not yet, I don't think."

The aircraft's parking spot on the ramp had been near the runway midpoint. He cursed to himself. With a runway this short, three passengers and a high-density altitude, he would need to use the full field for takeoff. But as soon as he started taxiing, he was sure to draw the gunmen's attention. He didn't have a choice.

Max throttled the engine and they began rolling forward on the taxiway, towards the far end of the runway.

"What about now? Are they following us?"

"I can't tell," Trent replied, careening his neck and looking back through the side windows of the plane.

Renee leaned forward from the backseat and opened Trent's door, peeking her head out to look behind them. She immediately flung herself back in and latched the door.

"Hurry up," was all she said, her face pale.

Max tapped the brakes to slow down in the turn, then pressed forward on the right pedal to bring the aircraft around to face the runway centerline, switching his flaps to fifty percent.

To his horror, he saw not one but two pickup trucks racing towards him down the taxiway. They were still a good half-mile away, but that would change fast. Still turning, Max immediately pushed the throttle all the way forward, felt and heard the 310-horsepower engine ramp up.

The airspeed was picking up. Fifty. Sixty.

He glanced to his left and watched the pickup trucks change bearing and turn as they overshot their mark. He could make out silent yellow flashes of gunfire in his peripheral vision.

He pulled back on the stick as the Cirrus hit its seventy-knot takeoff speed.

The ground dropped beneath them, and Max banked sharply away, climbing and accelerating to safety.

Renee squeezed Max's shoulder. His heart was pounding. The geometry had been in their favor, but barely. The gunmen had been only a few seconds away from having a much better shot.

Trent put on his headset and keyed his mike. "Someone really needs to teach those mooks how to lead the target."

## CHAPTER 15

THEY LANDED at David Wayne Hooks Airport, near Houston, less than an hour later. After talking about it during the flight, Max made the decision that they would not call Wilkes to check in.

At this point, they didn't know who they could trust.

They got fuel at Gill Aviation, the local FBO, and Max checked over the weather, still deciding where they should go next. Trent used the showers and changed into a pair of spare clothes Max lent him. Renee sipped hot tea while working on her computer in an empty pilot's lounge. The two men joined her in there after a while, and Max closed the door.

Max figured that Wilkes had probably been calling and texting each of their phones after the attack, but Renee had mandated keeping all cell phones off until now. She didn't want the devices pinging cell towers along their route. Despite her confidence in the security program she had installed on their hardware, none of them were one hundred percent sure how the hit team had located Rojas.

Renee said, "I ran some checks. I'm ninety-nine point nine percent sure that it wasn't us. It's extremely unlikely that anyone could have been eavesdropping on our calls or tracking our devices."

Trent looked at Max. "How well do you know Wilkes?"

Max shook his head. "I don't see it. Why would he have us go through all that down in Mexico, just to set us up?"

"Then who talked?"

Max said, "I don't know."

"Ian Williams knew about Wilkes's Mexican agent. And now a professional hit team takes out an interrogation unit and their prisoner on American soil. Both of these events have Wilkes as the tie-in. So I ask you again, how well do you know him?"

Max shook his head. "I'm not disagreeing with you that there's a leak. I'll grant you it's possible that Wilkes was even responsible for it. But since we don't know how many people were read in to both operations, none of us can say that with any confidence."

Renee spoke gently. "What do you think, then?"

Max said, "I suspect that if Wilkes was hunting a mole, he might have let them get *some* information on purpose."

Trent looked sideways at Max.

Renee said, "Why would he do that?"

"You remember last summer in Florida, Renee. Wilkes didn't tell us the whole truth until we absolutely needed to know. As good as Caleb Wilkes is at his job, he views his assets as expendable. He told me that he wanted to find out why the Sinaloa cartel and Pakistani intelligence were working together. What if that wasn't his real objective? Or what if it wasn't his *only* objective?"

Max saw Renee's eyes moving as she worked through the problem. "You think he's purposely allowing leaks of our operation to occur so that he can achieve a different objective. What, then?"

"I can think of three reasons. One is what's called a blue-dye operation."

Trent massaged his tired eyes with his thumb and forefinger. "Enough with this spook shit…this is why I said no to the CIA recruiter when I retired from the Army. I just want to shoot bad guys. Not have to wonder if they're really bad guys or not…"

Renee said, "I'll bite. What's a blue-dye operation?"

"It's when you have a leak and don't know where it is, but you're able to see your adversary's reaction, or maybe even what information they receive. So you insert multiple variations of some important story into the information stream. Whichever variation shows up in your enemy's inbox, that's the version your mole heard. You can use this technique to narrow down your field of suspects."

"But it requires you to provide information to a mole."

"Among others, yes. Normally one would provide information that isn't harmful to an ongoing operation. But the juiciest worms make the best bait."

Renee said, "You said there were three reasons why Wilkes would knowingly leak information. What are the other two?"

"The second reason is that he may already know who the mole is. He could be intentionally leaking information to suggest to the mole's handlers that the mole is still reliable, with the eventual intention of using the mole to provide false or misleading information."

Trent said, "I'm gonna say that's not what's going on here, based on the fact that we almost just got blown up. He wouldn't have done that intentionally. Right?"

Max nodded. "Agreed. I highly doubt Wilkes would have knowingly risked an attack on Rojas."

Renee said, "And the third reason?"

"I could be wrong about the whole thing. Wilkes could be the enemy."

The group turned their attention to the buzzing phone on Renee's armrest. She had powered it up while they were talking.

She looked at the caller ID. "It's him. Wilkes."

* * *

Max lifted up the phone and answered.

"Where have you been? Are you with the others?"

Max ignored the question. "How did they know where Rojas was being held, Caleb?"

"We're working on that. We think the ISI may have access to some very high-end satellite tracking tools. It's possible they tracked our aircraft from Mexico to the US. We thought we were being careful, but if the cartels and the ISI are coordinating that closely...Syed may have passed the location along."

"To Williams?"

"Yes. The FBI thinks the Sinaloa cartel flew in a squad from Mexico to do the wet work, using local gang members as support. The gear was Mexican military-issue. They used an antitank weapon on the HIG team's trailer. Are you guys alright? I assume both Trent and Renee are with you?"

The second time he'd asked that question, Max noted. Out of concern? Or to gain intel? Max kept his voice steady.

"Caleb, I think we're just going to lay low for a while."

A pause.

"Max, there are new developments. I appreciate the danger you were in, but I'm afraid I need you guys to find someone for me."

"What new developments?"

"We got a new name from Rojas. I need this person located and brought in ASAP."

Max looked at the others in the room, both of whom could

hear the conversation. Max could see that they shared his concern about going on another of Wilkes's assignments.

"Caleb, twice in the last week, we went where you told us to be. Both times, someone nearly had us killed."

The phone when quiet. When Wilkes finally spoke, his tone was softer. "I understand your concern. I hope you trust me enough to know that I value the well-being of each one of you."

"Like you valued your Mexican agent? The woman?"

Trent turned away. Renee didn't flinch.

Wilkes said, "That was unfair. Do you really think I don't regret that?" His tone showed a rare burst of emotion.

"I'm sorry. But you understand where our apprehension is coming from here. Caleb, there must be hundreds of capable people that could go find this person for you. Why do you need—"

"*Because we had a leak.* Why do you think I used you that night at Wolf Trap? Why do you think I needed you to go to Mexico? I was trying my damnedest to get this thing done without tipping off our mole. I apologize that it didn't work out so well."

There it was. Max understood why Wilkes was so frustrated. He couldn't use just anyone for this. He needed to keep the information tightly controlled. Everything that had been reported through the normal intel streams had been leaked. That was how his agent had been killed in Mexico.

But something still tugged at Max. Over a decade of instinct, telling him that Wilkes wasn't being completely transparent. He pushed the thought aside for the moment.

"You say you had a leak. Past tense. You've found the mole?"

"It looks that way," said Wilkes.

"Who?"

"The day before yesterday I sat in on an interview at the FBI. The man was a political aide named Ronald Dicks. He had access to classified intelligence, including the cryptonym and area of operation for Ines Sanchez. Ron Dicks likely passed information to Joseph Dahlman, the lobbyist you saw killed, who in turn passed information to the ISI."

"Damn. So you think Syed knew her identity before we even went down there?"

"Or at least provided Ian Williams enough information to figure it out for himself."

Max looked at the others. "Caleb, please give us a moment, I'm putting you on mute."

Max pressed the mute icon on the phone. Trent and Renee looked back at him.

"Are you guys convinced? We've been burned twice in the past two days. If either of you wants to walk away, I'll tell him to pound sand."

Renee stood with her arms folded, biting her lip. "I don't think Wilkes meant us any harm. And I assume that if he wants us to do something—to find this person Rojas mentioned—it must be important to stopping Ian Williams. If that's the case, then I think we should do it. I think we should continue to help."

Max suspected that Renee was thinking of Ines Sanchez's corpse, lying on the beach.

Trent said, "You know I'm up for it." In Trent's eyes, Max saw an eager willingness to continue the fight.

"We don't know that this will lead to Williams."

Trent shrugged. "I'll go anyway." His was a thirst that would never be quenched. A quest for revenge. One in which any satisfaction attained would be hollowed out by the sadness of loss.

Max nodded and unmuted the phone. "Alright, Caleb, we're in. But I do have one question. If Ron Dicks is the source of your leaks, and he's dead, why do you still need us to find this person for you?"

"Speed and operational security. We're on tight timeline. You know the mission details and the players involved. You've got a team read in. I don't have time to brief a new set of operators. And this is still being run out of the CIA's counterintelligence division. The more people we involve, the less secure it gets. Because of that, I want to keep this operation within a very small crew."

"What's the timing?"

"We already knew that Ian Williams and the ISI were preparing for an important meeting. This meeting, we believe, is also the deadline to complete their kill list. Rojas gave the HIG team a date. We don't know where, and we don't know with who, but he said that Ian Williams's big meeting was going to be held on the twenty-eighth. So we can assume any further hits will be executed by that time."

"That's only a few days away."

"Correct."

"May I ask why you aren't trying to find this person yourself?"

"I'm headed to Oshkosh."

Oshkosh? Max frowned. He looked at his watch to check the date. This was the last week in July. Each year at this time, the Experimental Aircraft Association hosted the largest air show in the world at Oshkosh, Wisconsin. Max's father had taken him there countless times when he was a boy.

"Why Oshkosh?"

"Rojas gave up two names before he was killed by his own men in Texas. It was a partial list, he said."

"Of Ian Williams's kill list?"

"We believe so, yes. Two on the list are already dead. Joseph Dahlman and Ron Dicks, our mole."

"Who are the other two?"

"One is a US senator. Herbert Becker, of Wisconsin. He'll be in Oshkosh this week. His daughter is one of the performers.

And he's the reason I'll be in attendance. My view is that he's the highest-priority target."

"My father knows him."

"Does he?"

"Yes. They've golfed together, I believe. I actually know his daughter too."

"I see."

"You've informed him that he's in danger?"

"He was already aware. Ron Dicks was his chief of staff. It was his interview I sat in on at the FBI headquarters. He's accepted additional security but refuses to go into hiding. I want to personally monitor his security while we try and find out what Williams and the ISI are up to. If the senator is on Williams's hit list, then we know where they'll be headed. If we can take down one of their hired guns, perhaps that can lead us to one of our targets."

"What's the last name on the list?"

Wilkes said, "This is the person I need you to locate."

"Who is he?"

"It's a she. Jennifer Upton. She's a political operative. Forty-seven years old. Single. She is based out of Cincinnati, but during my cursory attempt to locate her, I've learned that she hasn't been seen during the past twenty-four hours. She was once an aide to Senator Becker, and worked with Ron Dicks. No known connection to Dahlman."

"Why would Ian Williams want to kill her, or the senator?"

"It seems that the ISI is wrapped up with some group of investors in the opioid industry. Senator Becker was once a champion of the pharmaceutical industry but has shifted many of his political stances. My analysts tell me that this is in preparation for a future presidential run. He's now the cosponsor of a bill that will gut the legal opioid industry's profits within the United States. We're talking billions of dollars."

"So Ian Williams and the ISI want to kill the Senator to what…cancel his vote?"

"Possibly."

"If they kill him, does the bill die?"

"Possibly."

"But it sounds like you're talking about legitimate businesses here. A big corporation wouldn't be involved in something like this. It would be financial suicide."

"Agreed. We don't fully know the ISI's involvement yet, or how it plays into the legal opioid marketplace. My understanding is that the Big Pharma companies are not directly involved in this themselves. The ISI seems to be working with a group of shadow investors."

"What about this woman you want us to find, Jennifer Upton? Why would Williams want her dead?"

"That's what I need you to find out. I suspect she's our missing piece. My hope is that she'll be able to illuminate much that we currently don't know."

"Does she know she's in danger?"

"I don't know, considering that we've yet to make contact. But assuming you're able to locate her, your top priority is to bring her in and get her to a safe house. Once you do that, contact me."

"Williams may already believe that we have her name, since we spoke to Rojas."

"Correct. This all assumes that she hasn't been killed already. The fact that she's out of reach right now could mean either that she's dead or that she's gone underground. Consider this me being optimistic. Please do what you can to find her."

## CHAPTER 16

THE ASSASSIN HAD USED many names over the years, but Hugo was his name by birth. He'd first killed a man at the age of sixteen. For revenge.

Hugo's father had taught him how to hunt in the wilderness of Quebec. Together, they'd shot black bear, white-tailed deer, and moose. Some of their hunting trips would last days, involving deep treks into the forest using snowshoes. That had made hauling the animal carcasses back to their home difficult. But often the most difficult tasks in life could be the most rewarding. Especially when conducted in the company of one's father.

Their town was very small. Everyone knew each other. The winters were long and harsh.

Sometimes hellishly so.

One afternoon, Hugo and his father were returning from a hunt when they heard screams coming from their home. They left the sled that carried their prize and hurried into the house.

Hugo's mother was on the bed and on her back, eyes wide and face battered. The town drunk stood over her, holding a large curved blade. The man was a thuggish brute who had been thrown in the town jail twice for assault.

Hugo's father ran to the man but was cut down, blood pouring from his wounds. Hugo tried firing his hunting rifle from the hip but missed. The drunk ran out of the home, and Hugo tended to his father's wounds. But they were too deep. His father was dead within minutes. Hugo called the police and an ambulance. They took his mother to a hospital and apprehended the town drunk.

Hugo's mother was a mess, crying hysterically at the loss of Hugo's father. The local prosecutor wanted to interview Hugo and see if he would testify in court. But Hugo had no intention of letting the courts decide the fate of his father's killer. It was a small town. And Hugo knew the cops. His killer would be transferred to a larger prison the next day, so Hugo had to act fast. When the jailer went to the bathroom, he left the jail cell master key set on his desk. Hugo took his hunting bow and seven arrows with him.

From a range of less than ten feet, he unloaded the arrows into his father's murderer. Shafts of death plunging into his flesh. The screams of pain lasted only a moment as the arrows entered his lungs and made it too hard for the man to make a sound.

It looked incredibly painful.

It was immensely satisfying.

That night, Hugo took out several thousand dollars from various ATMs—his life savings—bought a ticket from Quebec City to France, and disappeared.

A few weeks later, he would join the French Foreign Legion under an alias, and his real training would begin. Hugo spent ten years in the Legion, traveling to various parts of the globe. He became an expert soldier, deploying to Afghanistan and several nations in Africa.

It was in Africa that he'd been approached by his first private employer. Half a month pay for two hours of work, he was told.

Hugo shot a man who hours earlier he did not know. Even when he was killed, Hugo didn't know his name, only a face and an address. He placed two bullets into his chest as he entered his home. Then one bullet in his head, before he walked away.

The employer appreciated the quick, reliable work, and Hugo found that he would rather become a contract killer than stand any more guard duty for a nation he wasn't particularly loyal to, on a continent he didn't care for. But it was Africa where he stayed, for a time. Working for another two years, refining his technique and gaining experience, before being picked up by the European placement agencies. That was where the real money was. Russian, Turkish, and Italian organized crime seemed to have a never-ending desire to kill each other off. And they were willing to pay top dollar to do so.

Eventually, the Pakistanis found him, and Hugo became exclusive.

Most assassinations in first-world countries required creating as much separation from the crime scene as possible. But killing someone this close to Washington, D.C., had been a unique challenge. The security cameras and sophisticated tracking technology put in place to track terrorists meant that any movement Hugo made would be a potential red flag to American government eyes. The Ron Dicks assignment had taken twelve hours to plan, and six hours to execute. Other than that, Hugo stayed put in D.C., remaining in the same rental unit he'd secured a week earlier. Enjoying the sights. Going to bars and restaurants.

It was in this small flat near Dupont Circle that he'd received the most recent message from Syed, his Pakistani contact. The main job. The reason that the ISI had sent their most prolific international assassin to the States.

Hugo had gone to the dead drop site and picked up his message within three hours. At the dead drop, he obtained another of their special thumb drives. After returning to the flat, he connected the thumb drive to his computer and entered the passphrase, which then brought up a series of screens. A sort of timed quiz, one in which he had to answer each question quickly and correctly or else the information would self-delete, which it would do anyway after thirty minutes.

When he was finished, he read over the file. It was a mission brief. The Pakistanis were playing a dangerous game by being this bold. But that wasn't his decision to make. The fee was very good, and that was what mattered.

Hugo deleted the files and then checked his watch. He would sleep here tonight, then fly out in the morning.

To Wisconsin.

* * *

Ian Williams's convoy pulled up to the Gulfstream, his security men eying their surroundings as he walked up the ladder to the jet and got in.

His assistant handed him a phone.

"It's him."

Williams nodded. They used the best antitrace software and encryption programs. The hardware was purchased in China and flown over by Williams's men. He didn't trust American companies. Williams had heard too many rumors of NSA agents embedding their own little surprises into US-sold devices.

But even with all that sophisticated technology, Williams never spoke to Syed directly over the phone. Too high a risk of the world's intelligence agencies listening in.

For calls to his ISI handler—business associate might be a better description of their current relationship nowadays—Williams used a system of trusted voice-relay personnel. Handwriting messages, holding them up to be read aloud over the phone. Even using this procedure, phone calls were rare forms of communication for the two as the climax of their ambitious plan drew near.

A woman's voice—Pakistani with a British accent, Williams thought—said, "We are worried that recent events may bring unwanted attention."

Williams scribbled something on a pad of paper, which would be placed in a burn bag as soon as they were finished. When he finished writing, his assistant read it aloud into the phone. It was a dreadfully tedious way to communicate. But it kept the conversation secure and anonymous.

"It was regrettable but necessary."

"The meeting is imminent. Will we be ready? How many more names do you have on the list?"

"That work will be finalized on location. We are sending our best people to complete the task."

"We have received word that some of the participants don't want to go. They are nervous about travel to America."

"Please assure them that we've chosen this venue carefully. The meeting location keeps everyone safe and ensures peace during the negotiation process. Use the secure entry points and procedures as directed. Arrival inspections won't be a problem. There will be ten thousand flights in and out of this airport in a few days' time. Passenger manifests can be manipulated. Security will be lax. And tell them that if they are too scared to show up for this meeting, then they will be cut out of our new agreement."

"What about the politician?"

"It is being handled."

"Very well. Good luck."

Williams signaled for his assistant to end the call. As the jet took off and headed north, a moment of panic seized him. What if Syed was right? Had the killings near Washington been too brazen? Had it tipped their hand? That Max Fend character had shown up right in his backyard. What information had Rojas given them? It couldn't have been much. He didn't know much. What if the Americans did know more than they were letting on?

No. That was impossible. The mole had given them accurate operational details as recently as the past few days, and the assassinations ensured that there would be no further link to him or the ISI. Williams licked his lips, thinking of what lay ahead. Only a few more days of risk.

After Oshkosh, things would be easier.

## CHAPTER 17

AFTER THE CALL WITH WILKES, Max, Renee and Trent agreed they would travel to Cincinnati to start the search for Jennifer Upton at her place of work. It would have been evening if they had flown straight to Ohio, and Renee wanted a night to do research before they arrived. So they made a pit stop in Memphis for what Max considered the most crucial elements of their success: fuel, ribs, and pulled pork sandwiches. "I'm afraid I must insist on the barbecue," Max had said. They had remained overnight in Memphis and had flown the final leg in the morning.

Max landed them at Lunken Airport, just to the east of the Ohio River, outside of Cincinnati.

"Is it always this busy?" Trent asked as Max taxied them to the ramp.

The flight line was filled with small aircraft. Mostly Cessnas and Pipers, some of which had smiling owners standing next to the planes, talking with each other as they waited. A lone fuel truck was slowly making its way through the aircraft.

"I doubt it. They must all be on their way up to Oshkosh. The fly-in starts in earnest today."

Max waited for fuel while Trent and Renee went inside.

Trent's mission was to secure them a rental vehicle. Renee was in the conference room on her computer, hunting for possible hints as to where Jennifer Upton might be. All they knew with certainty was where she lived and that she worked at a political nonprofit in Cincinnati.

"Nice Cirrus!" said a man standing beside the plane in the parking spot next to Max. He had sandy blond hair and wore wraparound sunglasses and a sweat-stained polo shirt. He stood beside two teenage boys who had trouble maintaining eye contact.

"Thanks," replied Max. "You guys headed up to Oshkosh?"

"Just like everybody else here. It's our fifth pilgrimage. Name's Jake King. These are my sons, James and Jack."

Max waved politely to the family with oddly similar names, keeping his smile to himself. "Nice to meet you."

"That Cirrus have a parachute in it?"

"I sure hope so. I hear they come in handy."

The man laughed. "Are you flying up for the air show today?"

"To Oshkosh? I'd sure love to go, but we don't have any plans to right now."

One of the sons—Max wasn't sure which was James and which was Jack—said, "We spent the last three months planning for the flight in. If you don't already know, I don't think—"

His father whispered, "You don't need to tell him that, James. I'm sure he knows all the planning required." Mr. King then looked up at Max. "Well, if you find yourself there, come see our gyrocopter. It's being shipped up by truck today. We'll be flying it on the ultralight field every day starting tomorrow."

"Well, that's pretty neat."

One of the boys said, "Yeah, but the best part is the remote-control function me and my dad built in."

The father looked proud. "Well, it's not that special. With

the advancements in drone technology, it was a relatively simple upgrade."

"Yeah, my experience hasn't been the best with remotely controlled aircraft."

The man squinted. "Say, you kind of look familiar. Have we met?"

Renee was waving at Max from the FBO building, trying to get his attention. Max noticed that the two King boys saw her and gave each other looks of approval.

"Looks like I've got to run."

As he was leaving, he heard Mr. King say, "I swear I recognize him…"

Max stopped at the fuel truck and told the man operating it, "Hey, the blue-and-white Cirrus is mine. Please top her off." The fuel man nodded, and Max headed towards Renee.

"We've got a vehicle," she said. "Trent's waiting in the parking lot."

"Great. I want to run by her home and office. Maybe we can talk to someone who knows how to find her."

* * *

They drove through the heart of the city, passing the Reds and Bengals stadiums and the Procter & Gamble headquarters building. Renee had Trent take the Liberty Street exit off I-71 towards a neighborhood known as Over the Rhine.

"Well, this is charming," said Renee, inspecting the homes.

"That's one way to put it." To Max it just looked like an old inner-city neighborhood. Spray-painted graffiti art on brick exteriors. Some blocks filled with boarded-up windows. A large billboard for domestic beer. Telephone wires and power lines overhanging the street. Older-model cars in need of body work.

"Okay, well, not everything looks great, but look at these buildings up here."

Max saw what she was looking at. Some of the shops and residences had been refurbished. As they drove, he saw cleaner and more modern-looking exteriors. Their new paint jobs provided splashes of color among the old brick.

At last they came upon the central square. A clock tower stood in one corner. Large potted plants and bright red metal picnic tables were spaced out over a wide concrete sidewalk. While much of the shopping was outdoors—there was a busy farmers market on one side—there was also a great hall with several dozen shops, delis, and bakeries inside, forming the center of the plaza. The building was crowned with a turquoise-lettered sign reading FINDLAY MARKET.

"There's the office," said Max. "Drop me off here. I'll text you if I need longer than fifteen minutes."

Renee and Trent parked in a lot a block away from Jennifer Upton's workplace. They sat in the rental, engine running, air conditioning humming, Trent behind the wheel, Renee's laptop open as she continued to research Upton.

Max was going fishing, trying to glean information from coworkers on where she might be. Jennifer Upton worked for a 501c nonprofit firm based in Ohio. Max went into the office, falsely claiming to have a meeting set up with Upton. He would dangle a new and high-profile client: Charles Fend, Max's well-known billionaire father, who was known to contribute his funds to causes that would help his business. With any luck, the members of the firm would eat out of his hand, and while they were trying to make a new client happy, Max would be asking seemingly innocuous questions about Upton.

"Here he comes."

Max was walking back towards their vehicle. Fifteen minutes, just like he'd said.

Renee rolled down her window. "Anything?"

"I might have some info for you, but no obvious location." Max handed Renee a sheet of paper with keywords written down. Upton's cat's name. Past employers and clients. Things Max had noticed on her office desk.

"I might be able to use some of this for potential usernames or passwords."

Trent said, "You guys mind if we get lunch?"

"Sounds good."

Trent and Renee got out of the vehicle, and the three of them began walking towards the marketplace.

"Crowded," said Max.

Trent hummed agreement.

Findlay Market was packed. Throngs of people—families pushing strollers, grandmas shopping at the flea market, yuppies wearing athleisure wear while sipping mimosas over brunch. There were a lot of nice-looking restaurants, bars, and even freshly renovated office space.

Max elbowed Renee. "Okay, maybe you are right. This place looks pretty cool."

Renee smiled up at him, pulling him close to her in a loving gesture as they walked. He could tell she was still tense by the way she was looking around.

"How are you holding up?"

She said, "I'm alright. It's just a lot to process, all of this. The shooting in Mexico, and in Texas…"

"I know. I'm sorry. We'll be okay." He felt her arm squeeze his waist. They walked past a little row of vendor shops that were situated along the sidewalk. The corner tent had big freezers and a long line of smiling customers. A variety of delicious gelato flavors were written on a chalkboard sign standing next to the tent.

The market square was lined with colorful two- and three-story attached mixed-use units—homes, businesses, restaurants, and stores. Max didn't like the number of opaque windows looking down on their meeting spot. Or the hundreds of casuals walking every which way around the marketplace. He told himself to relax. They weren't in danger here. At least, he didn't think they were.

"I'll grab a table here and wait."

Renee came back a few moments later and plopped down in the seat across from him. She liked to order for him without asking what he wanted, and Max didn't mind. Renee took two paper-wrapped submarine sandwiches out of a bag, smiling as Max examined his lunch.

"What did you get?"

"Banh mi. Vietnamese sandwiches. Have you ever had one?"

Max opened the paper wrapping. A French baguette, pork, little slices of jalapeños, cilantro by the look of it, thin slices of cucumbers and carrots, and some type of pink spread.

He took a large, brave bite, chewing and salivating as the combination of tastes hit his mouth. "My God."

"I know, right?"

"This is so good. Why the hell haven't I tried this before?"

"There's a Vietnamese place in Charlottesville that I go to all the time. They make great ones. But this isn't bad at all..."

Trent came back with a Styrofoam plate of Greek food. Lamb, spiced potatoes, onions, tomatoes, pita, and cucumber sauce.

Renee was eating with one hand and tapping on her open laptop's trackpad with the other. Her eyes widened, and she held up a hand. "Got it!"

"Excuse me?"

"I'm done. I've found her."

"Found who?"

She looked triumphant. "Your missing woman, *mon cheri*. Well, sort of. That is to say, I know where she will be."

"How?"

"I just went on one of the overlay networks where you can

buy people's usernames and passwords. You probably know this as the 'dark web.' Spooky name. I found an old email account that Miss Upton barely uses. It's not linked to her home or work IP addresses or her devices. She must have some software that she runs to avoid detection. And it's not under her name anymore. It's an alias. But this account is hers. I purchased her account data from one of the dark web sites. Max, you owe me twenty bucks for that purchase, by the way. We can work something out later." She winked. "Since no one ever changes their passwords—except for me, of course—I tried the same username and password on all of her other accounts. I also tried a few variations with the information you gave me. The winner was her current pet name, mixed with the numbers and symbols from one of her old passwords. I got a match, read through some of Miss Upton's emails, and found that she recently reserved a hotel."

"Nice work."

Trent, chewing a big bite of gyro, said, "Remind me to change my password."

Renee said, "Her check-in is at three p.m. tomorrow." Renee peered at the screen. "Hmm. Well, now, that's quite interesting. Guess where the hotel is?"

"Where?"

"Fond du Lac, Wisconsin. Which, I should point out, is suspiciously close to Oshkosh."

The table went silent for a moment.

"Really? Where Senator Becker is headed?"

Trent's face contorted into a confused expression. "Pretty suspicious that the only two names we know of on the kill list are both headed towards the same place. Why do you suppose that is?"

Max stood up and began picking up his food and stuffing it into the bag. "We'll have to ask her when we get there. Come on, we can eat in the car."

The others stood and began doing the same. Renee said, "And you don't want to just call up Wilkes and have him take care of it? Didn't he say he was going to bring a team to Oshkosh too?"

"Yeah, but the last two times Wilkes knew where we were, so did Ian Williams. How about this time, we wait to tell him until after we pick her up?"

Trent shrugged. "Works for me, man. I like air shows, and I like guns. This gives me a unique opportunity to combine the two."

An uneasy feeling overcame Max as he thought more about the situation. "If Jennifer Upton is on the kill list, then we could be facing cartel or ISI hit teams when we try to grab her."

"If she shows up," Trent said. "It's possible she made this reservation but was then taken or killed by Williams's men, right?"

Renee was looking at her computer. "Well, according to the monitoring program I now have running on her accounts, she just checked her email from her phone an hour ago. Her phone accessed cell towers in Chicago, but now it's powered off. It's *possible* that someone else is doing this. But my guess is that it's still her."

"Good. Please keep monitoring her electronic communications. Let us know if she tries to contact anyone or changes her plans. I think we should assume that our first opportunity to take her is when she arrives to check in at her hotel."

"Logical," said Renee. Renee closed her laptop, stuffing it into her handbag, and they began walking back towards the car.

Max said, "If Williams is going to send a hit team to get Upton, we need to get to her first."

\* \* \*

Max was in the flight planning room at the FBO. It was packed. Filled with more smiling recreational aviators on a break from their cross-country flights up to Wisconsin. He recognized the two King boys, who looked like they were packing up.

"You guys heading back out to your plane?"

"Yes, Mr. Fend."

"Ah, so you figured out my name, huh?"

"Our dad did, yes, sir."

"Say, you guys mentioned it took you a long time to plan your flight to Oshkosh. I've never flown in there myself, but I was thinking about doing it today. Could you give me the two-minute version of what I need to do?"

The boys looked at each other, wide-eyed. "Uh. Mr. Fend, respectfully, it's really complicated…"

"Actually, why don't you just let me see your flight plan for a second? I'll go make a photocopy."

One of them handed a copy to Max. "You can keep it. I have three copies."

"You're a great American, my friend."

"But, Mr. Fend, if you're really going to do this, you'll need to read the NOTAMs."

Max shrugged. "No problem." The Notice to Airmen was the advisory that alerted pilots about hazards or changes along their route of flight, including the airports. It was usually a quick read, only a few lines.

"You can take my spare copy of that, too." He handed Max what looked like a small book.

Max raised his eyebrows. "Okay. Great. Thanks…"

Renee and Trent were in the lobby. Renee had caught Max's eye and was giving him a concerned look, nodding towards the TV fixed to the wall.

The national news had interrupted the daytime TV programming and was showing footage of Washington, D.C., outside the Capitol Building.

US SENATOR RECEIVING DEATH THREATS AFTER AIDE
KILLED

Max walked over to Renee. "What is it?"

"They're talking about Senator Becker. A news story just
broke that he's been getting death threats because of an anti-
opioid bill he's sponsoring."

"Death threats from who?"

"They say there are international investors connected to
organized crime who are trying to stop his vote."

"Organized crime? What's that supposed to mean? The
cartels?"

"I don't know. The story's only just broken. But if it was the
cartels, why would they care about a law passing?"

The newscaster interrupted their conversation.

"Senator Becker has put out a statement saying that he
won't be deterred by brutish thugs who want to scare America
into submission. He still intends to be in public this week,
while watching his daughter perform at the Oshkosh Air Show
in his home state of Wisconsin."

Max and Renee looked at each other. Max said, "Well, if
there was any doubt as to where they could find him, that's
gone now."

# CHAPTER 18

TRENT SAT in the backseat of the Cirrus, Renee and Max in front. Max had filed the exact same flight plan as the King family. In a way, it was kind of like copying someone's homework. But since he wasn't getting graded, and they all had the same destination, he didn't think it was an ethical dilemma.

They were airborne about thirty minutes after Max had filed their flight plan. After they cleared Cincinnati airspace, the three of them conversed over the internal communication headsets. Max asked Renee if she wanted to do some of the flying, and she said yes.

"You won't stall us this time?" he joked.

"I'll do my best."

Trent said, "You guys make a pretty cute couple."

"Thank you." Renee looked at Max and pinched his cheek.

Max said, "It's not all roses. She can be very tough on me. We have major disagreements on how we see some things."

Trent looked skeptical. "Like what?"

Max said, "Trent, there are two types of people in this world. Those who like Tim Tebow, and those who don't."

Renee turned her head. "I didn't say that I don't *like* him. He just didn't have an NFL-caliber arm, that's all."

"You take that back. He's flawless in every way."

Trent said, "Renee, you like football?"

Max smiled. "Uh-oh. Here we go."

She turned to Trent, pulling her sunglasses down and narrowing her eyes. "And why wouldn't I like football? Because I'm a girl?"

Trent tapped Max on the shoulder. "I see what you mean."

The flight was several hours long, but it provided some much-needed downtime for the group.

"There's Chicago," Renee said into the mike. They were flying north along the shores of Lake Michigan, the skyline at their eleven o'clock. Max looked down at his chart display and dialed up the local air traffic control frequency, checking in and requesting visual flight following as he traveled to the north. He could hear dozens of other aircraft speaking to the controller every few seconds. It was busy airspace here all the time.

Trent keyed his mike from the backseat. "Pretty cool." Renee was all smiles as well. Max was glad.

"Maybe on the way back, we can stop there and hit up Lou Malnati's."

"Now you're talking."

After getting clear of Chicago airspace, Max banked the aircraft left, ensuring that they would take Kenosha and Milwaukee off their right side as they continued north. He had pre-dialed in a set of checkpoints and was scanning his GPS to ensure that they were on course.

"Okay, this is the tricky part." Max handed Renee the white booklet he had stapled together. A picture on the front cover showed a small airplane in a shallow climb, trailing aerobatic smoke.

"What's this?" Renee asked.

"That's the NOTAM. The Notice to Airmen. I haven't had a

chance to read it all yet, but I convinced one of those teenage boys to lend me their extra copy."

Renee said, "NOTAM? But you showed me those the other day when we were flying in Virginia. I thought NOTAMs were only a few words long."

"Normally they are."

She turned the pages of the booklet. "This is almost thirty pages!"

"Yeah. Well, ten thousand aircraft are all arriving at the same time. So, they probably don't want us to run into each other. Now, turn to page..." Max tried to keep his altitude while he flipped to near the end of the booklet, where he had placed a bright orange sticky note. "There. Please read that part the kid highlighted. I'm not sure what it says, but those kids seemed sharp, so we should probably read the highlights."

Renee moved her forefinger over the words as she read. "Ensure lights are on and set transponder to standby."

Max flipped a switch and scanned his instruments. "Check."

Renee kept reading the procedures, her eyes growing wider as she read. She looked over at Max. "It says find an aircraft of similar speed and type and follow them."

"Okay."

"Is that a joke? Ten thousand aircraft are flying here at the same time, and they tell you to find someone at the same speed as you and follow them?"

Max scanned outside for other aircraft. "Hmm. Well, maybe we should drop a procedural improvement into the Oshkosh suggestion box when we land. But for now, keep reading..."

Max spotted a Cessna out the window. "Traffic, three o'clock, level, no factor. He's going slower, so we'll overtake him."

More and more aircraft appeared outside, some just little white specks in the distance, others close in, and much larger. Some of the aircraft were above their altitude, some below.

One little orange-and-white helicopter chugged along to their east.

They found a white Cessna at about their same altitude, and Max adjusted his speed so they wouldn't overtake it. He then fell in a loose trail position, partly making sure he was following the map in the booklet and partly making sure he followed the plane ahead of him.

The ground below was carved into an endless expanse of brown and green fields. Roads and houses, trees and barns. Grain silos and cow pastures, and a highway filled with cars headed towards the air show. Another highway filled with planes above it, doing the same. Soon Lake Winnebago appeared, shimmering in the afternoon sun off to the east.

Renee said, "Okay, we're coming up on the part where we have to talk."

"I've always been a good talker."

"I feel like you aren't taking this as seriously as you should be."

Trent said, "Are couples allowed to fly and navigate together? Should I be worried here?"

A moment later, they arrived at the main entry checkpoint, and the Oshkosh aircraft controller called out Max's aircraft. The man spoke incredibly fast. He was probably taking a break from his normal job, which Max assumed must have been as an auctioneer.

"Blue-and-white-Cirrus-at-half-mile-south-of-Fisk, rock-your-wings."

Renee said, "What the hell did he just say?"

Max moved his yoke to the right and left in rapid succession, making the aircraft roll back and forth.

"Half-mile-south-of-Fisk, blue-and-white-Cirrus, good-rock-sir, continue-northeast-bound-along-the-railroad-tracks-for-a-right-downwind-runway-two-seven, maintain-one-thousand-eight-hundred-until-turning-your-downwind, monitor-tower-one-one-eight-point-five...*welcome-to-Oshkosh.*"

Renee looked at Max. "He was talking so fast! *Merde*. What did he say? He wants us to follow railroad tracks?"

Max shushed her. "Honey, can you be quiet for a moment? I need to concentrate." The aircraft ahead of them was turning sharply. Max felt like each plane was on an infinite conveyer belt that couldn't stop. Everyone had to perform their maneuvers at precisely the right moment. Otherwise, the entire line would get fouled up, which ended badly with airborne conveyer belts.

Max could see the line of planes landing in front of them, and the giant airport itself. Enormous green fields filled with cars, pup tents, Winnebagos, and, of course, planes. Rows and rows of aircraft of all colors, shapes and sizes.

"Oh my God," Renee said. "There are so many..."

Max had switched up the radio frequency to tower. After finishing his turn, he heard the tower controller say, "Clear to land." A beautiful phrase.

The white pavement of the runway grew larger in the windscreen as they descended on their approach. The rows of aircraft already on the ground zoomed by as their altitude decreased, and the world seemed to move faster and faster.

Then, with a squeak, the wheels touched down, and Max began pumping the brakes, decelerating as fast as he could. Max turned off at the appropriate taxiway, and a guy wearing an orange vest and holding orange batons directed him to follow the line of planes inching along ahead of him.

Max exhaled.

"Nice work. I knew you could do it." Renee patted him on the shoulder. She wore a wide smile, looking pretty in her aviator sunglasses, her dark hair held back by the aircraft headset.

Taxiing the aircraft seemed to take forever. They crept at a snail's pace, past the waving crowds of people in lawn chairs, sitting in the shade under the wings of their Cessnas, past the rows of old warbirds, and past the forest of covered pavilions where lecturers were speaking about aviation-related subjects.

Finally they arrived at their parking spot on the lawn, and Max shut down the Cirrus.

Max said, "Welcome to our new home."

Trent said, "I hope we like our neighbors. They got us packed in like the parking lot of a pumpkin patch."

Max shut down the engine, and they opened the doors. It was hot—a good eighty-five degrees—but nothing compared to the Tex-Mex heat they'd been exposed to last week. The aircraft behind them had just parked, and its prop was winding down. Pup tents were scattered among the aircraft in front of them. The field behind them was clear of aircraft for the moment, but it would be filled up soon.

"So where to first?" asked Renee.

Max said, "We probably need tents, a few supplies, and a rental vehicle. Then I say we spend a few hours getting the lay of the land here. Find out where Becker is going to be, and then work out our plan to bring in Jennifer Upton without consequence."

"How are we going to find the senator? This place is huge. You want to call Wilkes, let him know we're here?"

"Not yet. They have VIP tents set up. My father used to hang out in them. We can start there." Max gave Renee a funny look. "And I might know someone here who can get us to meet with the senator."

"Who?"

"His daughter."

"How do you know his daughter again?" asked Renee, her voice suspicious.

"Well, my father and Senator Becker knew each other. You know that. And there was a brief period where…"

"Wait, did you *date* his daughter?"

Max went red. "I mean…technically…uh…"

Trent saw Max's face and said, "Hey, man, you need a shovel?"

"What for?"

"'Cause I think you're gonna need to dig yourself out of a hole pretty soon."

## CHAPTER 19

THE VAST MAJORITY of attendees at the Oshkosh Air Show either camped out on the airport's vast grassy plains or slept in a Winnebago or trailer. Max, having been to Oshkosh when he was younger, knew that there would be little chance of getting a hotel room now that the air show had commenced. This was why he had dispatched Trent to secure a rental car, tents, and camping supplies.

Renee and Max walked along rows of aircraft to get to the central hub of the air show. Max had fond memories of this place from when he was younger. His father made it a point to show up almost every year. As the figurehead of Fend Aerospace, Charles Fend was a fixture of the event. Sort of like Arnold Palmer taking the first tee shot at the Masters.

Fend Aerospace was also one of the biggest sponsors of the show, and they often displayed their latest and greatest aircraft in the central area, renting giant tents and schmoozing with potential buyers. The air show was a place for aviation fans and history buffs to tour, but it was also a place for aviation businesses to wheel and deal. It wasn't quite the Paris Air Show, where the focus was more on the business side of things. But there was still a lot of that.

"It's hot." Max wiped sweat from his brow.

"Maybe we can stop and get something to drink?"

Max and Renee arrived at the main static display area in the center of the air show. There were a variety of giant jumbo jets, military fighters, and old warbirds set up for viewing in the central plaza. A double-decker commercial aircraft, an Airbus A380, dominated this year's static display. An Air Force AC-130 gunship was also a big crowd-pleaser.

"There's a DC-3 over there," said Max. He pointed to another. "Oh, look. Check out the paint job on that B-17. Impressive."

Renee smiled at him. "You love this stuff, don't you?"

"Doesn't everyone?"

"It would probably be more enjoyable if I wasn't worried about people trying to kill us."

He placed his hand on the small of her back. "You alright?"

"You don't need to keep asking me that. I'm fine. Just eager to meet this old girlfriend of yours."

Max took solace in the fact that if Renee was focused on the whole girlfriend-jealousy thing, it was probably a positive signal as to her current mental health. However, it was also a negative sign for Max's.

"So…the weather…pretty hot out, huh?"

Renee smirked at his obvious attempt to change the subject. "Yes. I need to pick up some sunblock or I'll turn into a lobster."

They walked into an air-conditioned minimart and Renee purchased some sunblock. Both of them threw on gobs of it while taking refuge under the shade of the overhang outside. Next, they walked over to another vendor's tent and ordered two giant lemonades, extra ice. Max handed one to a grateful Renee, and they continued along.

Max was interested in the planes, but his mind kept turning over the problems at hand. He thought about what they'd learned about Becker's connection to Upton. About Becker's chief of staff being killed. About the cartel attack in Texas. About Ian Williams learning of Wilkes's agent in Mexico. These were all pieces of a puzzle. Clues he needed to put together before…

Before what? Before Senator Becker was assassinated? Or before the ISI and Ian Williams commenced their mysterious meeting of minds? What were they meeting about? Who was attending? Where was the meeting being held? Why would they need a list of people killed before the meeting occurred? A list that involved one of the most powerful politicians in America?

And would Caleb Wilkes really let it get that far? Was he really so bold as to use a US senator as bait? Then again, it wasn't Wilkes who had forced the senator to come here to this public stage. Becker supposedly knew that he was in danger and was choosing to flout the warnings he'd been given by attending the Oshkosh air show anyway.

Max watched Renee sucking lemonade from her straw and again felt guilty for exposing her to this dangerous world. And to men like Ian Williams.

While she had volunteered to go to Mexico, Max realized that her reason wasn't the same as his. Max felt a calling to the trade. Partially a call to serve and protect or whatever the hell you wanted to call it. But it was also for himself. This mixture of adrenaline and noble purpose was his own addiction. Max needed his fix.

Renee was different. She was motivated by selfless compassion. The tugging at her heartstrings she'd felt when Josh Carpenter died, leaving little Josh behind. The unjust killing of Ines Sanchez on the beach in Mazatlán. And more than any of that, Max knew that Renee's original and most important reason for being here was because she loved him.

That was what had gotten her on that flight to Mexico. She

wanted to help keep Max safe. Walking next to her now, he realized that he felt the same way. Max loved and admired everything about her. Her infectious laugh. Her passion for life. Her love of learning and relentless work ethic.

Max looked at her now, at her dark shoulder-length hair with traces of white sunblock smudged in. Her fit yet curvy figure. Her Mona Lisa smile that seemed to come more and more often lately. The feelings he had for her made him vulnerable, which frightened him. And while he regretted that Renee was in danger, she was also proving extremely valuable to the operation.

Max once again promised himself that he would do a better job of protecting her. And when this was over...well, maybe he'd finally have that serious relationship talk he knew she wanted to have.

They sipped their drinks and walked along the crowded taxiway, which was being used mainly as a pedestrian sidewalk right now.

They came across a very old black man who was propped up on an elevated wooden chair on the side of the walkway. The set-up was official looking—the chair looked like a short lifeguard chair, complete with a large orange umbrella to keep the man shaded. A World War Two fighter plane rested in the grass behind him. Another black man of about sixty stood next to him. By their manner and proximity, Max guessed the second man to be the elder's son.

Max took Renee's arm and they stopped.

"Hello, sir. Excuse me, but did you fly that aircraft back there? The P-51 Mustang?"

The old-World War II fighter aircraft, silver and gleaming, had the word TUSKEGEE painted in blue on the engine compartment. The old man's hat read 332nd Fighter Group, TUSKEGEE AIRMEN.

The man's voice was slow and raspy with a bit of a Southern accent. "Why, yes, sir, I did."

"My father was one of the Tuskegee Airmen," said the son, a proud grin as he looked at his old man.

Max saw Renee's eyes widen. She mouthed, "Wow."

Max stuck out his hand, speaking slow and clear. "It is an honor to meet you, sir." Renee smiled widely and also shook the man's hand.

"Why, thank you both." He looked tired but pleased to be here. His smile widened at Renee. "My, my. Your wife sure is pretty." They all laughed, and neither Max nor Renee bothered to correct him.

The man's son said to Max, "Hey, don't I know you?"

Max shook the son's hand. "My name is Max Fend."

"Sure. Your father—"

"Yes, my father owns Fend Aerospace."

"I thought I recognized you. I've seen you on the news."

"Yeah, those weren't my finest moments."

The man laughed. "Well, if I recall, it all worked out in the end, didn't it?"

Max nodded. "It did." He looked back at the elderly man sitting quietly in the chair. "Are they going to let you fly that here?" Max was smiling, trying to make small talk.

"They promised me a ride on the Ford."

"The Ford?" said Renee.

Max smiled, knowing that she probably thought the old man was going senile.

The old Tuskegee Airman lifted up a shaky hand and pointed his finger down the taxiway to the south. "The old Ford Trimotor, ma'am. I come here almost every year, yet I still never rode one of them. I'm ninety-four years old now. This might be my last year. I'd sure like to fly one of them Fords."

A boxy silver aircraft rested on the active taxiway one hundred yards away. Next to it, inside the fence, was a long line of people waiting to take a ride. It was one of the first ever mass-produced passenger planes, Max knew. It had three extremely loud engines —one on each wing and one on the nose—all making puttering, scraping noises as they ran, like an old jalopy in need of a tune-up.

The nose angled sharply skyward due to the fact that the rear of the aircraft was balanced on a tiny tail wheel.

Max said, "You don't see too many passenger aircraft that are tail draggers anymore." Rides on the Ford Trimotor were a staple of the Oshkosh air show.

Renee offered the old man a big smile. "Well, that looks like it would be a lot of fun. I hope you get to take a ride."

Max and Renee bade farewell to the pair and kept walking. They headed through the central static display area, passing modern military fighter aircraft, giant commercial planes, and several large US Air Force tankers. They kept walking and arrived at the ultralight aircraft field. Small aircraft in a variety of shapes flew over that section of the airport. Some had hang glider wings. Others floated on parachutes, with rear-mounted props that reminded Max of Everglades airboats.

"Hey, look. There's the King family."

"Who?" asked Renee.

"The kids I met at the Cincinnati airport. The ones who I stole...I mean, the ones who *gave* me their flight plan."

She smirked.

The two teenage boys and their father were standing at the edge of the ultralight field, which was a few hundred yards long, south of the main exhibit, and fenced off from the crowd. Mr. King was placing a tablet computer and a joystick on top of a fold-up table. The boys were unfolding the arms of a white helicopter-like contraption about half the size of a car.

Max checked his watch. They still had another half hour before they were supposed to meet Trent near the VIP tent. They had time to kill.

"Hello, boys."

"Hey, Mr. Fend." They waved back, their teenage eyes magnetically drawn to Renee.

"Ah, Max Fend. I knew I recognized you when we met in Cincinnati." The father shook Max's hand. Max introduced him to Renee. "A pleasure."

"This your gyrocopter?"

"It sure is. Jack here was just going to take it for a spin."

The teenager wore a white helmet and was now strapping into the driver's seat. The gyrocopter had a tall, thin rotor overtop, like a helicopter. But the rotor was much smaller than a helicopter's—it must have only been about ten feet in diameter. The rear of the contraption had a propeller that rested just aft of a small engine. There was no glass canopy surrounding the driver's seat. The pilot would be sitting in the open air. It was like a cross between a bicycle and a helicopter, with a prop in the rear.

"That motor looks about the size of a lawnmower," Renee said, then covered her mouth, hoping she hadn't said anything insulting.

Mr. King smiled wide, looking quite proud. "It was! Well, it was a big mower—a tractor—but that's what we converted it from."

Jack's brother was helping him strap in. A moment later, his brother out of the way, Jack started up the gyrocopter and began rolling along the grass, taking off in a buzz, both the top rotor and rear prop spinning.

Renee clapped her hands. "Well done."

"Thank you," said Mr. King.

"Dad, show them the RC."

Mr. King walked over to a table they had set up behind the fence. He placed on a headset and said, "Okay, Jack, now fly it back over here to where I am. We're going to demonstrate the remote-control feature."

A moment later, Jack had flown the gyrocopter in a race-track pattern and landed in the grass directly in front of the fence before them.

"The rotors on top move very slow compared to a helicopter."

"Yes, a gyrocopter flies using a different aerodynamic principle than a helicopter. A helicopter forces its rotor blades through the air, but a gyrocopter uses a free-spinning rotor to generate lift like a glider."

"Fascinating."

"It sure is."

"So, your son will stay in the aircraft while you operate it remotely?"

"Yes. We aren't certified as a drone, so this is sort of a gray area, what we're doing. But Jack can easily take the controls and overpower the inputs I'll be making if anything doesn't look right to him."

Max turned to Renee. "Where have I heard that before?"

Not hearing the comment, Mr. King said into the headset, "Hands off, Jack, I've got it." Then he took the joystick on the table and pressed a few buttons on the tablet. The gyrocopter took off into forward flight.

James King said, "My brother and I wrote the program. We used the same code that most of the off-the-shelf helicopter drones use. You can see the readout right there."

Max watched as Mr. King maneuvered the gyrocopter forward in a slow hover. It was like playing a video game. He just tapped forward on an arrow on the tablet, and he could also use the joystick to turn.

Renee said, "This is incredible. You boys did such a great job."

The kid went beet red. "Thank you, ma'am. It's also got a really cool feature that we added that will bring it right back to you if you've got it far away."

"Let's see it," said Max.

"Sure."

Mr. King used the tablet to maneuver the gyrocopter to a spot about one hundred yards away. "See this button?"

A yellow button on the tablet read "GO TO SET COOR-DINATES."

"Yup."

"Press it."

Max pressed the button, and the tiny aircraft immediately turned and nosed over, skimming the ground as it headed towards them at a surprisingly high speed. Just before Max was about to move them out of the way, the gyrocopter decelerated. It settled down on the grass fifty feet in front of them, with Jack once again holding the controls, a big smile on his freckled face.

Max said, "Pretty neat."

"Thanks."

"So you can program it to fly anywhere?"

"Pretty much. As long as we have a latitude and longitude, and enough fuel. But you still need a pilot at the controls to make sure we don't fly it into a tree or anything. The program is very rudimentary."

"It's impressive."

They shut down the gyrocopter and Jack ran over to the table, removing his helmet. Just then a loud buzzing filled the air as a sleek black-and-red aerobatic plane zoomed by them on one of the airport's main runways. It pulled straight up into a climb and began rolling on its longitudinal axis like a spinning Olympic figure skater.

"Is that her? Is that *her*?" one of the King boys asked.

"Yeah, it is," said the other.

The two boys took off towards the runway. Renee looked at Mr. King, who was shaking his head.

"What are they so excited about?"

"Oh, they're really interested in this aerobatic performer for some reason."

"Who is it?"

The speakers mounted throughout the airfield answered Renee's question. "Ladies and gentlemen, if you'll turn your attention to runway two-three, flying the Blonde Bombshell, may we present...Karen Becker!"

## CHAPTER 20

A SPOTLESS GLASS canopy covered Karen Becker's head. It was a beautiful day to fly. Bright sunshine and blue sky above. An immense crowd of several hundred thousand onlookers standing on the grass to her right, just beyond the taxiway. She wore wraparound shades to dim the intense glare of the sun. A headset fit snugly over her bleach-blond hair.

Already motoring forward on the taxiway, Karen pressed down with one of her feet, turning her black Extra 300L aerobatics plane onto the runway and aiming it down the centerline.

Her plane was adorned with the inscription "The Blonde Bombshell." Karen's likeness, wearing her signature pink flight suit, the front zipper pulled down enough to show a bit of cleavage, was painted underneath. The bleach-blond hair from her cartoon image flowed back along the length of the aircraft and was artistically transformed into bright reddish flames.

She quickly checked her engine instruments, and then the healthy whine of the engine grew into a strong buzz as she pushed the throttle forward. The grass, runway, static display aircraft, and sea of onlookers transformed into a blur as her aircraft increased speed.

The bouncing and rumbling of the aircraft changed into a steady floating sensation as she went airborne. She felt loose, light, and in complete control of her machine. Karen kept forward pressure on the stick, purposely staying low to the ground, her wheels mere feet above the runway, building speed, going faster and faster until just the right moment, when she tugged back hard on the yoke.

She flexed her stomach as the world pitched back and the Blonde Bombshell went vertical, climbing straight up, engine humming. Karen could practically hear the crowd cheering for her as she rolled hard left on the stick, and the world blurred again as the aircraft began spinning, a tornado of color.

Karen's lip microphone slipped out of place from the strong g-forces, and she stopped her turn halfway through a roll. She used her left hand to place the mike back tight against her lips, then yanked again and began her show.

Red smoke trailed from her aircraft—a red dye combined with a white smoke base. The smoke was created by pumping a paraffin-based biodegradable oil directly onto the hot exhaust nozzles of her piston engine. The oil vaporized to provide the stunning visual effect of a crimson column of cloud following along after her aircraft.

Karen kept her rapid scan flicking between the outside world and her instruments, seeking out visual cues on the ground to note her position, then forcing her eyes back inside at the instrument panel to check her airspeed, altitude, and engine instruments.

One moment she was one thousand feet in the air, upside down at the top of a loop. The next she was diving down to the earth. Then back up at eight thousand feet, throttle all the way back, using her foot pedals and yoke to send the aircraft into a spin—transforming the aircraft into a giant metal leaf, twirling as it fell from the sky.

Karen had practiced every maneuver countless times, both

in the air and on the ground, "chair-flying" for hours in a windowless room, with only her coach, using hand gestures, body position, and her imagination like she was practicing a ballet routine.

That's just what it was like, in a way. Aerobatic performances were carefully scripted, and very dangerous. The g-forces alone could force a pilot into unconsciousness in the blink of an eye. Some of the maneuvers Karen performed placed ten g's on her body, so her one hundred and twenty pounds became over half a ton.

During those intense turns, gravity tried to force her blood towards her extremities. Through practice, she had become proficient at special breathing techniques performed while flexing her legs, butt, thighs, calves, and stomach during high-g maneuvers. These techniques, and her g-suit, allowed her to keep her circulation under control. The g-suit contained water-filled tubes that ran from her shoulder down to her ankles. They would compress as the g's came on, keeping her blood pumping into the upper body and head, which allowed her to retain consciousness.

Karen had to keep in great physical shape to be able to withstand this repetitive physical toll on her body. She had to be mentally tough as well. For the past five years, she had trained like an Olympian, and now she understood the physics of aviation as well as some aerospace PhDs.

She had worked hard over the years to become one of the top aerobatics performers in the world, and now she was here, at the pinnacle of her career.

Karen pulled out of her final maneuver and touched down smoothly on the runway. Then she taxied up to the flight line next to the central static displays. Karen shut off her engine, and her propeller spooled down. She opened her canopy and removed her headset, shaking down long waves of blond hair.

All eyes were on her. And that was just the way she liked it.

Karen Becker was a marketer's dream. She climbed down from the cockpit and walked out onto the stage that had been set up for her. Karen wore ruby-red lipstick, custom steel-toed flight boots made to look like leather cowgirl boots, a bright pink flight suit, always zipped low enough that it showed off a bit of her ample bosom. Her blond hair was topped with her customary Stetson hat, handed to her by her agent. Change up a few items, and she could have easily been a Nashville country singer about to take the stage.

The aerobatics world had never seen someone quite like her. If Amelia Earhart were still around, she would probably either be blushing or shaking her head in disapproval. But as much as Karen was an entertainer on the ground, in the air, she was a professional. After leaving her father's political staff, she had enrolled at Embry-Riddle University and earned a second degree. At first she'd thought she might go into airport management. Something far away from politics. But while she was there, she'd learned how to fly and fallen in love with aviation. She'd earned a series of progressively more advanced pilot ratings and had eventually been hired as a flight instructor in Daytona. After meeting a few pilots at air shows and taking a few aerobatic lessons, she had found her passion.

Karen absolutely loved the thrill of going up and hearing the full-throated sound of her three-hundred-horsepower engine as she yanked and banked the aircraft into submission. It was like riding a roller coaster but actually being in control.

As she marched towards her post-flight reception tent, she saw that the line of fans coming to get her autograph and picture wound around the VIP tent over one hundred feet away. She noticed several old ladies in line with their husbands, eying her like she was the Leg Lamp from the movie *A Christmas Story*. Well, maybe she was. But sex sells. And she challenged anyone else performing at the air show to pull a tighter split-S than her.

\* \* \*

"Is *that* her?" Renee asked Max.

Mr. King said, "Yup. My boys are big fans. I tried to get them to come with me to the aerospace engineering lecture that's scheduled now, but they seemed to want to get her autograph instead. I don't see why. One of Burt Rutan's engineers is going to be here."

Max said, "It's a mystery."

Renee and Max bade farewell to Mr. King and walked over towards the air show's VIP tent, watching as Karen Becker finished up signing autographs.

Karen was a stunner. Max didn't realize he was wearing a silly schoolboy smile until Renee elbowed him. He turned to face her. "What? Did you say something?"

She rolled her eyes.

Trent appeared out of nowhere. "There you guys are. Our rental car is parked in the grass lot, and I've got all the supplies we need. What are you guys looking at…?" Trent followed their gaze. "Holy mother of mercy…"

Renee said, "Well, I see we've found the Medusa of Oshkosh. Ugh. If that's what men are really looking for, then I give up. For a moment I thought she was one of those models hired by an advertising firm or something. You know, the kind that stand there smiling next to the racers at the Formula One or walk across the ring at a boxing match. Are you telling me that she was the one who was just flipping and rolling above their heads? I guess I have to give her a little respect, but why in God's name would she wear an outfit like that?"

Max said, "I'm just going to keep my mouth shut."

Renee patted him on the chest. "Good idea."

Karen Becker emerged from a crowd of smiling fans. Max tried not to look at what was probably the most marvelous décolletage ever to appear in a flight suit—if flight suit was indeed what you called the tight-fitting pink outfit that Karen had painted on her—but that proved challenging. Max remembered that she had always been a looker, but it had been a while since they'd last seen each other.

Karen had been a fling. They had been introduced by their fathers years ago at one of these air shows—her father a prominent politician and a strong advocate for the aviation industry, his father an aviation industry CEO and icon.

Karen had many such flings, Max suspected. He was just another notch on her belt. Which was a funny thing to say about a woman, he thought. But Karen was a unique woman. A wild and sexy thrill-seeker. A beautiful and buxom…

"Uh-hum."

Max realized that he was staring at Karen again, and Renee was staring at him. The damn permasmile had returned, too. The same look seemed to have afflicted all of the other men within twenty feet of Karen, most of whose spouses were rolling their eyes or shaking their heads.

"So are you going to go talk to her or what? She's your ticket to meet her father, right?"

"You know, to be honest, I'm not even sure that she'll remember me."

"Max!"

Karen waved excitedly from across the taxiway, jogging towards them, bouncing and jiggling as she did so. One man nearby was mid-sip on a soft drink and began coughing, then looked away.

Before Max knew it, he was being wrapped in Karen's arms, her chest mashed up against him. Renee stood quietly by his side, tongue in cheek, her face a mix of jealousy and amusement. Max imagined laser beams from her eyes carving into the back of his skull.

When Karen finally released Max, she shot out her hand, saying in a sweet voice, "Hello, I'm Renee."

"Oh, hello, I'm Karen. I'm sorry, I didn't know Max was with anyone."

She stuck out her hand, and Renee shook firmly, looking her square in the eye. Two female spiders, ready to fight over a mate before they killed him and devoured him for dinner.

Renee said, "And how long have you known Max?"

"Oh, we go way back. Right, Max? What would you say? Ten years at least. Was that when you were at Princeton?"

"Oh, how interesting." Renee's eyes squinted, her face bunched up into a forced smile. Max and Renee had also met while they were at Princeton. Max looked at Renee with pleading eyes, thinking he might have been safer back in Mexico.

"That's right," Max began. "Our fathers are friends, and they introduced us at one of these air shows back when they were here on business. And that's how Karen and I met...and became friends."

Trent, who had remained silent until now, stuck his thumb backward, saying, "So I got that shovel back with the camping supplies..."

Renee mercifully moved on. "So, Karen, that was you performing just now?"

Karen said, "Yes, that's right. This is my first time at Oshkosh. I've been doing the lesser-known air show circuit for years now. But this is as good as it gets."

Max said, "Renee, Karen's father is Senator Becker, of Wisconsin. Around here they joke that this is his air show. He's been a huge proponent of general aviation and the aviation industry since he's been in Congress."

"Oh, yes, Dad is famous here. But I've been hoping that maybe if I do a good enough job, I can outshine him someday."

"And where is your father? I assume he's coming."

"Oh yes, he wouldn't miss this for the world. He's back in

Washington for a vote but promised to catch my Thursday performance."

They talked for a moment longer, with Trent asking such deep questions as how Karen liked being an air show pilot. Max had to admit that he was impressed. Aerobatic flying at this level was no joke. She was all at once a top-level entertainer, athlete, and aviator. So whatever he thought of her on a personal level, he respected her professionally.

Karen said, "Well, let's make our way into the VIP tent. I've got the night off, and I don't perform again for another two days. That means I'm having a cocktail."

Trent made an excuse and headed back to the campground. He whispered to Max that he wanted to scout out the area a bit more.

Renee, Max, and Karen walked into the tent, and Max saw several aviation business executives he knew through his father, a few A-list actors that he knew to be general aviation aficionados, and a lot of people in flight suits. They made the rounds, Max introducing Renee to the people he knew from his father's network.

The VIP tent was closed off from the outside and had a mildly effective air-conditioning unit, but people were coming in and out of the plastic curtain door so often that it was still quite warm. The grass floor had a thick coat of hay to avoid getting too muddy. The atmosphere reminded him of a horse race.

Except for the noise. There was always the drone of aircraft overhead. Right now, it sounded like a crazed bumblebee. Out of one of the tent's transparent patches, they could see an aircraft doing spins, one after the other, puffy white smoke trailing from behind.

Max grabbed them all drinks from the bar. They gathered around a tall cocktail table that was affixed to the grass with stakes.

"Wow. That looks pretty dangerous," Renee said, looking up at the plane. "Do you do all that, Karen?"

Karen said, "I'll do quite a few spins, yes. I have one part of my routine I'll do this week where I basically go up to eight thousand feet and spin until I get close to the ground, then I chop a ribbon in half with the prop. First time I took Max up like that, he puked all over my aircraft. He ever tell you about that?"

"Oh, you've flown together, too? No, he didn't mention it. I'm sure there's a lot that he left out." Renee shot Max another look. "If you will excuse me, I'm going to run to the ladies' room."

When Renee was gone, Max swore that Karen moved a few inches closer to him, and her tone became a bit more mischievous. "You're not exclusive with her, are you, Max?"

Max laughed nervously. "I have to admit, it is getting kind of serious."

"The single women of the world shall weep. And probably some married ones too." She winked. "Well, don't worry. I'll behave."

"I appreciate that."

Just then, the tarp entrance of the tent opened and in walked a tall white-haired man, followed by two men in suits. The members of the VIP tent gave a slight cheer.

One of them said, "There he is!"

Max's father had arrived.

* * *

Renee was delighted that Charles Fend had shown up. Max expected that he might see him here, but he hadn't spoken to his father since last week, and at the time Oshkosh wasn't something Max had planned on attending.

"Hello, son."

"Hi, Dad."

Father and son embraced, and then Charles held Renee by the shoulders, beaming at her like she was his long-lost daughter. More like his dream potential daughter-in-law. Charles's increasingly effusive worship of Renee over the last year was an embarrassing hint to Max that his father thought they should get married. Renee adored him right back, and the two had developed a sort of annoying teaming-up-on-Max relationship.

"Has he been treating you well?"

"It's been an adventure," she said. "But Max is always the gentleman."

"Good. You'll tell me if he ever hints at trouble. I'll make sure to disown him."

Renee laughed.

Charles turned to Karen. "Ah, Miss Becker, you are a vision in pink." He took her hand and kissed it.

Karen gave a toothy grin. "Good to see you again, Mr. Fend. My father will be here tomorrow. I'm sure he'll want to say hello."

"Excellent. How is your father? I've seen him on the news. Horrible circumstances, I'm afraid."

"Yes, well...he's got security assigned to him now, so I feel better about it."

Max said, "Oh yes, I saw that on the news. They say his chief of staff was killed? What happened? Is your father okay?"

Karen nodded somberly. "It's still being investigated. He asked me not to talk about it until the investigation is over."

"Oh, of course."

Charles stood erect and proper, listening closely, genuine concern in his voice. "Well, if there is anything I can do to help..."

Charles Fend's presence in the tent was felt by every one of the attendees, many of whom were clamoring to speak with him about a business proposal, or to get their picture taken alongside him. While Karen Becker might have been dazzling, Charles Fend was world-famous.

"If you'll excuse me, dear, I shall make my obligatory rounds. Max, Renee, why don't we plan on meeting up for brunch?"

"Sounds great," Renee answered, and Charles left their circle.

Renee squeezed Max's arm. "We should probably get back and set up our tent. Was there anything else you wanted to do here?"

Max turned to Karen. "You said your father is arriving tomorrow?"

"That's right."

"Perhaps I could say hello."

"Of course. Just find me tomorrow—or text me. My number is still the same."

Max and Renee said their goodbyes to Karen and then walked out of the tent. They walked through the main static display area in silence. An enormous concert stage was being set up. A crowd of thousands had gathered around it.

Renee said, "This place is impressive."

"Are you mad about Karen?"

"Do I have a reason to be?"

"No."

"Then don't be silly. Of course not. Like you said, we need her to gain access to her father."

"Although it sounds like my father will be with the senator too."

Max wondered if that was a coincidence. Caleb Wilkes had once run his father as well. Charles Fend had been a CIA asset during the Cold War, helping the American government to pass on false information to the Soviets. And as Max had learned last year, Wilkes still called on him from time to time.

When Wilkes had recruited Max, he had been cast as the replacement agent for his father. The heir to the throne of Fend Aerospace. With that title came the power, access, and privileges that would be quite helpful to American intelligence. Max's background as a DIA operative was a huge plus.

Max's father hadn't looked surprised that Max was here at Oshkosh. Had Wilkes asked his father to come here? Why would Wilkes do that without telling Max?

They walked through the crowd and saw a giant drive-in-style outdoor movie theater towering over a grass field, a grove of trees in the background. Kids and families sprawled out on the lawn, waiting for the sunset movie to play.

"When do you want to head down to Fond du Lac and scout out the hotel area?" Renee asked.

"I was just thinking about that. I think we should go tonight."

## CHAPTER 21

TRENT WAS WAITING at Max's Cirrus. He was sitting in a lawn chair, whittling a piece of wood into the shape of an eagle.

"That's pretty good."

"Thanks."

Renee said, "I thought we were setting up the tents. Where are they?"

Trent rose and folded up the chair. "Probably not smart for us to camp out here. I got us a camping spot next to the rental car. It's listed under an alias, and there's no GPS installed. I checked. If we stayed by Max's plane, it would be easier for someone to locate us."

"Good thinking."

"Come on, follow me. I'll take us there."

They walked at least a mile over rolling grass fields, past thousands of cars, recreational vehicles, and tents. Campfires and little gas grills. Diesel generators motoring next to trailers. Kids playing football and playing tag. All the while, airplanes soared overhead, one giant parade in the big blue Wisconsin sky.

"Have you heard from your family at all, Trent?" Renee asked.

"No. They know me. With the type of contract work I get, sometimes I sort of go off the grid for a few weeks at a time. They know not to worry."

Max said, "You're doing private security work?"

"Stuff like that. Sometimes personal security. Bodyguard detail for celebrities, things like that. Not exactly the role you had me play." He smirked. "But I'll head back to PA once we're done here. I promised little Josh I'd take him fishing down at Harvey's Lake."

They arrived at a section of lawn with two new pup tents and a three-foot-high mound of firewood. Several grocery bags of supplies and a stocked cooler rested in between the tents.

"There's showers and bathrooms about one hundred yards that way." He pointed towards a few wooden buildings near a grove of trees. "I figured you guys wouldn't mind sharing a tent."

Max sighed. "Aw, man, she snores."

Renee pinched the skin of his tricep. Hard. Max tried to keep it together.

Trent unfolded three lawn chairs and then started a campfire. They ate cold sandwiches from the cooler and drank bottled waters.

The sun had set, and they spoke in hushed voices over the crackling fire. Max laid out his plan for how they should handle Jennifer Upton the next day. Trent and Renee chimed in with their thoughts. After an hour of working out the details, they took the rental car south and scouted out the area near Upton's hotel.

Renee dialed the front desk from the parking lot.

"Holiday Inn Fond du Lac, how may I assist you?"

Renee said, "Yes, hello, I have a reservation at your hotel tomorrow, but I need to cancel."

"Of course. May I have your name, please?"

"Yes, it's…" She read the alias Upton had used from her notepad.

The sound of fingers kitting a keyboard. "Just a moment… okay, there you go. Unfortunately, ma'am, you are within the twenty-four-hour cancellation window…but I tell you what. I'm sure that we'll be able to get someone to fill the slot. I'll see if I can get my manager to waive that fee."

"That would be great. Thanks."

"Okay, take care."

Renee hung up the phone. Max waited ten seconds before dialing the same number.

"Holiday Inn Fond du Lac, how may I assist you?"

"Yes, I was hoping to get a room for tomorrow. Do you have anything available?"

"Why, we actually just had a room open up. You're lucky. Everything is booked solid for the air show."

"Oh, what a surprise," said Max. "I'll take it."

\* \* \*

The stakeout was tense, as they didn't know if they were the only ones who were waiting for Upton to appear. There were two possible street entrances to the hotel. Max covered one side from the car. Trent and Renee observed the other entrance from the window seat of a coffee shop across the street.

Renee, still monitoring Jennifer Upton's personal email, had promptly deleted the automatically generated message from the hotel, confirming that she had canceled her room reservation. Now Renee was using software on her computer to look for signs that Upton's electronic devices might be pinging local cell towers.

Renee wore white earbuds, and her voice was being transmitted to flesh-colored earpieces that both Max and Trent were wearing.

"There it is. Her phone is local." Renee checked her watch: 3:30 p.m.

"She could be anywhere within a five-mile range. Expect her to head into the hotel any minute now."

Trent tapped the table and rose. He would start walking around the hotel, looking for any unwanted surveillance.

Max said, "I just got off the phone with Wilkes. I asked him to get us a safe house in the area."

"What did he say when you told him you were in Oshkosh?"

"He didn't sound happy about being kept in the dark. But he also didn't sound surprised. I told him that we had an op in progress and had to go. He'll get us the safe house."

Ten minutes later, a middle-aged woman wearing stiletto pumps and a fashionable pantsuit strode into the hotel entrance. She was pulling a small rolling suitcase, its wheels bumping along on the pockmarked lot. The automatic double doors of the hotel slid open and she disappeared inside. Trent followed her in.

Five minutes after that, she was outside again, red-faced and cursing as she pulled her car keys out of her pocketbook and walked into the parking lot.

"Okay, she's headed back to her car," said Max. "I'm moving. Renee, connect me please."

"Okay, it's going through. Remember, just speak normally. The software will do the rest."

Renee was running Max's voice through a new program being tested by a Silicon Valley–based artificial intelligence company. Renee knew one of the lead technologists, who had granted her partial access to the program. They claimed to be able to take five minutes of recorded voice data on any person and clone the voice signature.

Now, as Max spoke, his voice would be transformed into someone else's. Someone who Jennifer Upton knew very well.

Upton, feeling her phone ring, dug it out of her purse and answered the unknown caller. "Hello?"

"It's me."

"Herb?"

"Where are you? Are you at your hotel?"

"What? Yes...why are you calling me? Herb, you weren't supposed to—"

"I'm sending a car. My colleagues should be there now. I've got to go."

Max didn't want to mess around. The longer they attempted to impersonate Senator Becker, the more that could go wrong. It was a risk. He wasn't completely certain that Upton and Becker were still in touch, but they were both headed to Oshkosh, and his gut told him they were still connected. Not to mention, it was all he had to go on. He would only need a few moments' hesitation on her part.

Upton kept walking staring in confusion at her phone.

"Thirty seconds," said Max over the earpiece, now only speaking to Trent and Renee. He was driving the car into the hotel parking lot.

Trent was several paces behind Upton, having followed her out the door. He tapped his earpiece twice to acknowledge Max, the noise transmitting two consecutive thumping sounds. Trent pretended to be reading something on his cell phone while he walked a path parallel on the other side of the parking lot, following his target.

Max's car inched up behind Jennifer Upton's parked vehicle. Trent's pace sped up. Upton had put her phone back in her purse and was now in the process of collapsing the sliding handle of her suitcase. She glanced at the car now stopped just behind her.

Max rolled down the passenger window. His car was only a few feet away from her.

"Ma'am, Senator Becker sent us to pick you up. Could you come with us, please?"

"Excuse me?" She stared at Max, looking confused and worried. Her head jerked, seeing Trent approach from behind her.

Shit. She was going to be noncompliant. Max could see it in her eyes.

In one quick movement, Trent opened the rear door of their rental car, grabbed Jennifer Upton around the waist, and moved her into the rear seat. He climbed in after her, then reached for her bag, pulled it inside and shut the door as Max drove away, trying to calm her down.

"We're here to help you, ma'am," said Max, quickly making eye contact with her in the mirror.

Trent sat close, and leaned toward her, his finger over his mouth, signaling her to be quiet.

Jennifer Upton looked with wide eyes at Trent, the chiseled ex–Special Forces man, all muscle and clenched jaw, a menacing figure hovering over her tiny frame. She kept quiet long enough for them to give her an explanation.

"Ma'am, we're with US law enforcement, and we're here to protect you from an imminent threat. Senator Becker should have given you a call letting you know we were on the way." Not technically truthful, but it helped hold down her urge to scream.

Hearing Max say this, Renee shut down her laptop and headed out the door of the coffee shop. She walked quickly around the corner, and down the back alley. One block away, Max's car stopped abruptly just in front of the curb. Renee stepped out of the alleyway and hopped in the passenger seat, and the vehicle sped away.

\* \* \*

Hugo's plan had been simple.

He was going to wait for the woman to enter her hotel, then pay a visit to her room and kill her. Her death would be swift and quiet. Made to look like a fall in the shower, or a tragic choking. Perhaps a suicide? It really just depended on the situation. Hugo considered himself to be a creative—like an artist or a musician. He had learned from a career of contract killings that sometimes good art just comes to you in the moment. One can't plan for all the materials available or all the external influences that might affect an operation.

Like just now.

Hugo hadn't entered her hotel. Instead, he had stayed put. Watching an unexpected team tail the unsuspecting Jennifer Upton, apprehend her, and depart. This would cost him money and time. It would also anger Syed.

Hugo had been scouting out Jennifer's hotel from an empty apartment across the street for five hours. From Hugo's years of experience, he knew a fellow professional when he saw one. He had seen the first man casing the block an hour before Upton's arrival. Hugo had taken several snapshots, which he would later show to Syed.

Not long after the first man had gone out of sight, a second man had appeared. This second man was tall and walked with a military swagger. Hugo had observed all the comings and goings within two blocks of his position. This second man had entered the coffee shop across the street from the hotel and remained inside for several hours. The fact that he had emerged just as Jennifer Upton arrived on scene could not have been a coincidence.

That left several questions in Hugo's mind. Chief among them, who was this team of operators? Their moves were quick and professional. He guessed that they were Americans, which alarmed him.

Hugo had watched most of the activity through his rifle

scope. If he had wanted to, he could have executed a perfect headshot against his target while she was strolling through the parking lot. For a brief moment, he'd toyed with the idea of taking all three of them out, but that course of action would pose several problems. For one, he didn't have a clear shot of the driver, and he didn't want to risk missing one of them. Secondly, the two unknown men weren't part of the assassin's assignment. It was always possible they were allies to Syed, and that the ISI had communicated poorly. Or perhaps Williams had sent them. Unlikely, but possible. Yet the most important reason Hugo stayed still was that a triple homicide with a sniper rifle would have attracted a tremendous amount of attention. It would have required him to go into hiding, and it would have made it nearly impossible to achieve the larger objective here at Oshkosh.

So Hugo had taken several pictures with his long-zoom lens as the team drove away. Then he'd taken several more as the woman emerged from the coffee shop. A strange feeling of recognition hit him afterwards, when he reviewed the pictures of the woman on his digital camera.

Where did he know her from? Dark shoulder-length hair. Skinny and toned. Very pale complexion. The beginnings of a tattoo visible on one of her legs. Hugo couldn't place her. But these images might be useful to Syed.

Hugo packed up his rifle kit and camera, then walked out the back of the building. Within minutes, he was driving a ten-year-old Ford Focus south along I-41. Along the way he used a burner cell phone to send a text message. In code, the text message informed Syed that the mission to kill Upton had been aborted. An immediate response provided Hugo with a coded meeting location. Hugo deleted the message and powered off the phone, then threw it out the window while he was taking the highway exit.

An hour later, the assassin was safe in his hotel room. He

would have more driving to do when he headed to Oshkosh to meet his handler later that evening, but for now he would rest.

Hugo kicked off his shoes and flipped on the news.

"Authorities have not ruled out whether the violent attack on a federal interrogation team in Texas several days ago, which left six dead, is related to terrorism. From the steps of the Capitol Building earlier today, Senator Becker of Wisconsin, said this: 'Whether it was terrorism, narcoterrorism, or just some thuggish drug kingpin, the people who did this will be hunted down and prosecuted. The American people will not stand for it.' Senator Becker, whose chief of staff's death has now been ruled a homicide, has himself reportedly been the target of death threats due to his strong stance against the opioid industry. While no one has claimed responsibility for these death threats, authorities believe they are tied to international criminal organizations intent on influencing Senator Becker's controversial Opioid Epidemic Bill. Experts believe that this bill could drastically affect both the legal and illegal markets for opioid pills. Senator Becker had no comment on these death threats before he left for his home state of Wisconsin earlier today."

Hugo listened carefully, changing the channel to different news outlets, still on the lookout for any sign that authorities might be tracking him after the hits in Virginia. This trip to the United States would end with quite the body count. Some of them very well known. Hugo worried that the Pakistani intelligence service was getting too careless, working with this Englishman, Williams. Hugo had met the man before. An odd cat. But very efficient at his work. And while Hugo respected that, he didn't like taking unnecessary risks. He would have to be careful there. Perhaps Hugo would take a long vacation after this weekend.

The former Legionnaire set his watch alarm, shut his eyes and slept for an hour. He then rose and drove north to the meeting location. A crowded grass parking lot at the air show. The recreational vehicle lot.

Hugo smiled to the air show staff, who happily took his money in exchange for a weekly parking pass. He then parked his car and walked through the rows and rows of Winnebagos sitting in an endless grass field.

Overhead, the sky had come alive as a squadron of World War Two bomber aircraft flew by, their deep, guttural engines droning on. Massive dark silhouettes flew in formation as the hordes of spectators watched, using their hands as sun visors.

At last Hugo came upon a smaller RV with a brown-skinned man in shorts and a tee shirt sitting just outside the door. He sat in a folding chair, under the shade of a tall beach umbrella. Hugo kept walking, double-checking the area for surveillance before he approached.

The Pakistani ISI operative couldn't have looked more out of place if he'd tried. Syed was monumentally stupid for coming here. It was very unlike him, which further concerned Hugo. Why were they taking so many risks? Was this really that important?

This security guard had on clothing that looked like he'd just purchased it off the clearance rack at a local sporting goods store, tags probably still on. He appeared grumpy and mean, not even paying attention to the air show. Instead, he was scanning the area, diligently performing his security job, and sticking out like a sore thumb.

The Pakistani man rose up, looking at Hugo as he approached the Winnebago, a suspicious look on his face.

"I'm here to see Syed."

Movement in the window of the RV, and then the thin door swung open. "Let him in," came Syed's voice from the dark interior.

Hugo walked past the security man and entered the RV. It was cramped and looked barely used, aside from an electronics suite that was set up on the small kitchen table. The Pakistani intelligence officer shut the laptop on the table and motioned for Hugo to sit in the seat across from him.

"I thought you were worried about surveillance. I understand your men needed to come here, but what are you doing here in this thing?"

"We needed to blend in. This is what people at the air show do. Besides, there weren't any available hotels within an hour's drive. This was the best we could manage for now."

"Well, call your man inside. He's not blending in with anyone."

Syed grew visibly annoyed. "I appreciate the concern. He has been in here all day and just went out to look for you. We'll only be here for a short while longer. The meeting begins soon."

Syed flinched as a twin-engine fighter jet thundered overhead. The noise was loud enough that it set off car alarms in the parking lot. Hugo still couldn't believe that Syed's organization held this meeting at an air show each year.

Well, this would be the last time.

Hugo said, "What does Williams think he is doing, killing so many in Texas like that? It's not just his own skin that he's risking."

Syed ignored the question. "What happened earlier? You weren't able to get to Upton?"

"It was not possible. There were others present. Two men and a woman. They looked American. They were very efficient." Hugo described what happened in detail.

Syed said, "Who were they?"

"I was going to ask you. I was under the impression that your operation was still clear of American law enforcement and intelligence eyes. I took a few photos."

Hugo took out his camera. He had removed the zoom lens, so it was less cumbersome. He preferred to use cameras instead

of phones. Better resolution, better zoom, and most importantly—no connectivity. Hugo didn't normally carry a personal
phone, only the occasional burner. He'd known too many
competitors who were dead because they'd used a cell phone.

Syed's face darkened as he looked at the images. "One can
never assume oneself to be completely clear of surveillance.
Those who do usually wind up dead or compromised."

Hugo hummed agreement. "So you think it is the CIA
or FBI?"

"Most likely, yes." Syed said something in Urdu that
sounded like a curse. "You are sure that you weren't followed
here?"

"As sure as I can be. Have you handled the arrangements I
asked you to make inside the air show?"

Syed nodded. "Everything you asked for has been set up.
My contact will meet you tomorrow morning. He'll have a spot
for you here."

Syed pointed to a spot on the air show map.

"That will do perfectly. I should have a clear line of sight to
the target. I will re-check when I am there."

"Good."

"I will have free time tonight. Are you sure that you do not
want me to locate Upton? If it is the Americans, I assume that
they've moved her to a safe house and will interrogate her. Is
that a problem?"

"Yes. It is a problem."

"Then do you want me to solve your problem?" Hugo's tone
was filled with impatience. He liked the fees the ISI paid him,
but sometimes they were slow to act.

"No. Williams wishes to be involved now."

"I thought he was your agent. Now he tells you what
he wants?"

"Our relationship has evolved over time."

"Perhaps our relationship should evolve."

"Not if you want to keep getting paid."

Hugo snorted. "He already knows that I don't have Upton?"

"He does."

"Will he now use the same men he used in Texas?"

"Don't concern yourself with that."

"The woman was my target. I don't get paid if I don't do the job. Of course it is my concern. And Williams's men will make a public mess. I don't want to deal with the hassle when I lose you as a client because you ended up in an American prison."

Syed tilted his head, smiling like he thought this was a joke. The Pakistani man rose. "I appreciate your concern. Come with me. We will go now."

Hugo said, "Where are we going?"

"To see Williams."

# CHAPTER 22

HUGO FOLLOWED the Pakistanis in his car. They drove along Route 45, paralleling the shore of Lake Winnebago. They passed an inlet with a sign that read "Seaplane Base." A multi-engine aircraft was visible from the road, floating in the water, its props spinning as a gathered crowd took pictures.

Ten minutes further south, Syed's RV turned left onto a long gravel driveway. The vehicle stopped at a wrought-iron gate, an eight-foot-high stone wall spreading out on either side and surrounding the property.

The gate was being guarded by two Hispanic men, who approached both vehicles and inspected them carefully. Hugo saw that the first security guard was carrying a holstered pistol. A third man stood inside a small guardhouse positioned just behind and to the right of the entrance gate. He held some sort of small Uzi-like weapon. Hugo couldn't tell the exact make, as the guard was half-hidden behind the doorway, his sharp eyes watching the new arrivals with interest.

The gate guards allowed them to pass and then instructed the drivers of both vehicles to park on a gravel lot just behind and to the left of the wall. They were instructed to walk the rest of the way to the home, a quarter mile hike down a peninsula. The home was an impressive Victorian-style mansion. Three black Suburban SUVs were parked in the roundabout driveway in front of the mansion. A handful of armed Latino guards stood next to them.

The Pakistanis and Hugo were each searched and disarmed, which annoyed Hugo. But Syed nodded for him to comply. The guards actually had a tent set up in front of the mansion entrance. Under the tent was a folding table with numbered bins to hold weapons, phones, and electronic devices. One of the guards filled out a notepad to keep track of the owners and equipment.

"You will get it back when you are done," said the humorless Mexican man who placed Hugo's pistol in a plastic bin.

Hugo shook his head but gave up his weapon. "I need to keep this," he said, holding his camera. The guard looked at what Hugo presumed was his supervisor, who nodded.

They were escorted through the main floor of the mansion and onto the back deck. Ian Williams stood in the backyard, tall and lanky, chatting with an eclectic group of men. The group sat on expensive outdoor furniture, cocktails in their hands, laughing and apparently enjoying themselves. Just a backyard cookout in Wisconsin. Surrounded by cartel gunmen. Hugo wondered what the hell was going on. Syed wouldn't tell him who these men were, but to him it looked like happy hour for the United Nations. Every ethnicity was represented, and all were dressed in expensive business casual attire.

Seeing Syed, Williams rose and walked to him. "Abdul. It is good to see you. Your men can wait inside." He yelled something in Spanish to one of the guards. "They'll take care of them." Seeing Hugo, Williams pointed. "This is your specialist?"

Syed nodded. "You may call him Hugo."

Williams said, "Ah. Please remain with us, if you would. I wish to speak with you." Williams turned to the half dozen men enjoying themselves in the sun. "Gentlemen, if you'll excuse me." Nodding heads and several held-up drinks in response.

Williams and Syed whispered to each other as Williams led them east on the property, towards the water's edge. The tip of the peninsula ended with a long wooden dock and over-water gazebo.

Williams brought them to the gazebo and had them each sit. Then he said, "What happened with Miss Upton?"

Syed recounted what he knew, and Hugo filled in the gaps. Then Hugo showed Williams the images he had taken with his camera. Ian Williams's eyes went wide.

"These were the people who apprehended Miss Upton?" His eyes locked on to Hugo.

"Yes. I assume you know them?"

"I do."

Syed said, "Who are they?"

"You and I can discuss that momentarily."

"Do you want me to retrieve the woman? Upton?" asked Hugo.

Williams shook his head, clicking his tongue. "Forget her for now. Your other work here is much more important."

"Very well."

"Have you made your preparations?"

"I have been training for weeks."

"You understand the critical nature of the timing?"

"I do."

"There will be an increased security presence. Will that be a problem?"

"It will be factored in to my approach."

Ian Williams glanced at Syed and smiled. "Good. Tomorrow, then."

* * *

Jennifer Upton barely spoke during the car ride to the safe house. This was understandable, considering the abrupt way they'd taken her in the hotel parking lot. Max had explained that she was in danger, that they were moving her for her own safety, but she looked skeptical and was hesitant to cooperate. She hadn't brought up why Senator Becker was involved, but neither had Max. He didn't want to press his luck before earning a little trust.

Wilkes had given them the address of a farm forty minutes to the west of Oshkosh. Now their sedan bumped along a rocky dirt road, beyond fields of sweet corn.

"Knee high by the Fourth of July," said Trent, looking out the window.

"What?" asked Upton, seeming more angry than scared at this point.

"Something my brother always used to say. If the cornstalks back home were knee high by the Fourth of July, it was going to be a bumper crop."

Upton looked at Trent like he was crazy.

Max parked the vehicle in the driveway of a small ranch home surrounded by weeping willow trees. An old white barn stood next to a grain elevator one hundred yards to the south. A rusty charcoal grill collected dust in the backyard. The shrubs needed to be trimmed. The front door opened, and a serious-looking kid in his early twenties stuck his head out, evaluating them while keeping his right arm behind the door. When the kid recognized Max, he placed the pistol he'd been holding down on the coffee table by the door and walked outside.

"Mr. Fend, Caleb Wilkes asked me to convey his apologies for not being able to make it here himself."

"What's he doing?"

"He's otherwise engaged."

After an awkward introduction to Jennifer Upton, Max and

crew headed inside the home. The CIA kid introduced himself as Mike Barnaby. By the look of him, Max figured he was maybe a year out of the Farm, if that. Wilkes was scraping the bottom of the barrel for this op.

Mike showed them into the living room and offered them something to eat and drink. Still looking angry, Upton requested only a glass of tap water. Mike did a quick search of her person and took her phone and an e-reader device that was in her purse. "Sorry, Miss Upton, but this is for your own safety. We'll give it back as soon as we know that you're no longer in danger."

Trent and the CIA kid waited in the kitchen, watching the surveillance feed that had been set up around the house and eavesdropping on the interrogation that would soon commence.

Max asked Renee to stay with them, hoping that a kind-looking female face might help to instill trust. Renee and Max sat on the couch, opposite Jennifer Upton, who plopped down on a love seat. The room was quiet, dark, and cool. They were miles away from the drone of aircraft engines and crowds of the air show here. But the clock was ticking. Tomorrow was the twenty-eighth. According to Rojas, it was the day of Williams's meeting. Max needed to find out why Upton had gone off the grid. What had made her come up here? Was she connected to Ian Williams and the ISI? More importantly, he needed to know what was critical enough about this mysterious meeting for the ISI and the cartel to kill multiple Americans in a series of brazen attacks within the US.

Upton squinted at him, as if trying to work something out. "You're Charles Fend's boy, aren't you?"

"I am."

Her expression softened. "I've met your father."

"Did you? When was that?"

"Maybe a decade ago, at a fundraiser. He contributed to a campaign I was working on."

"May I ask who you were working for at the time?"

She hesitated, then said, "Herbert Becker."

"You were on Senator Becker's staff?" Max asked, already knowing the answer.

"He was a congressman back then. But yes," replied Upton. She looked out the window. It was getting dark now. "How long are you planning to keep me here?"

"Since we have reason to believe your life is in danger, it'll be at least a day or more, until we can find a more suitable arrangement."

"What if I want to leave?"

"We'll get you out of here if that's what you want. But you need to be under our protection. It's for your own good."

"Why am I in danger?"

"Tell me, Jennifer, does the name Ian Williams mean anything to you?"

Jennifer's smile faded. So, she knew him.

"It rings a bell, but..." She looked like she was searching her mind for a memory...or a lie. "No. No, I don't think I know him."

"Really?" Max's voice was even-keeled. His piercing blue eyes studied her face for the slightest microexpression that might give away the truth. "We received information that Ian Williams may want to cause you harm. Are you sure you don't know him?"

She shook her head.

"What about a lobbyist named Dahlman?"

"Who?" Her eyes narrowed.

"Your name was on a list. The only other name on that list was a lobbyist named Joseph Dahlman. A few days ago, he was killed in Virginia."

Jennifer went pale. "Killed?"

Max nodded somberly.

"You knew him?" Renee said.

"No," she said, her face twitching. "I'm sorry, but what is this list you're referring to?"

"What about Ronald Dicks? You knew him."

She looked down at the floor. "Yes. I knew Ron. I was very sad to read about what happened."

"They're calling that a homicide."

"I know."

"When was the last time you spoke to Ron?"

"Years ago. We've lost touch. I worked with him. That was all."

"What are you doing up here in Wisconsin, Miss Upton?"

"I...I came to see Herb."

Renee said, "Becker? You came to see the senator?"

"That's right."

"Why?"

She looked away. "It's somewhat embarrassing. A woman my age running around like this, trying to stay out of the lime-light just to see a man."

Max said, "It was a social call?"

Upton said, "Senator Becker is a very high-profile individ-ual, obviously. And unfortunately, based on our past...and the feelings of certain members of his family...we need to be discreet about our relationship."

"So you and Becker are *with* each other? In an ongoing rela-tionship?" Renee asked, as diplomatically as she could manage.

Annoyance flashed on Upton's face. "Yes, darling."

Max said, "Miss Upton, I hope you don't mind if I pry, but it may be relevant...why do you feel the need to keep the low profile about the relationship? What do you mean about the family members? Do they not approve?"

Upton's voice grew ugly. "It's mostly just his damned daughter, Karen. She has too much influence with him. Always has. When Herb's wife found out about our little fling, she divorced him in no time. He wanted to be with me. At least the wife was reasonable. She wasn't going to make a big fuss about it and ruin his name. The senator's daughter, on the other hand—"

"Karen Becker?"

Upton nodded. "She was the one who caught us together in the first place. Our relationship had been easier to keep under wraps when we were traveling internationally, but our travel had slowed down. It was an election year, of course, and Becker was running a mere two points ahead. This was back before he switched parties. The girl said the only way she wouldn't tell the press about the affair was if I agreed to leave his staff. I mean, the nerve of that little brat. Their marriage was in shambles anyway. What the hell did it matter to her?"

Max said, "When was all this?"

"That was a long time ago. It was when I was on his staff, so...2006? Yes, that was it."

"So you are telling me that you're here in Wisconsin to see Senator Becker socially. And that you're keeping a low profile because Karen Becker still doesn't approve?"

Max could see Jennifer Upton's mind racing, trying to work out how to answer the question. Max knew this story was all bullshit, of course. If she was just hiding from the daughter, she wouldn't have kept her phone switched off for hours at a time. No one does that. Not unless they're worried about someone tracking their movements through their phone.

"Karen Becker is a very opinionated woman. And Herb wishes to keep his family life and his social life separate. There's nothing wrong with what we are doing." Another flare-up in her tone.

The conversation went on for another ninety minutes. Jennifer Upton continued to be evasive. She denied trying to avoid detection by turning her phone off. "Sometimes you just need to disconnect." She also brushed off any meaning behind making her hotel reservation with a seldom-used account, under a fake name. "I told you, I like my privacy."

Upton claimed to have no idea how Ian Williams was connected to Senator Becker, or if he even was. She said she'd never met anyone from Pakistan and laughed nervously when Max asked about foreign intelligence services. "What, now you think I'm a spy? I don't think so."

Eventually, Max suggested they take a break for the evening. It was getting dark, and they were getting nowhere with Upton. Max was ready to try more aggressive tactics, but first he wanted to check in with Wilkes.

Jennifer Upton was given one of the bedrooms for the evening, and Mike the CIA operative was joined by his partner, who had brought them all food.

On the ride back to the Oshkosh campground, Trent and Renee both verbalized Max's feelings.

"She's full of it," said Renee.

"Agreed," said Max.

"What are you going to do?" asked Trent.

"She was surprised that I knew the name Ian Williams. And she was pretty disturbed at the death of Joseph Dahlman. Rightfully distressed at the mention of Ron Dicks. I don't know what worries her more—that we'll figure out what she's really up to, or that someone might be trying to kill her. Either way, let's let her stew for the evening."

## CHAPTER 23

THE NEXT MORNING, Max and Renee crawled out of the tent to see Trent doing push-ups in the grass, a steely-eyed determination on his face, his muscles rippling and sweaty, huffs of exertion coming as he continued to pump out perfect-form reps.

"Morning," he said to them as he switched to sit-ups.

Renee smiled as she tied her sneakers. "We were going to go for a run. You want to come?"

"I'm good, thanks."

She glanced at Max. Renee was worried about Trent. A veteran of multiple wars who had lost his brother to a drug overdose. He was strong, but she could see that he was struggling with his inner demons.

"You sure?" Max said.

"No, it's alright. I was up early and ran around the perimeter of the field. Looks like they're going to have a 5K there on the runway. Would have liked to do that one."

"Maybe next year. Wilkes sent us a message. He wants us to meet him this morning."

Renee and Max began their jog, winding through the grass parking lots, campgrounds, and groves of trees surrounding the airfield. Droplets of dew coated the grass. A buzzing flock of ultralight aircraft skimmed the treetops on a massive morning flight, the rising sun painting them with reddish-orange light. It was a peaceful scene, and it felt good to sweat.

The pair ran for forty minutes, stretched, then showered at the campground's public showers. It felt like a vacation, but Max kept getting reminders that it wasn't. Everywhere he looked, he saw a potential conspirator staring back at him. A man leaning on his car, talking on a cell phone as he and Renee strode by. A middle-aged Latina woman, walking along the road next to the air show entrance. Everyone looked suspicious, and Max was getting twitchy.

Trent had grabbed a few breakfast sandwiches and handed them out when they arrived back at the tents. Renee was drying her wet hair with a white towel. Max sat on one of the lawn chairs surrounding the ash from last night's campfire. Renee sat on the chair next to him. She had taken out her computer again and was connecting to her sat link.

Through a mouthful of bacon, egg, and cheese biscuit, Max said, "You're working now? We've only got about fifteen minutes before we're supposed to meet Wilkes."

"I just had an idea come to me when we were running. I wanted to check it out really quick." She hit a key and said, "Bingo."

"What is it?" Max craned his head around to see her screen.

"Something Upton said to us last night was bothering me. She said that it had been easier for her and Becker to have a relationship when they traveled more. So I wanted to see where they were traveling to."

"And?"

"Afghanistan."

Trent looked up.

Max said, "Ian Williams was stationed there with MI6, right? I'd be very interested to know whether the two met. The

ISI has a big presence in Afghanistan as well. Good work, Renee. We can grill Upton on this later."

Together they walked through the main entrance of the air show, under a tall blue sign with flags flapping on top. Even this early in the morning, the crowds were impressive. Groups of retirees in baseball caps, families with strollers, and young aviation enthusiasts walked over the expansive concrete walkway towards the aircraft static displays. In the distance, they heard the whine of aircraft engines starting up, then a rumble of thunder overhead as two dark F-15 Strike Eagles joined the empty runway pattern.

"Wow, they're really loud!" said Renee, holding her ears.

The twin-engine Air Force fighters were doing touch-and-goes—landing on the runway, rolling for a few seconds, and then gunning their engines and taking off again. Each time, they banked hard, exposing their underbellies in the turn, throttling their engines, tongues of blue-yellow afterburner shooting out, and then smoothly flattening out in the downwind.

"What are they doing?"

"Showing off," Max said.

"You've got that schoolboy grin again."

"Can't help it. They're magnificent beasts. Someday I've got to get a ride in one."

Trent said, "That him?"

Wilkes was standing under the nose of a KC-10 aerial refueling tanker, its monstrous nose towering over him. Seeing Max, he motioned for them to follow.

"Ladies and gentlemen, good morning."

They said their hellos as Wilkes brought them to a pair of motorized golf carts. Wilkes drove one and Max the other, and they scooted off down the taxiway, driving all the way to the opposite side of the field. It took them a good ten minutes to get to the area of the airport where the private jets were parked, but Max recognized his father's personal jet from afar.

They parked the golf carts outside the sleek aircraft and walked up the stairway. Max didn't say anything to Wilkes about his father's participation in this morning's conversation, but he was a bit annoyed. Until now, neither Caleb nor his father had said anything about working with the other at Oshkosh. Add it to the list of actions that Caleb Wilkes had taken without giving Max a heads-up.

"Renee, good to see you again," Charles greeted her at the entrance to the aircraft, holding a glass of juice in one hand as they hugged. She smiled and said hello, but Max caught a questioning glance from her as the group walked to the central area in the jet's cabin. She was also wondering how his father was involved.

The inside of the aircraft was quite luxurious, and appropriately set up as the mobile office of a billionaire industrialist. A long leather couch on one side. A computer terminal with the latest communications. Several flat-screen TVs, each tuned to a different cable news business channel.

In one section of the cabin, a meeting area had been set up. Rotating cushioned seats had been turned to face towards each other. In between them was an impressive breakfast spread laid out on a glossy maple table.

"Coffee, tea, anyone?" asked Charles's personal assistant.

"We'll be fine, thank you. No calls or visitors for now," said Charles. The cabin door was shut, and Caleb, Charles, Max, Trent, and Renee all sat down. "Help yourselves." Charles waved towards the pastries and coffee cups on the table.

Wilkes began, "Max, I read your report. So far it sounds like Upton isn't cooperating." Max had typed up a short summary of the Upton interview on Renee's computer the night before and sent it to Wilkes.

"That's my opinion. But as I wrote, I think she's hiding

something."

Wilkes nodded. "She claims she's here as Senator Becker's secret lover?"

"That's it."

"And no connection to Ian Williams or the ISI?"

"Correct. According to Miss Upton," Max said skeptically. "But Renee did some research and uncovered something interesting this morning." Max filled Wilkes and his father in on what Renee had uncovered relating to the international trips then-congressman Becker had made to Afghanistan back in the 2000s.

Wilkes didn't look very surprised.

"Excellent work, Renee," Wilkes said. He turned to Charles, who was quiet. "What was your read on the senator, Charles?"

Max looked at his father, who was staring back at his son, a look of admiration in his eyes. So, Wilkes was indeed using his father to probe Senator Becker, eh? It made sense, Max thought. The senator and the CEO had known each other for decades.

Charles said, "He's worried about something, I know that much. I ate dinner with him and his daughter, Karen, last night. When I wasn't at the table, they engaged in a tense private conversation. Were you going to share that?"

"In a moment, yes. Charles, if you would, please continue to shadow the senator today. Try to keep him in your sight as much as you can, and keep your guard up. His daughter performs this afternoon. The senator's official schedule has him heading back to D.C. this evening, after his daughter's performance."

Max said, "You think they'll target Senator Becker while he's here at Oshkosh?"

Wilkes folded his hands in his lap. "I do. Max, I think it's time that I provide you with a bit more about the senator's history."

# CHAPTER 24

IT BEGAN during the Cold War.

When the Soviets had occupied Afghanistan in the 1980s, they'd accused the CIA of helping the Mujahideen smuggle opium out of the country in order to raise funds. While a connection between Western intelligence agencies and the Afghan drug trade had never been proven, the various Afghan factions had increased opium production in the country after the Soviets fled in 1989. This was partially due to the loss of alternative sources of financial support from the West.

Opium production continued to flourish as the Taliban rose to power in the 1990s. That was until Mullah Omar, the effective leader of the Taliban, declared it un-Islamic in the year 2000. For a brief period, the Taliban enforced the eradication of poppy farming in Afghanistan, which resulted in a sixty-five percent drop in global heroin production during the year 2001.

Then, on a clear sunny morning in September of that year, Al Qaeda terrorists hijacked four commercial airliners and the world changed forever. Soon after the attacks, the United States demanded that the Taliban hand over Osama bin Laden. The Taliban responded that they would not extradite bin

Laden unless the United States provided "evidence that bin Laden was behind the September 11 terrorist attacks."

The US military soon began deploying to Afghanistan, and the Taliban was removed from power.

Afghan farmers quickly returned to growing opium, which was much more profitable than anything else they could produce. Soon Afghanistan was supplying ninety percent of the world's heroin and expanding its production each year. Opium was the lifeblood of the Afghan farming economy. In 2007, when Afghan leader Hamid Karzai addressed all thirty-four provincial governors in Kabul, he began his speech by denouncing the drug trade. The line was greeted by a few polite claps and many looks of concern. Later in the speech, he admonished the international community for wanting to spray Afghan opium crops. The room erupted in cheers.

Wilkes said, "By the late 2000s, more than half of Afghanistan's economy—around three billion dollars—was based on the drug trade. Three billion. That's a lot of money, right?"

Max said, "Sure. It's a lot of money."

Wilkes leaned forward. "But it isn't. Not compared to what it turns into. That's damn pocket change. From there, the drugs flow across trade routes through Iran and Turkey on their way to Europe. In the opposite direction, they flow through India and by sea to East Asia and Australia. The drugs gain value every inch of the way. The closer they are to the customer, the more middlemen, the higher the risk, which needs to be built into the price. The heroin is sold on the streets for twenty times the original price. The Afghans only see a tiny piece of the action. So, who gets all that money?"

"The international criminal organizations who traffic it and sell it on the streets."

"Yes. But that's not all. Who else gets the money?"

"I don't know, who?"

"Ask the ISI. Ask Ian Williams."

Max looked at him sideways. "What do you mean?"

Wilkes smiled. "When Williams was still in good standing with MI6, he was working in their Pakistan field office, where I now believe he was recruited by our friend Abdul Syed of the ISI."

Trent said, "So Ian Williams got recruited by the ISI. That fits with what we know of him."

"Some of our sources confirmed that Williams was kicked out of MI6 for unethical and possibly illegal actions involving Afghan drug lords. He was also reportedly spotted meeting with an ISI operative, and he didn't disclose the meeting to MI6. He was kicked out of MI6 as the investigations began. But he fled the country. MI6 tells us that they think he contacted his old buddies in Pakistan and went to work for them."

"What did they have him doing?"

Wilkes said, "That's where it gets interesting. For several years now, we've suspected that Pakistani intelligence is helping to run a substantial portion of the illicit drug trade in Afghanistan. Williams was already connected to many of the players in that business. But this was back in the early 2000s. The demand for opium—both the legal and illegal demand— was only a fraction of what it is today."

"The ISI saw an opportunity."

"Exactly. The ISI knew the benefit that type of business could have for them. Behind the scenes, the ISI runs Pakistan. Taking over Afghanistan's heroin trade allows them enormous power and international influence."

Renee shook her head. "How?"

Max said, "Think about it. If Pakistan controls the economy of their neighbor Afghanistan, they own that country. And all that cash is off the books, so they can do whatever they want with it. Influence elections. Buy policy. Pay for black ops. That's why so many intelligence agencies around the world sometimes deal with narcotics traffickers. It's the darker side of the intel business."

Renee said, "The US doesn't do that, do they?"

Wilkes smiled. "We use taxpayer money to fund our black ops."

Polite laughter followed. Except for Renee, who looked slightly horrified.

Wilkes said, "And it isn't just influence in Pakistan. Remember, the trade routes for Afghan opium run through Iran, Turkey, India, and dozens of other nations. The more the ISI gets their hands in different international pots of money, the more power they have in those countries as well. The ISI wanted Ian Williams to help them grow the pie, and to make sure they got a huge piece to themselves."

Max tried to put it all together in his mind. "So what are you saying? That the ISI recruited Williams to somehow spur on the global opium market? How?"

"Pakistani influence could only go so far by itself. They needed men like Ian Williams. People with connections. Dark salesmen who wouldn't mind stuffing a politician or businessman's back pocket with illicit cash in exchange for a big favor."

"How did he do it?"

"Back in the early 2000s, after the international coalition went in and collapsed the Taliban government, the United Kingdom was put in charge of the farming and drug policy in Afghanistan. Officially it was supposed to be run by their diplomats. But Ian Williams had huge sway with them, thanks to all his backroom deals throughout both Afghanistan and Pakistan. Between Williams and a group of other ISI agents, they were able to ensure that Afghan opium farming would grow rapidly. Maybe it wasn't completely official, but there were winks and nods. And Williams and Syed didn't stop there. Recognizing the huge growth opportunity in opium, they knew that they could expand to other markets. Other regions.

And we think they got involved in the legal side of the market-place as well."

Max frowned.

"What do you mean?"

"Then-congressman Herbert Becker first met Ian Williams in Afghanistan in 2002. Becker was on a diplomatic fact-finding mission. That same year, research came out that supported the use of narcotics like opioids to treat long-term pain. This was a new development. The research was paid for by Big Pharma. A year later, Becker voted on legislation dereg-ulating the use of prescription opioids in the United States."

Max's thoughts were a swirl of ideas and facts. "Are you trying to tell me that the ISI, along with a rogue British agent and a dirty US politician, intentionally orchestrated the opioid epidemic?"

Renee said, "That seems far-fetched."

"I thought the same thing at first. But around this time, Becker made a lot of changes. He ran for Senate. He got a ton of money from outside contributors, many of whom had ties to the drug industry."

"That doesn't mean he was working for the ISI. Every politician gets supported by some special interest."

"You're right. But you have to ask yourself, how does Afghanistan end up producing ninety percent of the world's heroin? That's a multibillion-dollar operation. You always hear about the Colombian and Mexican drug cartels and how they operated like Fortune 500 companies, right? Guess what, the Afghans *aren't* running their drug trade by themselves. There's too much money in it. A business that size needs to plan the supply chain, distribution, sales. To seed demand among millions of customers…"

"A conspiracy of this size would have to be huge."

Wilkes said, "You have no idea. Afghanistan makes a few billion dollars a year from their opioid farming operation. But the global market for illicit heroin is closer to *fifty* billion. Add in *another* fifty billion for legal opioids. Add in more money for all the treatment programs. For insurance companies. Tax dollars. Opioids are an economic juggernaut."

"And Afghanistan grows ninety percent of all of that?"

"Not quite. They grow ninety percent of the *illicit* opium. The legal stuff is grown by licensed opium producers—mostly in Australia, Turkey, India, and France, and a few other countries. These are the suppliers for the pharmaceutical companies. But the illegal and legal opioid demand is related. They feed off each other."

Trent cleared his throat. "That's how my brother got started. Josh used both. He got a prescription for pain meds. The prescription ran out, but he was hooked. Couldn't stop. And it wasn't like he was a weak guy or anything. Hell, he'd been to war."

Renee was making the same connection. "All the statistics I looked at online showed the trend of increased heroin use in the US following the increased use of legal opioids."

Wilkes nodded. "And that trend line began right after Becker met with Williams."

The group went silent for a moment.

Trent said, "How is Senator Becker in on it?"

"We don't know that he is, exactly. Our intel suggests he may have been unaware of many details," Wilkes replied. "Last night, using a device we provided, your father was able to record part of the conversation between Senator Becker and his daughter, Karen."

Charles pressed his lips together and nodded in acknowledgment.

"What did they say?"

Wilkes placed his cell phone down on the coffee table in front of him. He tapped a button, and a conversation began playing.

Karen: "I think you should go back to the FBI."

Senator Becker: "I've spoken with them already."

Karen: "Dad…"

Senator Becker: "We've had this discussion."

Karen: "I'm worried for you. I think it's time for you to tell them everything."

Senator Becker: "Let's not talk about it now."

Karen: "You made one mistake a long time ago. And that was listening to Ron and Jennifer. You shouldn't have to pay for that forever."

Senator Becker: "I'm going to take care of it."

Karen: "No more deals with Ian."

Senator Becker: "I told you I'm done with him and I meant it."

Karen: "Are they here again?"

Senator Becker: "Karen, I promise you. I have ended it once and for all."

Karen: "But Ron…"

Senator Becker: "Ron kept going without my knowledge or approval."

Karen: "And they're just…*killing people*? Now, after all this time? All for that stupid bill?"

Senator Becker: "Yes."

Karen: "Why is it so important to them?"

Senator Becker: "Money."

Karen: "Can't you just drop the bill or change your vote or something? Give them what they want?"

Senator Becker: "I could. But my career would be over, and they would have won. And our problem wouldn't end there. They would still own me."

Karen: "So what are you going to do?"

Senator Becker: "I don't want to say. I don't want you knowing any more than you have to. But they won't have anything on me after this week. Trust me, Karen."

Karen: "Fine. But if you run into trouble, you go right back to the FBI, Dad. Alright? No matter what happens, it's not worth getting killed for."

The recording ended and Wilkes picked up his phone.

Renee said, "So the senator knows Ian Williams?"

"Yes," Wilkes confessed.

Max was confused. "If they were once collaborating, why would the ISI be trying to kill Becker now?"

"Becker has changed his stance on a policy that's making them billions."

"Okay, but why? Don't politicians usually want to make the guys bankrolling them happy?"

Charles said, "May I offer a thought? In business, joint ventures often end when one party no longer needs the other. Perhaps the senator benefited from the ISI's support for a time, but now he has outgrown his britches? He has excellent name recognition and a host of donors. His eye is on the big election in a few years. He's had to make a strategic choice to part ways with some of his original fundraisers."

Renee said, "How is it even possible that foreign government agents gave him money?"

Max said, "Unfortunately, there are several ways to do it."

Charles said, "He's right. Although it is easier to do in smaller quantities. That could be another reason Becker is no longer interested in accepting money from this source. Foreign nationals wouldn't be able to give him a big enough contribution to matter in the presidential election. Not without the risk of getting caught. Those sums of money are too high. But in state races...that wouldn't have been a problem."

"Too big for his britches..."

"This assumes Becker knew about it all. He claims only his aide knew about recent contact with the foreign investors. And he knew nothing about the foreigners being tied to the ISI."

Max said, "Why would the ISI kill Dahlman and Dicks?"

Wilkes shrugged. "Perhaps they decided those sources were no longer of value."

"Why?"

"Becker wasn't playing ball. If you're a foreign intelligence service and one of your key agents stops producing for you, what do you do?"

"Try to get them producing again."

"And if that doesn't work?"

"Get rid of any evidence that can lead back to me, and put the network to sleep."

Wilkes nodded. "Some agencies have a more permanent view of what that means than others. As Renee pointed out, Upton traveled to Afghanistan with Becker. So did Ron Dicks. Senator Becker, in his conversation with his daughter, revealed that he knew an Ian. Let us assume that is *our* Ian Williams. It is quite possible that Ian Williams still has a connection to Jennifer Upton, who was—according to Rojas—on the cartel's kill list." Wilkes sighed. "Maybe the ISI wants to get rid of a rogue agent? Maybe Becker has been ignorant of ninety-nine percent of all of this, and they're just pissed off that he isn't playing ball? Either way, it certainly looks like Senator Becker is in danger. And he knows this better than anyone."

"He has protection?"

"The Capitol Police has given him round-the-clock security, even outside of D.C."

"What are the Capitol Police going to do in Wisconsin?" asked Trent.

"It's their responsibility to protect members of Congress. They've coordinated with local law enforcement. It's the Oshkosh police who are providing the senator with a protective detail. You'll see plainclothes officers here with the senator."

"How many?"

"Two to four, depending on the time of day. I also have a

few of my men keeping an eye on him, but our team here is small. And I have to provide at least one body to the safe house. But I've also reached out to the FBI and notified them that there may be a threat to the senator while he's here. They have over a dozen plainclothes agents who will be close to the senator for the duration of his stay at the air show."

Max said, "This would be a lot easier if he would just go to a safe house for a few days."

"The FBI and Capitol Police have both made that painfully clear. The senator has refused to alter his schedule. He insists on seeing his daughter perform today." Wilkes frowned, "I know this is ugly. We're doing our best. For now, I think we should assume that the senator is a target, and that either the cartel or ISI may try to take him out while he's at Oshkosh."

The thought was chilling. They were leaving a highly visible target out in the open. Max didn't like this at all.

Renee said, "I still don't understand something. Rojas said that the meeting was on the twenty-eighth, right? That's today."

"Correct," said Wilkes.

Renee shook her head. "But I guess I still don't understand why Ian Williams and the ISI need to kill anyone before it occurs."

Renee's question was answered with silence.

Charles cleared his throat. "She's absolutely right. The clock appears to be ticking. Yet you gentlemen don't know what happens when the minute hand strikes twelve."

Wilkes hummed. "Yes, thank you for that, Charles."

Charles turned to his son. "What do you think, Max?"

Max let out a deep breath, searching the faces of those around him. "Upton. Now that I know more about Becker's connection to Williams, I'll know where to add pressure. She's got to know more about this meeting."

Renee said, "Why can't we just go to Senator Becker and confront him with this?"

Wilkes shook his head. "If he's doing anything illegal himself, we don't want to expose ourselves. We'll want to uncover their network. And we can't do that if they know we're on to them."

Max said, "Caleb, if you're good with it, I'll head to the safe house now to continue my conversation with Jennifer Upton."

"Approved."

Max turned to Trent. "I think you should stay here and shadow Senator Becker. Ian Williams's sicarios are military-trained. He might be using them to execute a hit on the senator. If they were Mexican military, some of them may have even been trained inside the US by our own Special Forces. You're the most familiar with how they might operate."

Trent nodded. "Sounds good."

Max said to Renee, "You can come with me. Cross-reference every tidbit of information Jennifer Upton spills on us today. And let's dig into her phone and email accounts. Maybe we can find more hints about why she really came up here, if not for a lovers' rendezvous."

The group got up to leave. As they did, Wilkes said, "Remember, no phones. Syed and Williams have access to excellent crypto specialists. If you need to communicate, we'll either be set up here at Charles's aircraft or near the VIP tent on the main side of the airport. Good luck."

## CHAPTER 25

WHEN MAX and Renee got back to the safe house, they could see that something had changed in Jennifer Upton. She appeared more nervous, and Max began to put pressure on, telling her that they already knew Senator Becker and Ian Williams were connected.

Max brought up the very real threat of her and Senator Becker's assassinations. He told her how critical she was to saving the senator's life. And he promised her that he would help her. That anything she told them would be held in the strictest of confidence. He wasn't a cop, after all. He just wanted to avoid any further violence. Whatever she had seen or done, none of it mattered to him.

"I promise to help you, Jennifer. But you need to come clean and tell me everything."

It started off as a trickle. But as she got going, the vault cracked open, and gold coins began pouring out of her mouth.

"Williams was the match that started Herb Becker's political bonfire. Ron and I were both on Herb's staff at the time. Back when he was just in the House. Herb's political career was nothing special. He barely won his seat. Then September 11 happened, and the next thing we knew, Herb was making a name for himself in the international arena. We were all flying overseas on fact-finding missions and diplomatic trips to Afghanistan. It was like the Wild West. The war in Afghanistan was still young. Nobody knew what they were doing back then. Our congressional delegation was sent there to come up with a way to stabilize the Afghan economy. To try and bring peace to the region."

"How many trips?"

She placed her water glass on a coaster. "Three? Four, maybe? I went on three, he and Ron went on four, I think."

"And that's where Becker met Williams?"

"Yes. But Ron and I quickly decided to make sure Herb stayed clear of Ian Williams. We saw that Williams's connections to international business could present us with a huge opportunity. But with it came great risk. Ian Williams was in tight with a group of investors that desperately wanted to gain influence within the US government. But we suspected Williams might not have had the cleanest record. For that reason, Ron took point on all communication with Williams and the investor group."

"What was Williams doing that make you think he was dirty?"

"There were rumors about him accepting bribes from some of the Afghan poppy growers. The British diplomats there hated him, too. Thought he was a creep, if I recall. One of the Brits gave us a warning to stay away from Williams. Said he was getting some under-the-table payments or something."

"If you thought he was dirty, why'd you let Ron keep talking to him?"

She shot Max a sly look. "You aren't in politics, are you? Honey, there's all types. We didn't see Williams do anything illegal. It's good to have well-financed friends. Williams was offering us that. If you turn away every Tom, Dick, and Harry with a speck of dirt in their past, you'd have to turn away everyone. At the time, Williams just struck me as a wheeler and dealer."

"Tell me about this investment group that he offered access to. Were they connected to Pakistan? Pakistani intelligence, maybe?"

She touched her neck and pursed her lips. "I don't think so. Not that I'm aware."

That question flustered her, Max thought.

"But it was foreign money?"

Upton folded her arms and didn't answer. Okay, she didn't want to directly incriminate herself or her friends. Fine.

"What was motivating Williams to make these introductions between Ron and the foreign investors?"

"At that time, I think Ian knew he was on the way out of the British government. He was the subject of an internal investigation—we didn't find that out until later. My guess? The money came from people making tens of billions on heroin and other drugs. Ian Williams dealt with these people in the war on terror. He was MI6, after all. I imagine with the people he had to deal with, everything turned to shades of gray."

Max knew that Upton was close to home with that assessment. When he'd been under nonofficial cover in Europe with the DIA, he'd oftentimes met with men working for criminal organizations.

"So you think Williams was recruited by organized crime? The ones moving product from Afghanistan to the sellers' markets in Europe and Asia?"

"Maybe." She shrugged. "I just know that Ian was sharp. He knew how to play the game. He knew how to influence people. He was a power broker. He spoke several languages, and he didn't strike me as the type to worry about ethical considerations."

She looked uncomfortable. "You promised me that anything I say here won't get me in trouble, right?"

Max said, "I told you, I'm not a cop."

She frowned. "Fine, then. In the end, I knew Ian Williams was dirty because of the promises he made to Ron Dicks."

Max raised his eyebrow. "What promises?"

"Now, I only know what Ron told me in confidence. I don't have any firsthand evidence. But I believe Williams wanted Becker to help push certain policy stances within the US government. Becker represented some US agricultural interests, for instance. He could help make sure the US government didn't give subsidies that would turn Afghanistan into a farming competitor."

"Why would that matter?"

"Let me ask you something. You see a big black market for corn? Ian Williams was working with people who wanted to ramp up Afghanistan opium production. While the international community would never outright go along with that, there were ways that Becker could help. Like leaving Afghanistan no other option. Ian Williams worked through Ron Dicks to make Becker sway US policy."

"And Senator Becker was okay with this?"

"He didn't know everything. Our policy was to keep Becker in the dark. It would protect him. These agreements with Ian Williams were all on Ron Dicks back then. Becker trusted Ron to give him good advice. But Becker didn't know the details, and he didn't want to know, if you catch my meaning."

"But he must have been told enough to know it was going to be beneficial for him. What did Becker get?"

"Ron said that Williams had contacts in the business world that would start contributing to Becker's campaign."

So far Jennifer Upton's story was matching up very well with Caleb Wilkes's theory. "Quid pro quo?"

Upton said, "I'd rather not be so explicit in what I say, regardless of the fact that you aren't a cop."

"How long have these investors been investing, do you think?"

"Quite a while."

Renee said, "But this was foreign money, right? Wasn't this against the law? How could this happen without people finding out about it?"

Upton shrugged. "Campaign finance is a gray area. Super PACs and certain types of nonprofits can take money from foreign entities, but there are restrictions. The beauty of it is, though, that none of these restrictions are investigated or enforced. And some of the nonprofit types, under US law, can take unlimited money from any source, without having to disclose anything about that source."

"Dark money," Max said.

"That's the buzz word, yes. But I will tell you that politicians don't get anywhere nowadays without heavy financial backing. Each one of those TV commercials cost money. We used to think that the digital revolution would be great for politics. Lower spending and make things more efficient. Then the advertising cost per click rose as the market got flooded. Everything costs more now. It's insane. The research, the advertising. It's a political arms race. My company uses social networks and online analytics to microtarget our voters. Thanks to the tech companies, we can identify everything about a person and actually calculate down to the cent how much a voter is going to cost. So each election is just a simple matter of math. Does your candidate have the money or not? Ron got Ian Williams to help Becker with money."

"And the only thing Williams got in return was help in Afghan opium farming policy? That doesn't even sound like something Becker could pull off by himself."

"That type of help might have had a huge impact on the rebirth of Afghan poppy growth. Although you would never be able to prove it. And I seriously doubt that Ron was the only one Ian Williams was working with."

Max considered that. Who else was involved with Ian Williams? How big was his circle? *VIP meeting?*

Upton continued. "Afghan policy was just how it started. Ian Williams was like the drug dealer that starts you off on pot, only to trade you up into the hard stuff later. Williams wanted Ron to taste how good it could be. Three years after the two met, Becker won his Senate seat. And that's when Williams came calling again."

"What did he want then?"

"I don't know. I was no longer on staff."

"Then how'd you hear about it?"

She looked like she was stuck. Caught saying more than she'd intended to. "Ron mentioned it last year. I saw him at the party's convention. We had a drink and got caught up. Ron told me that someone working with Ian Williams had approached him, trying to push some new policy ideas. Perhaps that person was the lobbyist who was killed?"

"Did Becker play ball?"

She looked at Max with a cynical stare. "You keep asking about Becker. Again, I don't think Herb even knew about it. You need to understand something. Senators don't do the grunt work at that level. They have staff that brings them all of the information and big ideas. With a lot of 'em, politicians are just the monkeys behind the microphones."

"So if Ron was on board, the senator was too? Maybe without knowing why?"

Upton nodded. "Yes. If Ron was sure they would get more funding, and weren't at risk, my guess is he went along with it. You know the whole system works this way, right? Money makes the world go round."

Renee shook her head. "I don't understand. What's the problem, then? Why would Ian Williams be sending Senator

Becker death threats now, if Ron was still playing ball? And why would he want to hurt you?"

Jennifer's eyes darted around the room as she spoke. "I wouldn't know. This weekend was the first time I've seen Herb in a long time. My guess is that Herb found out Ron was still in contact with Williams somehow and told him to break it off, once and for all."

"Why would he do that?"

"Herb Becker is truly motivated by only one thing. Ambition. Like many politicians, he wants to be president. And Herb would do anything to become president. Herb is pushing this new Opioid Epidemic Bill. It's a political football. But it's definitely not compatible with Ian Williams's interests."

"Why not?"

"From what Ron told me, Williams's investors included members of Big Pharma as well. International companies that made billions in opioid sales in the US. So Maybe Ron was still playing ball with Williams behind Herb's back? Maybe Ron told Williams or this lobbyist he was working with that everything was great. That Herb was still on board. That might have worked as long as their policy agendas were aligned. Williams thought he had a big fish in his pocket. Then Herb decides he's going to make this new bill his big signature achievement. I have to admit, it'd look great if you were running for president. Everyone wants to help stop the opioid epidemic. Who wouldn't want their name attached?"

"Do you know where Ian Williams works now?"

She shrugged.

"Let me ask a different question. Does Senator Becker know where Ian Williams works now?"

A dark smile formed on her lips. "Ask yourself why Herb is going so hard against the drug cartels now."

Max stared at her, his face impassive. So she did know. And she was implying that Becker knew too.

"You tell me," he said.

"It's because he wants to counter any problems he might have if the Williams scandal comes to light. Now let me make this clear. Herb didn't do anything wrong. But just the mere association with someone who's now involved in a drug cartel could be catastrophic to a presidential campaign. Ian Williams is toxic now. Look at where he is. Herb must be terrified at that development. Then all of a sudden, Ron isn't returning Williams's calls. He's cut Williams off. Williams feels betrayed because Herb isn't playing ball. Herb doesn't need Ian Williams's shady friends anymore. But he sure as hell will need to make sure none of those skeletons fall out of the closet if he ever wants to become president."

"You keep saying Herb. I thought Ron Dicks was the one who was connected to Williams?"

She shrugged. "Excuse me. I misspoke. Ron knows the details. He knows not to bother the senator with them, I'm sure. He did back when I worked for him. Herb's clean. But Ron, God rest his soul, may have taken a few shortcuts."

Max frowned. "Who knows about Becker and Williams?"

"Almost no one. And I'll deny it, if you ever try to make this public. Herb Becker made one mistake. He didn't report his connection with Ian Williams in the beginning. But after that, everything he did was legal. And I'll say something else. Everything he did, he did for the right reasons. We won the war on terror, in part because men like Herb made deals to keep Afghanistan stable. Keep their economy going."

Renee said, "By growing heroin?"

"Don't give me that judgmental look, missy."

Max said, "Has Senator Becker had any contact with Williams in the past few years?"

"Absolutely not."

"You seem pretty sure of that."

"I am."

"How do you know?"

"Because I have, as you say, been seeing Herb socially again, every so often. I would know if they were still in touch."

"Do you know anything about a meeting Ian Williams is about to have?"

"A meeting with who?"

"Some important people."

She shook her head. "I don't know anything about any meeting. I haven't seen Williams since the 2000s. And even then, it was only a few times."

"Why do you think Ian Williams would need to kill a list of people before this meeting?"

Max thought she looked alarmed for a moment, but then she said, "I wouldn't know. I'm sorry."

"Let me ask you the same question I asked you yesterday. Do you know of any reason that Ian Williams would want to hurt you?"

She said, "Ian Williams could care less about me."

"What do you mean?"

"The only reason he would care about me is if he was trying to get to Herb. It's not me you should be worried about. From what I've seen, Ian Williams is a survivalist. If he's at the point where he's killing people, then he'll definitely take a shot at the senator." She sighed and looked at Max. "I lied to you yesterday. I was scared, and I didn't want to put Herb in legal jeopardy or hurt his career. But I care about him. He's a good man, and he's tried to do the right thing. This is the reason I've decided to talk to you about all of this today, even if it gets Herb in hot water. Please, Max. Don't let Herb Becker get hurt. You don't need to worry about me. It's Senator Becker you need to be protecting."

Max stood. "We'll continue this later." Looking at Renee he said, "I should get back."

She nodded. He left the house, got in the rental car and

drove away, leaving Renee, Jennifer Upton, and the other CIA man at the safe house. Max needed to get back to the air show to meet with Wilkes. While he didn't trust everything that Jennifer Upton had said, enough of it sounded right to him that he felt Senator Becker should be considered a confirmed target.

## CHAPTER 26

SENATOR BECKER WALKED up to the grassy area where Karen was busy preflighting her aircraft before the show. Karen walked around the right wing, checking for any popped rivets or loose fasteners. She checked the oil levels and landing gear, the prop and the engine, making sure that there was no foreign object debris anywhere in sight.

"You ready?" asked her father, looking stiff and artificial in his creased button-down shirt.

Her coach was nearby, still within earshot. "Could you give us a moment?"

The coach pointed at his watch. "Two minutes and you gotta start up."

She nodded, mouthing, "Thanks."

On the nearby taxiway, people were staring at both Karen and her father as they spoke, close and quiet beside her cockpit. Karen could see at least three security men, watching the crowd through their sunglasses.

"Have you decided what you'll do?"

Her father nodded. "Yes. I've made arrangements to speak to someone representing the group. I think we'll be able to work something out."

"How can you trust them after what they've done? What makes you think they'll ever leave you alone?"

"Don't worry about that now."

"You made a mistake. But you were trying to do the right thing. People will understand that. You might not be able to run for office again, but you don't need that. Tell them you're done, Dad. They'll just keep coming after you for more."

"I know, honey. You're right." He looked into her eyes, giving her that same warm smile that had soothed her as a child and annoyed her as an adult, when she realized he gave it to everyone on the campaign trail as well. "I'll end it. Once and for all. Everything will be alright. Why are you crying? Honey…"

She shook her head. "Dad, I can't be doing this right now."

"It's fine. We'll talk later."

Karen nodded. She wiped away a tear and hugged her father.

"Now good luck today."

Karen smiled and climbed into her plane.

* * *

Max walked under the air show entrance gate and towards the VIP tent area. Once there, he saw the other CIA guy, Mike, standing behind a vendor stand that was selling airplane vacation tours in New Zealand. A red "Display Closed" sign sat on the desk in front of him.

"How's everything going?"

Mike looked up at Max and motioned him to come closer. He pulled out a drawer and handed him an earpiece, which Max promptly put in.

"Trent and Wilkes are both up on our closed circuit. FBI and local police have about twenty personnel doing roaming security, most of them close in to the senator. They're both on separate comms freqs. They know we're here. Your father opted not to wear one of these since he'll be in the VIP tent. Have you heard the news on timing?"

"No, what?"

"Our SIGINT techies said they picked up some chatter. They think Williams has someone on the move right now."

Max's eyes went wide. "Shit. Where's Wilkes?"

Mike pointed towards the grove of trees behind the VIP tent. Max walked over there, tapping his earpiece as he did. "Comms check. Max is up."

"Trent hears you."

Max could see Wilkes give him a thumbs-up as he approached. Caleb Wilkes had a pair of binoculars wrapped around his neck but was using them to scan the crowd, not the five aerobatics planes flying in formation above them.

Max filled Wilkes in on what he'd learned from Jennifer Upton.

Wilkes cursed softly. "This is crazy. I don't care what the guy wants. We should move him. With this and the intel we received earlier, I think it's now too much. I'll get on the phone with my contacts at FBI and the Capitol Police. It might take a few minutes, but they'll put the word out to the security he's got stationed here. I expect they'll insist on pulling him out. You and Trent keep your eyes open until that happens."

Max said, "Trent, you got all that?"

"Copy."

Max could see his father and the senator through a plastic window of the VIP tent. They were holding drinks and talking with their hands, telling stories to a captivated group around them. The senator looked completely unaware of the danger he was in.

* * *

Trent walked along the alleyways and vendor tents of the air show, scanning for anything out of place. It felt weird to be using these skills here. In Middle Eastern and African countries and, during the final years of his Army career, in the streets of Mexico, he had grown used to having to blend in. But operating at an air show in Wisconsin was a first. He'd spent more than half his adult life deployed overseas. Where had the time gone? Just yesterday he and his brother had been teenagers, having pushup contests in the backyard and watching old Rambo movies on the VHS.

The thought of Josh brought a sting of sadness. He missed his brother like hell.

He shook off the thought and continued to walk the air show exhibits near the VIP tent, evaluating each face in the crowd through his sunglasses. This wasn't the kind of place where he wanted to get into a firefight. Way too many civilians around. He looked for possible IEDs, sniper locations, ambush spots. He profiled everyone he saw, paying particular attention to the younger, fitter men, anyone with Latin or Central Asian features. He also scanned anyone with clothing or bags capable of hiding a weapon.

He took a turn and saw Max walk by, evaluating the crowd in the same fashion. They gave each other barely perceptible nods and kept at it. Max looked tense. Trent had a hard time believing that the cartels would try something here. Especially against a US senator. Trent had worked in Mexico. He knew that the cartels could be brutally violent, but they also had rules. And one of them was not to poke the bear to the north. Assassinating a senator was definitely against the rules.

He checked his watch. Almost time for Karen Becker's performance. After that, Senator Becker would leave the air show, and protecting him would get a lot easier.

Trent flexed his fingers together against his palms, his eyes darting from one end of the central plaza to the other. Everywhere he looked, there were people. The atmosphere was jovial. Kids licking ice cream cones and holding their grand-parents' hands.

Trent realized that the crowd was now moving en masse, migrating the hundred-yard distance from all the aircraft exhibits toward the sprawling grassy plain situated just next to the runway. People were setting up their lawn chairs and blankets, grabbing the empty spots and looking up at the sky, which was, for the moment, silent.

Today's highlight was about to begin.

Karen Becker's show.

A golf cart bumping along in the opposite direction of the crowd caught his eye. Two men wearing gray flight suits with plenty of pockets. Sunglasses and dark blue ball caps. One white guy, one looked...Indian or Pakistani, maybe? Both looked to be in their thirties or forties. Neither spoke, and both looked deadly serious. Their uniforms made them look like they were part of a performance crew—maybe maintenance men or part of the air show admin team? But something seemed off about them. They didn't have those keycard IDs around their necks, for one. And he hadn't seen any of the other aircraft maintenance crews driving in pairs, only by themselves.

He kept watching them as their golf cart passed by the vintage air exhibit and came to a halt next to the now-deserted outdoor movie theater in the woods.

An odd destination.

As Trent had learned in the past day, nothing went on there until after sunset. His instincts tingling, Trent tapped his earpiece and said, "Max, meet me in the woods by the vintage aircraft hangar ASAP."

Max's reply was drowned out by the loudspeaker, which was fixed to the tree above Trent's head.

"Ladies and gentlemen, please turn your attention to the

south side of the runway as the Blonde Bombshell, Karen Becker, begins her takeoff roll!"

*　*　*

Renee sat in the living room of the safe house. Jennifer Upton was on the couch. She had the TV on and was watching bad reality TV. Renee had given her a questioning look, and the woman had actually hissed at her. There was something off about Jennifer Upton.

Renee had been sitting feet away from Upton while researching her testimony on the computer.

"Why can't I have my phone back?"

"It wouldn't be safe," answered the CIA kid from the kitchen. Upton rolled her eyes and heaved a hearty sigh like a teenage girl angry at her father's rules.

Renee had just connected with one of her hacker friends on an encrypted chat. He was helping her get access to the previous locations of Dahlman, Dicks, Becker, and Upton. They accessed the cell phone GPS coordinate archives of each person and overlaid that information with any known locations where Ian Williams or Abdul Syed had been stationed and associated dates.

Information about Williams and Syed was scarce. And what little they did have turned out to be a dead end.

But after about fifteen minutes, Renee saw a definite trend. When she looked at the four Americans' information and took the timestamps back three years, they were in the same location at the same time each year.

Oshkosh.

*All four of them at Oshkosh?*

They must have been together, which was not consistent with the story Jennifer Upton had just told them. She'd said she hadn't seen Ron Dicks in years, for one.

Renee thanked her hacker friend and signed out of the chat room. She glanced at Jennifer Upton to make sure she wasn't watching her. Upton was still busy messing around with her watch, only half-paying attention to the trashy TV show about whiny brides and wedding dresses.

Renee locked her computer and went into the kitchen, where the CIA operative was watching the security monitors.

"Anything going on?" Renee whispered.

"Nothing," the young man said.

She kept her voice very quiet. "I need access to her phone."

He nodded and opened up the safe under the kitchen counter. He removed Upton's cell phone and handed it to Renee. "You need a cable?"

"Won't be a problem."

Renee powered up the device and slid it into her pocket. Thankfully it wasn't an iPhone. Those were harder to crack. Sitting on the couch across from Jennifer Upton, Renee used her computer's near field communication and some special software to access the phone. She then searched through pictures, text messages, and any other data from the time period that overlapped each annual Oshkosh visit.

There wasn't much. It was almost like Upton was purposely not communicating or taking pictures during those time periods. The fact that all three of them were together at Oshkosh meant something. But now that Renee had that morsel of a clue, she was determined to find the missing puzzle piece.

She looked up again. Upton was looking at the TV.

Renee looked at the map on her screen again. The one with the overlay of locations. She frowned. It wasn't exactly at Oshkosh, was it? No. It was southeast. Near the water. Renee decided to try something else. She dug into Upton's cloud storage accounts. Sometimes they synced up photos without people realizing it, keeping images that were thought to have been deleted.

Nothing. Upton wasn't a big social media person. Neither was the senator, which made sense.

Renee typed to her hacker friend again. With his help, Renee was able to search through hundreds of thousands of images stored online with GPS stamps near the same time and location she was interested in. They put the images through facial recognition software and came up with several hits. One of the photos was particularly interesting. There was water on the lower half of the image. It might have been taken from a boat or across a small inlet, but the resolution was good. Renee was able to zoom in on a gazebo where a group of people were having some type of gathering. The photo was dated three years ago, and the GPS tag was within five miles of Oshkosh.

In the image, Senator Becker was standing next to Jennifer Upton and Ron Dicks. They were outdoors, drinks in hand, smiling. They seemed to be unaware the picture was being taken.

Ian Williams was in the background, on a cell phone.

They *were* all together at Oshkosh.

Becker, Upton, Dicks, and Ian Williams. Only three years ago. What did this mean? She needed to tell Max.

Renee got up from the couch and walked into one of the spare bedrooms, closing the door and locking it behind her. Damn the security procedures, she had to call Max. She dialed his phone, but it just went straight to his voicemail.

Renee left him a voicemail anyway.

Short and to the point. Hopefully he would get it soon.

Then she walked into the living room and sat back down on the couch. Renee looked back up at Upton, who was still playing with her watch...

But it wasn't just a watch, Renee realized.

It was a smart watch.

A connected device.

They had confiscated her phone but didn't notice the

watch. The design hadn't looked like a typical smart watch. They had glossed right over it.

She was communicating.

Jennifer Upton glanced up at Renee, and their eyes met.

Renee's heart pounded in her chest. She could feel herself breathing.

Renee turned at the sounds of the CIA man swearing from the kitchen. Then she heard the sound of vehicles arriving out front. Tires grinding to a halt on the gravel driveway.

Renee shut her computer and ran into the kitchen. The CIA man had his gun drawn.

On the security monitors, Renee saw several SUVs parked outside. Men wearing masks and holding assault rifles approached the home.

## CHAPTER 27

THE SAME ANNOUNCER broadcasting over the air show speaker system was on frequency with Karen as she began racing down the runway.

"Can you hear us, Karen?"

"I read you loud and clear! Good afternoon, Oshkosh!"

The crowd cheered and hollered as Karen gained speed, pulled back on her stick, and shot straight up into the air.

Karen's heart was beating fast. Adrenaline pumped through her veins. This was her Super Bowl. Nothing compared to performing at Oshkosh. It was her time to shine in front of hundreds of thousands of screaming fans. To leave behind the angst she felt about her father's mistakes and her own insecurities. Up here, she was alive and in her element, doing what she was meant to do.

She went through her routine with expert precision. She got on altitude and airspeed, checked her instruments, ran through her silent checklist, then jammed the stick hard left, cut the throttle and pulled through her dive upside down and gaining speed, the ground coming closer and closer, the spectators' mouths opening as they clicked pictures. Then she came to the bottom of her dive, airspeed rocketing upward, the g's hitting her body, flexing her legs and grunting and pulling in a bit more backstick, then slamming down one pedal and putting her aircraft into a sideslip, practically hovering over the ground at an impossible angle.

Her engine buzzed loud, its pitch changing to the ears below along with the dynamic stresses and speeds of her maneuvers, and she demanded all the power it could muster without redlining. Then she centered her pedals, dipped her nose, and began gaining speed again, diving towards the earth.

"How's it going up there, Karen? Ready to cut the tape?"

"Sure am, Oshkosh!"

Her eyes scanned her instruments again. She leveled off at eight thousand feet, the clear runways and colorful crowd huddled below her. Blue sky above. Each pull of the stick put enormous g-forces on her body, and she huffed and flexed to stay conscious as she performed loop after loop. Roll after roll. She couldn't hear the cheering below, but she knew that they were getting one hell of a show.

Now she would start her spin. Full left pedal, full back and slightly left stick...enter the stall...feel her stomach floating up, and then the green and red and blue outside the windscreen twirled into a blur and her aircraft departed controlled flight.

This was her most challenging maneuver.

An eight-thousand-foot controlled drop, plummeting and twirling seemingly out of control, like a maple leaf falling in the air, spinning and spinning towards the ground, all the while she was in control, taking a scalpel to the air and carving it up exactly how she intended.

Her spin would transform into a steep dive below two thousand feet, and she would once again pull herself out just feet over the runway, using her propeller to cut a thin plastic ribbon which had been set up just in front of the crowd.

\* \* \*

The two men in gray flight suits were just waiting there.

"What are they doing?" asked Trent.

Max spoke into his earpiece. "Caleb, if they're armed, they could be at the VIP tent in about thirty seconds. Trent and I are going to head over there. Has the senator been alerted to the threat?"

Wilkes shook his head. "Local law enforcement is passing on the warning now."

Max looked back and saw a man he knew to be a plain-clothes police officer assigned to the senator's security detail. He was speaking into the senator's ear, with Max's father looking concerned next to them. Max's father also had a body-guard, but if these guys had the same equipment they'd used down in Texas and Mexico, the best course of action was to evacuate the VIPs immediately and notify the police.

Overhead, Karen's aircraft was looping and swirling, a bright red stream of smoke trailing behind her.

* * *

Hugo had spotted several plainclothes security personnel during his time on the air show grounds this morning, but his risk would soon be minimal.

He had a clear line of sight to his target from here. Hugo fished into the navy-blue maintenance bag on his lap and took the black plastic transmitter in his hands. He had powered it up moments ago, making sure that the LED lit up green. Now he had to wait until his target was in just the right position.

He had trained for this for the past few weeks, working with an explosives expert to custom-design the charge and ensure that they had just the right weapon for this job.

There. His target was at the perfect spot.

Hugo flipped up the transmit switch and watched Karen Becker's plane.

\* \* \*

Just as she was about to take herself out of the spin, Karen heard a sharp mechanical pop underneath her, and her controls went slack in her hands and under her feet.

All the resistance pushing back against her right hand, which gripped the yoke, and against her boots on the pedals was now completely gone. Karen rapidly moved the yoke as far as it would go in all directions, alternating pumps with each foot. Moving it around in a big square. Slow at first. Then fast. Both directions.

*Nothing.*

A terrifying chill ran up her spine as her aircraft continued to spin, plummeting towards the earth.

What she didn't know was that Hugo and his ISI assistant, who had been trained by the Pakistani Air Force in small aircraft maintenance procedures, had accessed Karen Becker's plane at three a.m. local time. Together they had placed a trace amount of plastic explosive at three critical points that connected the plane's flight controls. A silver-colored patch was placed over the control rod, encasing a small receiver, trigger, and detonator. The charges had been painstakingly planted in a ring-shape around the control rod. The explosions would be small, but quite effective, snapping apart the linkage from the flight controls to the aircraft's control surfaces.

The work was almost invisible to the naked eye and had not been noticed by the maintenance or pilot inspections, as it was located inside the aircraft—a position only checked during scheduled maintenance tune-ups.

"Tower," she began, her voice strained.

"Say again, Bravo Sierra…" A different voice over the radio now. Deeper, and this man had used her call sign, all pretense of showmanship gone.

She tried again, moving her yoke in one big square,

attempting to fix the problem. She pushed and pulled both foot pedals all the way forward and backward, to no avail. Nothing was giving her control back. It was like the mechanical connections had all been severed.

Her altitude wound down with sickening speed, the colors of the spectators still swirling together as the ground rushed up to meet her.

"Tower, Bravo Sierra. Declaring an emergency. Loss of flight controls…"

* * *

Max and Trent made their way through the grove of trees towards the two men in gray flight suits. They were watching the aerobatics demonstration.

"Hold on," Wilkes said. "Are you guys listening to this?"

Trent and Max were farther away from the air show loudspeakers. The two men stopped and turned to see where the crowd was pointing.

One woman near Max was hugging her husband and wincing, saying, "Oh my God…" Another man was swearing over and over, seemingly unaware of the children next to him. Both were looking up at Karen Becker's aircraft.

What had Max missed?

Then he heard Karen's radio call, still being broadcast over the speaker.

"Did she say loss of controls?"

Trent looked alarmed, his head on a swivel, careful not to lose the men standing by the outdoor theater.

Max looked up towards Karen Becker's aircraft. Red and black, spiraling downward, lower and lower. His eyes widened as it became obvious she was in real trouble. She was too low. She should have recovered from that spin by now…

Max looked towards the VIP tent. He could just make out

the figure of Senator Becker pressed up against the translucent plastic of the tent, looking up at the plane, and then away at the ground.

Max looked up at the aircraft again.

"Something's wrong," Max said. "Something is very wrong…"

* * *

The last hundred feet felt like the aircraft was flying straight down.

Screams from the crowd the closer it got.

And the chilling cries of Karen herself, still broadcasting over the outdoor speakers as the aircraft slammed into the hard pavement of the nearest taxiway. A gaseous yellow fireball erupted from the concrete, transforming into plumes of thick black smoke.

A collective gasp of horror from hundreds of thousands of spectators, holding their mouths and picking up crying children. Men and women stared at the wreckage, held captive by their own morbid curiosity.

Sirens blared from a mile away as the crash crew activated. Giant versions of fire engines and heavy-duty ambulances raced to the scene. They sprayed water on the fires, but there was nothing anyone could do for Karen Becker now.

Max looked at the senator. He was on his knees, one hand still holding the plastic of the tent window, the other over his face.

"Hey." Trent tapped Max on the arm to get his attention. "Look."

The men in gray flight suits were on the move, riding their golf cart away from the scene. Max watched as they rolled through the nearest exit and headed for the massive parking lot area.

"They're gone."

* * *

Bullet holes filled the door.

Renee watched in horror as the CIA man standing behind it collapsed to the floor, his chest covered in crimson. Three men in black tactical gear stormed through the entrance, fanning out through the living room, their weapons trained on the two women.

Within seconds, Renee and Upton were on their stomachs, a boot in each of their backs, the barrel of a submachine gun aimed at their heads.

More men entered the house, including two who carried in a large plastic tarp roll. One of the gunmen flipped up the coffee table and threw it into the corner of the room, picture frames and glass shattering. Two other men pushed the couches and chairs so that the space became open. Then they unrolled the plastic tarp on the floor.

Renee became nauseous as she realized what was going on.

A tall Caucasian man appeared in the doorway, a thin smile on his face.

"Hello, ladies," said Ian Williams in his thick British accent. He said something in Spanish, and both women were hiked up off the floor.

Jennifer Upton said, "Ian, would you please tell your men here to release me? I'm the one who called you here, for God's sake."

"Yes, and it's much appreciated." One of the men set a toolbox down on the floor next to Williams.

"*Gracias.*" He opened the toolbox and removed a pair of pliers, a vise, and a small power saw, which he plugged into the wall.

Williams walked over to Renee and caressed her neckline

up to her cheek. His face twitched, and he pressed his lips forward and together like a deranged kiss. Renee turned her head away, shivering in fear and revulsion.

Where was Max? Wilkes must know that something had happened here. They would come for them. But how long would it take? The air show was more than a half hour away.

Williams seemed to be reading her mind. "Don't worry, dear, I'll have you out of here before your friends begin to worry. They're busy cleaning up another mess right now."

He kissed her on the neck and walked around her body, sliding his fingers over her bare arm. Renee wanted to lash out. She could feel her blood pressure rising and her face heating up as anger overcame all her other emotions. But there must have been six of his attack dogs in the room, each one holding a large black machine gun. Renee hated guns. But what she wouldn't give to get her hands on one of them right now.

"Renee. You don't know how happy it makes me to see us united again. If you please, my dear. Go wait in the car. I will join you momentarily."

He gave another command in Spanish, and she was escorted into the back of a large SUV outside, a gunman sitting on either side of her. They didn't even bother to tie her hands. She had no chance against men like these. They left the door open, allowing the airflow to cool them in the warm summer day. Through the open door, Renee heard the high-pitched sound of the power saw. Then she heard screaming. A loud, blood-curdling scream. Then nothing for a few moments. Then more power saw and screams, and an awful gurgling noise. Then nothing. Renee dry-heaved in the backseat of the car and one of the men guarding her laughed.

The whole thing took ten minutes, and then the men marched back out. This time the tarp was significantly thicker and heavier, with ties around each end as they shoved the remains of Jennifer Upton into the empty back of the lead vehicle.

Ian Williams sat shotgun in Renee's SUV. He looked back at her. "We're in good shape. Now let's go show you the lake house, shall we?"

He smiled at her, his white teeth contrasting with the rest of his face, which was covered in tiny crimson dots of blood.

## CHAPTER 28

MAX, Trent, and Caleb Wilkes stood talking in the CIA's faux vendor booth near the VIP tent. Charles had retired to his private jet after Senator Becker had left. Becker had wanted to mourn his daughter's death alone, and Charles Fend had to agree.

Max was still in shock after witnessing Karen Becker's crash. It had affected everyone watching.

Max spoke in a hushed tone. "So what do we think happened here? Was this another attempt to intimidate the senator? By targeting his daughter?"

Wilkes nodded. "It fits with the profile thus far."

"This seems different than the other killings."

"Are you sure it wasn't an accident?"

"Yes. It's too much of a coincidence not to be intentional. And with the men in the gray flight suits you saw disappearing after the crash…it's got to be foul play."

Max looked out at the wreckage, rubbing his chin. The thick plumes of black smoke had ceased, but there were still wisps of white and gray rising up into the air. The air show, being as large as it was, had a policy in the event that a crash occurred. All flight operations stopped, and a new tentative schedule was announced. There was to be a four-hour delay before flights would continue. The taxiway where the accident had occurred would be closed while safety and investigation crews did their jobs. When the day's events resumed, they would begin with a moment of silence.

Wilkes picked up his phone. "Go ahead."

His face went from annoyed to panicked. "When did you get there? Son of a bitch. Do another sweep of the place, then call the local police and notify the FBI. You'll have to stay there. Call me when authorities arrive. Don't provide any info on our ongoing operation. I'll contact my man at the FBI and give him a heads-up."

Wilkes hung up and looked at Max.

"What is it?"

"Mike just got to the safe house. Someone hit it."

"What?"

Trent shook his head and cursed.

Max said, "What the hell do you mean? Hit it? Where's Renee?"

"She wasn't there. My agent was dead at the scene."

Max felt dizzy.

"No sign of either Jennifer Upton or Renee. But there were several bullet holes near the door, the furniture had been kicked around, and there were a few traces of blood spatter on the walls."

Max's mind was on fire. Caleb kept talking, but he couldn't hear him. Max turned and walked away, fists clenched, breathing heavy through his nose and flexing his jaw.

Renee was gone.

Ian Williams had taken her. Was she still alive? If so, how long did she have?

Trent had placed his hand on his shoulder. "Max, you alright?"

The world was spinning all around him. Conversations and

memories of the past week flashed through his head in a vortex of images and emotions. Joseph Dahlman shot in the park. Breakfast with Ian Williams. Ines Sanchez killed on the beach. The attack in Texas. Flying in to Oshkosh. Karen's crash. Now Renee had been taken by these murderous madmen.

Then the flood of thoughts froze as he felt his phone vibrating. After the crash, he had turned it back on in hopes that Renee might have left him a message—before he knew she had been taken.

He hoped that she had been taken, and not worse.

There it was. A single voicemail. Max pressed the play button and held the phone up to his ear. Renee's voice was a mousy whisper, quick and nervous.

"Max, I know I'm not supposed to call, but this is important. What did Karen Becker say to her father in the conversation your dad recorded? She asked him if they were *here again*? That kept bugging me, the way she said that. *Here again*. I didn't think anything of it at first. Like maybe just that the bad guys were back. But now I think she actually meant that *literally*. Like here in Oshkosh. I found a picture from the internet dated three years ago. Get this. Senator Becker, Ron Dicks, Jennifer Upton, all smiling, and Ian freaking Williams is in the background. Max, they were at Oshkosh. Becker and Williams, Upton and Dicks. Oshkosh. Three years ago. Call me."

Max was stunned. He pressed the play button and listened the the message again. Thoughts racing through his mind.

When the message finished, he looked at Trent, who was watching him with a concerned look. Max said, "Karen Becker was killed right when they hit the safe house."

Trent said, "Yeah, I know, Max. Hey, maybe you should sit down, man?"

What had Senator Becker said to his daughter? *They won't have anything on me after this week.*

This was part of his plan.

"He knew about it," Max said.

"Knew about what?" said Trent.

"Senator Becker knew. That bastard knew his daughter was going to be killed. Becker didn't have a plan to escape Ian Williams and the ISI. He has a plan to cover up his involvement with them."

\* \* \*

Renee was shoved out of the SUV by Williams's gunmen and made to follow him up the large flat steps and through the mansion's entrance. The opulent home was empty inside, but Renee heard raucous laughter coming from the rear garden area. Through open French doors, Renee saw a group of six men sitting around an open fire pit.

A dark-featured man walked up the expansive lawn towards them. He looked at her with surprise and fear.

Syed, Renee realized.

"What is she doing here?" he whispered to Williams.

Williams, who was nearly a foot taller than the Pakistani man, craned his neck to look at him as he spoke.

"Don't worry about her. What happened at the air show? I heard on the radio there was a crash."

Syed looked at Renee.

Williams snorted. "I told you to relax. Say what you want. Did your man Hugo have any problems?"

"No, I didn't," came a voice from behind them. Renee turned and saw a younger man in a gray flight suit, two-day old stubble on his face. She thought she recognized him. Evidently, he was thinking the same thing, staring her down with menacing brown eyes.

Williams said, "She's dead?"

"Yes."

"You're sure?"

"One hundred percent. Now I need to clean up and collect my payment. Then I'll be gone."

Syed said, "I'll be leaving with you shortly. Mr. Williams and I need to take care of something first. You will need to remain in the house. Out of the backyard." The tone and look Syed used were ominous. The men in the room exchanged glances.

Williams said, "You can babysit her." He pointed to Renee. "Have a seat, darling. We'll be a few minutes."

Syed and Williams walked outside. The group of men around the fire pit were smiling and holding up their drinks. They were trying to get them to come join them, but the two men kept walking, out towards the lake. They walked down the dock and sat in a little wooden gazebo that stood over the water.

It was just the two of them now. Renee needed to find out what was going on. Understand who she was dealing with. Figure out more options. She was scared, but she was also raging inside.

She looked at the man standing in the room and said, "You were in Virginia, weren't you? Two weeks ago. In the park. I saw you get on your bike and ride away."

The man looked at her, expressionless. "Why has he let you live? Williams?"

"I don't know."

"I would be concerned about that if I were you. He's not a nice man."

Renee let out a scoff. "You killed someone. You're not a nice man."

"I've killed a lot of people."

"Why?"

"Money."

She spoke softly. "I can get you money. Help me. They're all outside. You could help me get away right now. I..."

He shook his head, looking at her with a skeptical eye.

"Don't waste your time. If I betrayed them, I would be hunted down and killed. And I wouldn't be paid. Nor would I get any more work. No offense, but your proposal is illogical."

She exhaled, looking outside. "*Baptême.*"

He turned and looked at her with renewed interest. "You're from Quebec?" he asked in French.

"Yes. I lived there until I was eighteen," she said, also in French. "You?"

"I've spent time there. Also in France."

For a moment, Renee thought she saw an opening, but then he switched back to English and turned away. "But that was long ago. What do you think is going on here?"

"I assumed you knew more than me."

"They only tell me what they need to."

"And you trust them?"

"No. But I trust money and leverage. Both of which are working in my favor. Syed knows what will happen if he double-crosses me. And I know the same. It's a healthy relationship."

Outside on the gazebo, Ian Williams and Syed were standing up now. It looked like they were talking to someone on some type of oversized phone.

* * *

The senator was numb, but he remained focused on the task at hand. Charles Fend had wanted to accompany him home, but Becker had insisted on being alone. Only the local police security detail had accompanied him back to his lake house after the crash.

The maid was in tears when he entered, and the police officers stood by the door with awkward and curious looks. Not wanting to intrude, but also keenly aware that the man they were tasked to protect was still at risk and shouldn't be left alone.

"Gentlemen, you can stand watch in the front yard, but I don't wish to be disturbed. Please keep off the property for the evening."

The police officers nodded and kept their vehicles where the long drive met the main road. The senator's backyard was on Lake Winnebago, so that was secure. The policemen figured as long as they monitored the entrance, the security risk was low. The man was in mourning. Anyone could see the despair in his eyes. He deserved his solitude.

"Your wife called, Senator."

The maid had been with the family for decades, although she was only asked to come occasionally now that the senator spent most of his time in Washington. She knew Karen's mom from before the divorce, and Becker suspected that she liked her better than him.

"No calls for now."

Senator Becker walked up the creaky stairs into his office, which overlooked the lake. He closed and locked the office door.

Alone at last, he allowed himself a moment of reflection. His daughter was dead. It wasn't his fault. It was her own. If she hadn't been so stubborn and nosy, like her mother. He told himself that the feeling of guilt would pass. He willed it to pass. This had been the only course of action, he told himself. His was too important a career to sacrifice.

Thankfully Karen hadn't told anyone else about the annual meetings with the cabal. While this was her first performance at the show, Karen was at Oshkosh each year, often in his presence. Because of that, she had seen things she shouldn't have. She had seen Dahlman, Dicks, and the senator together with Ian Williams. She might have even seen Syed there, once.

Four or five years ago, Ron had told the senator about a

conversation he'd had with Karen. After witnessing the group at Oshkosh, Karen had privately admonished Ron for the continued relationship with the international investors. Senator Becker had gone to her after that and apologized. He'd assured her that it was only a meeting. That no further partnership was underway. Becker partly blamed himself. He never should have told Karen so much. For a long time, Becker thought that Karen was like him. A future politician, sharp as steel and able to look past the rough spots of the game. But for that damned afternoon where his daughter had caught him with Jennifer Upton. The girl had changed after that.

After Ron's warning, Senator Becker had made Karen promise to keep what she had seen at Oshkosh to herself, and she had. But if scandal broke during a presidential election campaign, Becker couldn't risk her stubborn streak showing itself again. Perhaps if she hadn't threatened to go to the press about Jennifer Upton years ago, he would have been able to trust her. But no.

That was why Becker had had dinner with her last week. One final check to make sure Karen hadn't told anyone anything she shouldn't have. Her accident wasn't originally supposed to occur during the Oshkosh airshow. Until recently, it was to have been a target of opportunity. Scheduled to occur during any number of her summer air shows. But then Karen had been selected for this performance at Oshkosh. The other members of the cabal were to be eliminated at that time. So with all of Syed's assets in the area, taking care of Karen here had been the most efficient solution.

While he tried not to think about it, Becker couldn't help but wonder how the sympathy vote might impact him in the years to come. His beautiful daughter, lost in a tragic accident. Tearful interviews recalling how much she had meant to him. Even better would be if Syed's explosive residue was discovered by investigators. The cartels or some of the rogue agents the ISI was cutting loose would take the blame. Then her death would be seen as a horrific attack on the senator. A man beyond reproach, having paid the ultimate sacrifice in the name of our country.

A grandfather clock ticked behind him. The sands of time. The endless prompt of ambitious men. As he grew older, the scarcity of time filled him with fear. Fear that he would not achieve his goals. Fear that he would not be seen as great. Fear that his competitors would discover him and take from him that which he had worked so hard to achieve.

Senator Becker walked over to the liquor cabinet and poured himself a tall glass of Bombay Sapphire gin. He then took a large cube of ice from the mini fridge, dropped it in, and poured in a splash of soda water. He sipped it and looked out over the darkening lake. Here he would be alone with his pain.

And with his relief.

The hard part was finally coming to an end. The witnesses were being removed. The loose ends tied up.

Senator Becker took another sip from his glass and then placed it on the top of a knee-high black safe that rested next to his office desk. He spun the dial back and forth several times from memory, hearing a click as the final digit in the combination unlocked the safe. Then he slid the latch downward and pulled open the sturdy door. He reached inside with two hands and removed the small black device that the lobbyist, Joseph Dahlman, had given him three years earlier.

The point-to-point laser communication was very secure, and the device wouldn't store any traceable information.

Dahlman had been Senator Becker's only contact in Washington. They had rarely met face-to-face in the past year. Even the annual cabal meetings at Oshkosh were coming to an end now. Becker was getting too high up on the food chain. People were getting suspicious. Ian Williams had warned him that this might happen eventually if things went according to plan. Too much attention. Too many questions.

Too many loose ends. Even Karen.

He finished the drink and wiped his eyes, then poured some more gin in the glass. He took another sip, then put the glass down on the desk.

Senator Becker placed the black box on his desk and opened the window the way he'd been trained, making sure that the transmitter was aimed at the gazebo across the small bay. The cabal acquired the property through a cutout over a decade ago, using it as a vacation spot for visiting members during the annual meeting, and renting it out during the rest of the year so as not to look suspicious. The communications device connected to the receiver and began flashing, and Becker was prompted to place his finger down on the scanner and enter a passcode. The double verification allowed the encryption key, stored in the device's hard drive, to be transmitted to a similar device that had been set up on the gazebo.

Becker picked up his binoculars and looked towards the gazebo. There were only two men sitting there, as he expected.

Williams and Syed. Their final meeting. Risky, but they would have called it off if there were a problem.

The link established, Becker put on the headset and listened to their voices for the first time in a year.

It was Syed who spoke first. "We are sorry for your loss, Herbert."

"Thank you, Abdul."

"But your sacrifice and determination have once again proven to be unmatched."

"Yes."

He fought back the taste of bile in his throat, taking a moment to maintain his composure. "So, we are done now?"

"Almost."

"Almost?"

"Your government is under the impression that you are a target. Ronald Dicks is seen as the source of the intelligence leaks. But there is a complication. The CIA was interrogating Upton."

Senator Becker's eyes went wide. "What?"

"The CIA has a team here in Wisconsin."

"But I thought…how is that possible?"

"Herbert, be calm. It has been taken care of. We instructed Miss Upton on what to say. After speaking to her, we can confirm that the CIA is unaware of our true relationship. They are now under the impression that Ian Williams worked through Ronald Dicks, and that you had no knowledge of illegal activities. All others with knowledge of our relationship have been terminated, with the exception of a few members here with us now. Upton is no longer a problem. She is dead, and her body will not be found. You shall continue to say that Ronald Dicks was your only contact with Dahlman, and that you had no inappropriate foreign contact."

Becker simply said, "I understand."

He ran through the plans and possible options in his head. This was always going to be a complicated exit strategy. He simply had too many coconspirators and witnesses that were close to him.

Jennifer Upton had been naïve enough to think her personal relationship with him would protect her. That was what Becker had promised her. Syed had taken care of her now.

That she had spoken to the CIA was very worrisome. He should get off this device soon and get back to D.C. Syed would send a team into his house to empty his safe and clean up any evidence.

There still remained members of the inner circle across the bay that knew of his participation, however. The group of executives and politicians, of lawyers and executives from around the world. The men who had helped to orchestrate the opioid boom and reaped the rewards. Cash payments to numbered accounts, with a final large bonus payment expected today, as the new contract terms were settled. Williams could just make out some of these men, sitting across the bay in the backyard of the Pakistani mansion. Surrounding a fire pit. Drinking and laughing.

The final names on Ian Williams's list of participants. The last of the loose ends that must be dealt with.

Now it was Ian Williams's voice. "Herb, it's likely that you'll be interviewed by American counterintelligence."

He took another gulp of his gin. "I thought we were doing all this so that we could avoid—"

"It will be crucial that you maintain a consistent recollection of the facts. If you do this, you'll come out of it unscathed. You knew nothing about any quid pro quo on campaign contributions. You only met me briefly in Afghanistan. You didn't characterize your conversations with me as a recruitment, and you don't recall the specifics anyway. It was almost fifteen years ago. Even if we did speak, you never went along with anything I said. Anyone who says anything other than that is a liar. Ron Dicks was the only one we ever worked with, and he didn't tell you what he was doing."

"So that's it?"

"Yes. We have some housecleaning to do here tonight. But once that's complete, you will be in the clear, Herb. We will no longer contact you through unofficial channels."

Becker rubbed his hands together. This was good. Finally, he would be free. With no ties to this cabal, he could run for president without fear of scandal. The deaths of those near to him were tragic, of course. But they wouldn't be in vain. He would win the presidency and make this the greatest nation on earth. That was what mattered.

And if he was unable to attain the presidency, whether it be due to scandal or luck, he would still have the hundreds of millions of dollars piling up in several numbered accounts around the world. The investors' secretive dividend payments. Those financial updates were another reason the cabal met each year.

Senator Becker had made a pact with Ian Williams and Abdul Syed years ago. Together their fortunes would rise or fall.

Now it appeared their fortunes would rise higher than any of them had imagined.

"When will you two be gone?"

"In a few hours. We'll wrap things up here and clean up. This will be the last time we speak. Good luck."

Becker didn't need a handler anymore. He knew what Ian Williams and the ISI wanted. And they knew that if he ever decided to go back on his word, they could ruin him by bringing certain elements of the conspiracy to light. Perhaps someday, the other two would become leaders of their own nations. Someone always had leverage on you, Becker had learned over the years. But if your interests were aligned, it didn't matter.

Becker wouldn't double-cross them. He was getting what he wanted and would push policy that helped them all. It took ambitious men like him to change the world. Bargains and sacrifices had to be made. Too many people saw the world in black and white. But not him. He was a visionary, and he was willing to do whatever it took to win.

\* \* \*

Max now stood in front of Wilkes under the CIA's faux vendor tent. "You said Senator Becker went back to his home here in Oshkosh."

"That's right."

"Where?"

Wilkes narrowed his eyes. "Max, the man just lost his daughter. What are you going to do, barge in there and confront him?"

"At this point, I think that's the best idea."

Max dialed up his voicemail and played it on speaker phone so both Trent and Wilkes could hear. They looked at him, shocked.

"I think Becker knew his daughter was going to be killed. And I think this meeting might be here in Oshkosh. You said Syed disappeared. What if he's here?"

"He could be anywhere."

Max played the voicemail again.

"Karen Becker asked her dad if they had come back here. *Here*. As in, Oshkosh. Ian Williams is here, Caleb."

"That's insane. Why would they take that risk?"

"Ten thousand planes and nearly a million people all coming in and out of the same place, at the same time, once per year. Sounds like a great place to hold a meeting you don't want discovered."

"I don't know…"

"They took Renee, Caleb. Some of them must be here. Becker might be able to tell us how to find her. You said yourself that Ron Dicks was only a possible source of the leaks to Ian Williams. What if it wasn't him? What if it was really Becker?"

Wilkes lowered his voice. "The counterintelligence investigation is ongoing. It could have been twenty other people. We just don't know yet."

"Let's consider it," said Max. "What if Upton only gave us half the truth? What if Williams and Becker met, just like she said, but Williams actually bought in? He's been working for the ISI for more than a decade. He isn't a target. He's the mole. A traitor to our country."

"What about Ron Dicks?"

"A fall guy. Someone types up a bogus letter and mails it to the senator, right after they kill him."

"Why would Ian Williams and Becker both be coming here? That's crazy. And why would he let his daughter be killed?"

Max said, "You said that Senator Becker is going to run for president next election cycle, right? What if this big meeting is to get rid of witnesses? They're cleaning house so that they can get their man elected. Hell, even if he doesn't win the presidency, running alone will give him huge political influence."

"And this secret society decided to meet here at Oshkosh? Why?"

"I don't know. But Becker would. And I bet he knows where Ian Williams is. We get to Becker, we get to Williams. And to Renee…"

Wilkes looked unsure. "I can give you Becker's address, but—"

Max said, "Caleb, this isn't me operating on your behalf. I'm doing this whether you want me to or not."

Trent said, "I'm coming."

Wilkes said, "Very well. But it'll take you a while to get there. The traffic to exit this place is awful right now. Everyone wants to leave after witnessing that crash. There must be a hundred thousand people trying to drive out."

He was right. Max could hear the horns of static traffic in the distance.

The overhead speakers came on with an announcement. "Oshkosh flights will resume at six p.m. Aircraft are allowed to conduct maintenance ground turns prior to that time. Contact Base Ops for questions."

Max looked at Trent. "Follow me. I think I have an idea."

## CHAPTER 29

THE GYROCOPTER CONTROLS took a little getting used to. And Max was pretty sure that the King boys were going to catch hell from their father when he realized they'd allowed Max to take it. Max had received a five-minute orientation from the two boys.

"It's super easy," said Jack.

Then they set the destination GPS coordinates in the iPad, and Max and Trent strapped in. Trent had a bulky black duffle bag on his lap, which he had retrieved from their car. Max promised the boys he would get them a private tour of Fend Aerospace headquarters someday, and they were off.

Max started it up and saw Trent shaking in the seat next to him. "Will this thing really fly?"

Max shrugged and yelled back, "Think so." He pushed the throttle lever forward to add power, and they rolled forward in the grass, gaining lift at a very slow speed. Max banked left and headed towards the east, then tapped the button on the iPad to allow autopilot to take over steering.

An Oshkosh air show official was waving and yelling at Max as they overflew the runway. It was still an hour before the airfield reopened, and they were breaking the rules. Max realized that there were probably fifty thousand people watching him, including FAA officials who could take away his prized pilot's license. But he didn't care. Ian Williams had Renee, and Max had to get to her.

They puttered along, only feet above the power lines and treetops east of the airport, headed towards the huge lake on the horizon. Max scanned the iPad, careful to keep his hands on the controls in case the autopilot did anything unsafe. Even at the slow speed the gyrocopter was going, this trip would be much faster than driving.

"Where are you going to land it?" Trent yelled.

"There's a farmer's field about a half mile to the east. It looks like I'll be able to land it unseen if that grove of trees is thick enough." Max pointed at the map on the iPad. "I'll put you down and give you five minutes before I approach the security detail. If it doesn't look doable, just meet me out at the street and we can try to negotiate with them. If all else fails, I'll call Wilkes and see if he can pull some strings with the cops."

"That won't be necessary," Trent said with an air of confidence.

Max gave Trent a look, then turned his attention back to the landing, the rotor whomping above them as they passed a flock of surprised-looking geese headed in the opposite direction.

Ten minutes later, the dark blue expanse of Lake Winnebago spread out before them. A grassy peninsula jutted out to the left, with a two-story mansion capping the point. A row of nice lakefront homes was spaced out along the adjacent bay, each with long driveways and carefully manicured lawns. The street below had two police cars—one unmarked—parked at the gate of one of the homes. Max flew past them, hoping he was high enough that they wouldn't recognize faces, and if they did, that they wouldn't think about the fact that there were two passengers.

He saw the farmer's field, his intended landing spot, and maneuvered them around into the wind, lowering the throttle and making his approach on a flat patch of grass just next to the tree line. He quickly shut the engine down, and Trent disappeared into the woods with the duffle bag over his shoulder. Max walked along the field until he reached the street, then headed towards the senator's driveway gate. He kept an eye on his watch, making sure that he gave Trent at least five minutes to make his way through the woods and towards the house.

Eventually Max walked up to the police car outside Becker's property and waved. "Good afternoon." He must have looked like a drifter, coming down the street without a car.

"Can I help you?" asked the uniformed cop, approaching from the nearest police vehicle.

"Sir, my name is Max Fend. My father is Charles Fend. Perhaps you've heard of him? He's the CEO of Fend Aerospace and a good friend of Senator Becker's. I know the senator is in, and I wished to pay our respects and offer our services."

"The senator told us he didn't wish to be disturbed."

"Of course, I understand that, sir. However, my father and I have a personal relationship with the senator—"

The second cop got out of his vehicle and approached, this one in plain clothes. Good. Two cars, two cops. No one else watching the house. Max could make out a shadowy figure in the distance, walking fast from the woods towards the house, a black duffle bag over its shoulder. Moving quick enough to make up the ground at a good pace, but slow enough not to draw the eye's attention. Just another few seconds.

"What's going on?" asked the second officer. Max surmised that this was the senior man, based on the way he was posturing. Max relayed his request to pay Senator Becker a visit, adding, "Officer, our family is very close with the senator. My father, Charles Fend, owner of Fend Aerospace, is a good friend. I will only be a few minutes. My father wants to offer him a flight on his private jet back to D.C., where the funeral will be held."

The last part was total BS, since the funeral likely hadn't even been discussed, but Max figured where there was confusion, there was opportunity.

The two cops looked at each other. Max heard one whisper to the other, "Well, his dad is famous. I mean, what's he gonna do? I say let him at least go to the door."

The plainclothes cop shook his head. "I'm sorry, Mr. Fend. But the senator said—"

A yell from the home interrupted them, and for a moment Max panicked, thinking Trent might have run into trouble.

But it was the senator, standing in the doorway, waving. "Let him in, gentlemen! Thank you."

The police officers tipped their hats to Max, and he walked the fifty yards down the paved driveway and up the steps to the front entrance. The door was left cracked open, and the senator's face looked much less peaceful this close up.

"They still looking?" Max asked.

"Yeah," replied Trent from the dark hallway.

The maid was on the floor, her wrists and ankles bound with zip ties and her mouth covered with duct tape. Trent stood next to her holding a pistol, its suppressor nuzzled against the senator's back.

Max shut the door behind them.

"Hello, Senator. We'd like to have a quick word."

# CHAPTER 30

FROM INSIDE THE HOME, Renee could see Ian Williams's men moving closer to the group in the middle.

She spoke quietly, still trying to dig for information. The man was holding a weapon. A small black pistol. "Who are the men here, do you think?"

The assassin said, "I don't know exactly. But I don't give them much longer to live."

Renee gave him a concerned glance.

One of the men sitting on the patio furniture called out to Williams. Renee could hear him speaking Spanish and laughing. Then Williams nodded to one of his gunmen, and the rest happened quick.

She cupped her mouth as the gunman wheeled around and unslung his submachine gun. One of the tiny black ones, with a long cylinder on the end. A rapid spray of flame, and the group of men around the fire pit were cut down in a burst of red, their bodies littered with bullet holes.

Everything went quiet as the shooters surveyed the scene. Renee was horrified. She saw two of the gunmen rolling out the same blue tarp that they had used to wrap up Jennifer Upton's body. It looked like they were about to start cleanup.

The French-speaking assassin standing next to Renee suddenly cursed.

"What's wrong?"

He had been calm during the gunfire but was now agitated. He stood up quickly and moved towards the window, holding his weapon in both hands.

"What's wrong?" asked Renee again, wondering if he would go outside, leaving her alone in the room.

A chance to escape.

"Shhh."

The men outside were now upset as well, she saw. One of Williams's Mexican gunmen was down on the ground, dead and bleeding from his head. She heard Williams swearing at his men.

"Well, one of you must have bloody shot him! It couldn't have ricocheted from there! How the hell…?"

Then another gunman's face went missing, his body dropping to the brick patio.

For a moment everyone was frozen in confusion. By the time the third gunman was hit, they were scattering like ants. Williams and Syed sprinted towards the house, heads tucked low. Loud cracks of gunfire rang out as some of the sicarios began shooting towards the inlet.

At what, Renee couldn't see.

* * *

The senator hadn't known who Renee was or whether she was in captivity. But after Trent had held a gun to his head, Becker had done two things rather fast: wet his pants, and revealed Ian Williams's location.

Williams was—incredibly—just across the bay, at the mansion on the peninsula. Within Trent's rifle range. The senator's window was the only spot with a view over the stone wall of the peninsular property. Just as Max and Trent looked out the window, they witnessed several men in black gun down a group sitting on a patio.

Trent had taken out his suppressed rifle and gone to work. Max ran down the stairs and out the senator's front door, towards the police vehicles in front of the house. He had quickly called Wilkes, frantically filling him in. Wilkes promised to contact local law enforcement.

Now Max watched as the black-and-white police car put its lights on and sped out of the driveway, heading north on the main road. The plainclothes officer was halfway into his vehicle when he saw Max.

"We just got a call from our chief. It seems you misled us, Mr. Fend."

"Sorry about that," Max huffed.

They both turned as the sound of popping gunfire erupted in the distance.

"It was suggested to me that I let you tag along. You've got some three-letter agency affiliation."

"Please…"

The cop rolled his eyes. "Get in. Get in. We got to go."

Max hopped in the passenger side and the police vehicle accelerated down the road.

"Does Oshkosh have a SWAT team?"

"Yes, we do."

"They on the way?" The speedometer got up to eighty on the tiny road, the trees flying by. Then the police officer decelerated rapidly and took a hard right, following the lake road, the car bouncing as they drove.

"Most of them are on duty at the air show. But they've been notified to get here as soon as possible."

Ahead of them, Max saw the other police car parked outside of a stone wall with a wrought-iron gate. The cop had his pistol drawn and was standing behind the car. Max's vehicle came to a halt right behind the first vehicle, and both he and the plainclothes officer got out.

The gunfire was louder now that they were here, coming in rapid bursts. But they couldn't see anyone manning the gate. The whole property was surrounded by a tall stone wall. All Max could see through the wrought-iron front gate was a row of fancy SUVs parked on the lawn just inside the stone wall, and two more SUVs parked in the roundabout driveway in front of the mansion.

"What are you doing?" asked the cop.

Max was feeling his way up the stone wall, finding a grip and placing his shoe on a foothold.

"I need to get in there. I suggest you two wait here for your SWAT team. There's at least one hostage inside—a woman. Tell them to be careful when they arrive."

Max didn't wait for a response. He flung himself over, scraping his leg and ignoring the pain, landing on his feet on the grass. He then removed his pistol from his concealed carry holster and jogged towards the entrance of the house.

* * *

Trent had picked off seven of the twelve gunmen from the senator's office window across the bay when he'd decided to move his position. By then, some of the gunmen had located him and he was drawing fire.

He placed his weapon on safe and tucked it back in the duffle bag. Then he headed down the stairs. The senator and maid were both still tied up, sitting in the front hallway. The duct tape had been taken off the maid's mouth and placed over the senator's.

A knock at the door made Trent reach for his pistol. Mike, the young CIA operative, stuck his head in.

"Wilkes asked me to give you a hand here."

Trent looked at the senator, who was avoiding eye contact. "You babysit them. And give me your keys."

"Wilkes is outside. He'll drive you."

"Fine."

Trent jogged to the car and got in.

"Everything go alright?"

"For me. Not so much for them."

Wilkes hit the gas and they headed towards the fight.

Wilkes said, "Any word from Max?"

"I couldn't see him, but he should be there by now."

"How many?"

"At least five of them were left."

"That's not great odds."

* * *

Renee was wired with adrenaline and sheer terror as she witnessed the gunfire. Williams and Syed were now inside the room, both looking out at the carnage in the yard. The assassin was also looking that way, but he'd moved to an adjacent room, still holding his gun.

She decided it was now or never, and she bolted.

Renee raced towards the mansion's front door, pumping her arms and gritting her teeth, her limbs feeling like they were twice their usual weight. She was scared half out of her mind as she braced herself for a bullet in the back.

"Hey!" someone shouted from behind, and she heard the fast squeaks of footsteps on hardwood flooring.

Her sweaty palm pushed down the ornate door latch and pulled, but she felt resistance. She cursed, then flipped the deadbolt and repeated. The door flung open, and she could just barely make out a man running towards her with a gun in his hand. She almost panicked but then realized who it was.

She screamed, "Max!"

As she started to run out the door, what felt like a locomotive hit her from the side, knocking her out of the way and to the floor. The sound of gunshots and a slamming door and then more yelling and a searing white-hot pain in her temple.

"Take her with you."

Her vision was blurred, but somewhere in her mind she knew the voice belonged to Ian Williams. She felt herself being dragged away. She tried to squirm and fight, but the strong grip and multiple hands on her were too much to overcome.

Renee blinked away the haze and realized she was being carried into a garage, then thrown in the backseat of a car. The cough of an engine turning over and the familiar creak of a garage door opening. Then a lurch as the car accelerated and the deafening roar of gunfire coming from inside her vehicle. Ears ringing and a clang as the car must have hit something.

Then everything got quiet. She looked up, and Ian Williams's face was smiling over hers. Licking his lips in his disgusting way.

He whispered, "I told you that I would take you myself, dearie."

## CHAPTER 31

MAX CURSED from his hiding spot in the hedges in front of the house. He'd seen Renee at the door, screaming his name. She was so close, but then someone had tackled her from the side. Max had shot one of the gunmen square in the chest before the door had slammed shut. He was getting ready to break through a window when an SUV had emerged from the garage. Max was sure he could make out Renee's face in the backseat.

Someone from the getaway vehicle had fired at the now-substantial police presence on the main street in front of the home as it barreled through the wrought-iron gate.

Max got up, tucked his gun into its holster, and ran the fifty or so yards towards the police vehicles, hoping no one would mistake him for one of the cartel gunmen. He heard a pop shot behind him and the snap of a bullet going past but kept running, knowing it was his best course of action.

As he arrived at the now-bashed gate entrance, a man in SWAT tactical gear grabbed him and pulled him behind the stone wall. A few of the police cars were starting up, looking like they were getting ready to pursue the fleeing SUV.

Someone yelled, "It's okay, he's with us!"

A sedan came to a halt in the middle of the street and two men got out. Trent and Wilkes.

Max pointed down the road as the SWAT man released him. "Trent, they're about a half mile ahead. Dark SUV. They've got Renee."

Trent nodded and grabbed the keys out of Wilkes's hand, jumping in the driver's seat. Max opened the passenger door and threw himself inside.

Wilkes stared at the two from the street as Trent accelerated, and the world spun past. Max's mind raced as he thought of what Renee was going through. Of where she was headed. Of what they might do to her...

* * *

Renee felt the SUV jolt as they drove through a chain-link fence. She was sitting up in the center of the backseat, a Latino gunman to her left, Williams to her right.

"There," William yelled. "That's ours."

The SUV zoomed along the flight line, where the private jets were parked. It came to a halt outside a sleek white Learjet.

Williams talked to one of the pilots out the window, speaking rapid Spanish and getting angrier by the moment.

"He says we can't take off. Several of the private jets have been defueled by airport operations, this one included. They say the order came from the Department of Homeland Security. We need another way."

Syed said, "If we can get to Fond du Lac's airport, my aircraft is there."

"How do you know we won't face the same issue?"

"My men will not have allowed this to happen. If we can get there, we will be able to leave without problem."

"Well, we can't drive there. The police are everywhere now."

The younger man—the assassin—was in the front

passenger seat. He pointed out the front window. "That aircraft over there across the runway has started up. We can tell the pilot to take us to Fond du Lac."

"That thing is a relic. It's for tourists."

"It doesn't matter, it flies," spat Williams.

He said something in Spanish, and the driver raced across the taxiways and main runway as fast as the SUV would go. The vehicle slammed to a stop just in back of the running aircraft.

Renee recognized the plane. She realized it was the Ford Trimotor. The one the old Tuskegee Airman had been telling her about. A short line of passengers stood at the gate. Renee was forced out of the SUV at gunpoint, and the group began walking towards the old aircraft. Three loud external motors, each the size of a man, sputtered and rattled, their propellers spinning, angled upward.

The crowd in line for Ford Trimotor rides looked alarmed as the menacing group walked towards the plane. Some noticed that they were carrying weapons, and someone yelled, "Gun!"

A police officer wearing a bike helmet and a neon-yellow-and-black uniform shouted and began to draw his weapon. Ian Williams lifted his pistol and shot the man twice in rapid succession, the dark red holes appearing in the neon yellow uniform as the man fell backward.

Renee cringed and let out a yelp, the crowd around them screaming, running away.

As she was marched towards the plane, she saw the assassin get on first and point a gun towards the pilot. She walked up a short staircase and ducked through the entrance. Renee was made to sit in the front of the cabin. The rear door slammed shut, barely audible over the noise, and Williams and Syed sat in the seats behind and next to her. Then the engines roared louder, and she could barely hear a thing. She looked up at the cockpit of the plane, high up another set of stairs, bright white daylight from outside the cockpit windscreen contrasting with the dark cabin. The assassin stood there, pointing a gun at the head of the pilot in the right seat.

She realized the man in the left pilot seat was the little old Tuskegee Airman. For a brief moment she thought she was hallucinating, yet there he was, his wrinkled face looking up at the assassin's eyes and then down at his gun.

Renee felt a jolt as the aircraft's engine power overcame the friction of its own chocks, and they began moving slowly forward down the taxiway.

* * *

Max's vehicle raced across the runway as the Ford Trimotor began taxiing.

"We've got to stop them from taking off."

"How?"

"I don't know. The plane's passenger door is on the rear right side. See if you can get me on board."

Trent glanced at Max quickly. Maybe seeing if he was kidding. Then he looked forward, gripping the wheel tight, the gas all the way to the floor. "Roger. Get in the backseat."

Max hopped in the back-left seat and lowered the window.

Trent kept the speed up and stayed wide, maneuvering his vehicle around the aircraft's tail and then pulling in left, slowing and getting snug up to the aircraft.

Because the aircraft rested on a tail wheel, the fuselage angled up sharply. The cabin windows were just forward of the rear passenger door. Trent had the car positioned in a blind spot, just aft of the passenger door. Right now, Max and Trent couldn't see any of the passengers, and the passengers couldn't see them. But the vehicle would need to come forward in order for Max to reach the door.

"Get ready," said Trent. Max saw that he had his silenced pistol in his right hand, relying on his left hand to drive.

Max stood on the rear seat and prepared himself to exit out the window. They were only going about forty miles per hour, but looking at the pavement below, it still seemed fast. But they were running out of time. Max's best guess was that they had about twenty seconds before the plane turned sharply left onto the active runway and he missed his chance.

He stuck his head out the window and the wind met his face. Max looked forward along the length of the plane and could make out the pilot's eyes through the reflection of the aircraft's right side-mounted mirror. The pilot's mouth opened, and then closed as he saw the car driving along next to them and recognized what was happening.

Max continued climbing through the window, grabbing on to the car's "oh shit" handle with his right hand, balancing himself on the door frame and reaching with his left hand for the door latch of the Ford Trimotor.

Trent began moving the vehicle forward. Here it came. The leap of faith. Hot exhaust and deafening noise all around him. The taxiway pavement whizzing by below. A two-foot chasm waiting to break his bones.

Remarkably, the door opened from the outside without much effort. But keeping it open as the wind pushed against it was a challenge.

Then the gunshots sounded. The passengers had seen Trent. He was firing with one hand on the wheel.

Shattering glass and muffled yelling.

Time to commit. If any of the gunmen were looking back this way, he would be a dead man. But this was his only chance to save Renee.

Max pulled open the door with his left hand, reached out with his right, and dove forward. He landed with a sharp pain, his chest now on the floor of the aircraft cabin, then felt the terror as his legs began to fall, their weight starting to pull him back out the door.

Max dug deep and swung his legs up, pulling his body over the precipice. Then he used his arms to wriggle forward the rest of the way through and onto the aircraft cabin floor.

He was on board, heart pounding in his chest.

Max looked up to see one of the gunmen standing over him, aiming a submachine gun at his face. Then the man's chest popped with two red holes and he fell backward toward the cabin wall.

A burst of gunfire forward and a lurch as the aircraft veered left and Trent's vehicle slid away.

Yelling and cursing in Spanish. Max realized Trent had shot several of the men on board through the windows. Max reached across the aisle and picked up the weapon of the now-dead sicario from the floor. Then he craned his neck around the seat that had been concealing him from the front of the plane.

Max took a mental snapshot of the aircraft interior, then hid back behind the rearmost row.

The aircraft had a narrow column of seats. One seat on either side of the aisle. Five rows, ten seats total. An incredibly steep incline up toward the cockpit. No door between the cockpit and cabin. Max guessed he was looking at a twenty-foot ramp towards the bright white light of the cockpit windows. A difficult length to ascend.

Renee sat in the forwardmost left cabin seat, looking unharmed. Williams stood in the center aisle just aft of her. He was holding his hands to his face, bright red blood dripping through the cracks in his fingers. Glass from the window, or a graze, maybe.

Max saw two men on the ground, injured or dead, he couldn't tell which yet. But one looked like Abdul Syed. There was a white guy gripping the back of the right-side pilot's seat, holding a gun to the man's head.

Now all Max had to do was get past the gauntlet and tell the pilot to halt his takeoff.

Max felt the aircraft make another sharp left turn onto the runway. Then the engines roared to full power, and both of the remaining men in the cabin—Ian Williams and the man holding the gun to the pilot's head—tumbled backward along the steep aisle as the aircraft accelerated forward on its takeoff roll.

* * *

Renee felt her head press back into her seat as the aircraft throttle was moved to takeoff power. She felt like she was launching in the space shuttle the way she was angled up so sharply.

The assassin who'd been pointing his gun at the pilot hadn't been prepared for the force of the acceleration combined with that steep an angle. His only grip had been one hand on the pilot's seat, his other hand holding a pistol. The man fell backward through the air, landing on his back halfway down the aisle, rolling and then sliding towards the aft end of the aircraft. Renee saw the flying pilot look backward, the aircraft still rumbling through its takeoff roll.

A decisive moment. Would he abort the takeoff with two gunmen still on board and remaining runway disappearing before him? Renee hoped he would, but even she was fearful of the repercussions.

Her hopes were dashed seconds later when they became airborne, gliding up and banking slightly to the right, the air now rushing through cracked and broken windows on the right side of the cabin. Renee let out a breath of defeat. Out her window were thousands of planes parked next to each other in the grass. Rows of tents and the massive static display of jumbo jets and military aircraft in the center of the air show.

And Max.

He was down there. She hoped she would see him again.

Then she turned around and did.

Impossibly, Max was now locked in a wrestling match with the assassin who had just fallen backward from the cockpit. They were fighting for control of a gun.

She reached down and unlatched her seat belt. Taking a quick breath, she forced herself out of the seat, ready to vault down the aisle, past the bloody bodies on the floor, and pummel the man who dared hurt her beloved Max.

Then Ian Williams rose up from his seat. One of his eyes was a mass of crimson. His face was smeared with wet blood. His other eye was wide and crazed. Mouth open with white teeth clenched down in a mad rage.

Williams raised a black pistol towards Renee and fired.

* * *

Max heard a gunshot and involuntarily snapped his gaze towards the shooter. Ian Williams had fired up near the front of the aircraft. Renee had been up there, but Max couldn't see her now. A single shot rang out. Max kept trying to spot Renee but then felt a fist pounding him in the kidney.

He forced himself to fight one problem at a time.

The man was wrapped around him, off balance but trying to gain leverage. Max elbowed his opponent in the face twice and felt him go limp. Then Max got to his feet and brought his knee up hard under the man's chin, breaking his jaw and sending him to the floor, motionless. Unconscious.

*Renee.*

Max turned back towards Williams. The Englishman had dropped his pistol and was searching around on the floor for another weapon. Max sprinted towards him and tackled him from his blind side, putting all his force into his right shoulder and wrapping up the way he'd been taught to tackle playing football as a boy.

Williams slammed forward with a grimace, landing on his chest and already-bloodied face.

"Max!"

Max looked up from the floor and saw Renee standing at the front of the plane. Then she began to have trouble balancing herself as the aircraft tilted sideways.

Max looked beyond her. The pilot was hanging lifeless from his seat.

* * *

Renee watched a squirming Ian Williams as he tried reaching for a weapon on the floor. Renee had sent her forearm into Williams's shooting hand moments ago as he was trying to fire his weapon. He was half-blind from a vicious eye wound, and in his disorientation, she had managed to throw off his aim.

But while she was unharmed, it appeared that Williams had shot the pilot.

"Help the pilots!" Max shouted, pointing with one hand.

Renee frowned and turned around, still holding on to the edges of the aisle seats so she wouldn't fall over, the aircraft now in a sharp turn and an unusually steep climb.

The pilot was dead. Ian Williams's gunshot had hit him in the back of the head. Renee panicked as she realized the copilot was the ninety-something-year-old Tuskegee Airman. She climbed up the stairs as fast as she could, fighting the pull of the earth's gravity that seemed to want her to lie on the wall.

Renee heaved herself up to the pilot's seat and grimaced as she unstrapped the dead man and pulled his body into the center aisle. Then she got in the seat, strapped in, put on his headset and grabbed the…steering wheel?

The plane had a steering wheel.

She said over the headset, "Can you hear me?" Then she tried to do what she thought Max would tell her to do during one of her flight lessons.

"Yes, I can hear you," said the Tuskegee Airman. "I'm afraid I'm having a hard time seeing everything. I don't have my glasses." His hands were on his steering wheel.

"It's alright. I'm going to try and level us out. I think I should just turn the wheel left. What do you think?"

"Yes, I think you're right."

Renee turned the wheel to the left, feeling a good amount of resistance. But sure enough, the wings banked over to the left and now they were only in a climb, not a turn.

The Tuskegee Airman said, "Now I think you need to push the stick forward."

"Okay."

Renee pushed forward on the steering wheel and the nose tilted down until they were flying almost straight and level.

She looked at the Tuskegee Airman and smiled. "We did it!"

A series of gunshots rang out from the rear of the plane.

\* \* \*

Max had seen it coming. The man in the back, whom Max had thought was unconscious, rose up on his elbows and reached for a submachine gun that had been resting underneath one of the dead sicarios. Max released Ian Williams from his wrestling hold, reached out for the handgun four feet down the aisle, turned, and fired, single-handed.

Both shots missed, but they helped him gain the advantage over his opponent.

The man was now hunkered down behind useless cushioned seats. The only thing they did was put him out of sight. But Max knew exactly where he was. This was a thinking man's game. The one who solved the problem the fastest won.

Max drew himself up from the floor and balanced his weight between his left foot and his right knee, holding the pistol firmly with both hands, steadying his aim as much as possible in the maneuvering aircraft…

And pulled the trigger.

He saw a quick jerk in the shadows beneath the seat. Then the man's body collapsed into a heap on the floor.

Now it was just Ian Williams. Max saw Williams rise up in the middle of the aisle, standing defiant and unarmed. He started to turn and walk aft.

"Don't move!" Max yelled above the howling wind.

Williams turned and stared at Max with one eye, his other just a swollen slit now. "Shoot me, then." He slowly stepped backwards, holding on to the tops of the seats for balance. Looking Max in the face, daring him to fire on an unarmed man. And getting closer to the other weapons on the floor that had slid to the aft part of the aircraft.

*Fine*, Max thought. *He wants to go this way? He deserves it.*

Before Max pulled the trigger, he did a double take, looking down at the weapon in his hands. In the excitement of the moment he had missed it. The slide of his pistol was all the way back, the chamber empty.

He was out of bullets.

* * *

Renee had her head on a swivel. Just like playing defense on Princeton's field hockey team. Except now she was trying to fly an ancient plane and make sure that the love of her life wasn't being shot at.

"What is he doing back there?"

"What do you see?" said the Tuskegee pilot. He was holding the airplane's controls with her. She could feel his inputs every few seconds. Flying by sight, judging the horizon. Unable to read any of the dials, but his decades-old aviation instinct helping nonetheless.

"Max isn't shooting. I think the man who hijacked the plane is going for a gun. We need to do something."

Renee looked forward again, making sure that they weren't aiming towards the ground. They were probably thousands of feet off the altitude they had started at. Indeed, the air seemed cooler and hazier than a few moments ago. But her only real goal was to make sure they didn't crash until Max could come help.

But he wouldn't be coming to help if Ian Williams shot him.

"What can we do?"

"Land," the old man offered.

"I mean right now. Is there something we can do to help shake things up back there?"

The old man looked at Renee and said, "We could try some maneuvers."

She said, "What if we stall the aircraft? Maybe we can shake them up enough back there that..." Renee wasn't sure if it would work, or help. But she didn't have any other options. There was only one problem. "I have no idea how to stall this thing, do you?"

The old man said, "I would try to pull those levers right there. The throttle levers. No, not that. Yes, those ones. All the way...well, maybe not all the way..."

Renee pulled the three levers back to about one quarter of where they could be set. The engines wound down and became much quieter, and thankfully the propellers were still spinning.

"Now pull back on the stick as hard as you can. Don't let go. After we go through the stall, push forward hard. Then, when we get speed back, pull up hard."

Renee pulled on the steering wheel with sweaty hands. She reached her forearms around it to help. The nose of the large aircraft went up, and she could see the airspeed sliding back. A high-pitched whine sounded through their headphones.

She turned her head back and yelled as loud as she could. "Max, hold on!"

The airspeed slowed, the sun came into view, and then the bottom dropped out.

* * *

Max started running towards Williams but was going to be too late. Then he heard a female voice screaming about something, and Max realized the aircraft had changed configuration. As Ian Williams raised up the submachine gun from the floor, Max grabbed on to the metal base of the seat nearest to him and held on tight.

The next few seconds happened in slow motion. Ian picked up the weapon just as the stall began. As the nose of the aircraft dove down and they passed through zero g's, Ian Williams floated up into the ceiling. Then the g's came back on and he slammed to the floor, hitting it hard enough to stun him.

Max was crouched and holding on to the seats. He took two quick steps towards the rear of the aircraft.

Ian was now sprawled out right next to the exit door.

Which was fluttering ever so slightly.

The latch had taken gunfire, Max realized.

The only thing holding the door shut was the airflow over the fuselage. Which was considerable at this speed. But no match for the force of a man being kicked through it.

Before Williams could regain his balance, Max grabbed on to the two metal handles atop the rearmost aisle seats. He swung his legs forward and aimed his heels towards Ian's sternum, extending himself, kicking and squatting with all his might.

The result was Ian Williams flying backward, slamming through the unlocked exit door, screaming as he disappeared into the wild blue yonder.

* * *

Max took Renee's seat and contacted Oshkosh tower on guard, the emergency frequency for all aircraft.

The tower air traffic controller got one of the other Ford Trimotor pilots on the radio, and while the landing was definitely not Max's finest, they were able to talk him down to the runway safely.

Max taxied the aircraft up to the central display area of the air show and shut off the engines. Renee embraced him and kissed him on the lips.

Then she did the same to the Tuskegee Airman, who was smiling, despite the chaos.

Firetrucks and ambulances converged on the scene. Police cars and news crews. Crowds of people, stunned and taking pictures and clapping and pointing. Max, Renee, and the Tuskegee Airman were helped out of the aircraft and taken to the hospital under police guard.

Max's father Charles, Trent Carpenter, and Caleb Wilkes all met him there. After all the official interviews and medical treatment, Max asked Trent what had happened to the senator.

Trent gave him a look and said, "Later."

Max understood enough to be patient.

## CHAPTER 32

MAX AND CALEB WILKES sat across from Senator Becker, a recording device resting on the table between them. They were in the senator's home. The investigators were done with it, although they were still evaluating evidence at the mansion property across the cove. That was a crime scene, still being investigated several days after the events of last week.

No charges had been filed against Senator Becker yet. The problem was witnesses. For all of Ian Williams's faults, he had done a good job of covering their tracks. Almost everyone who could point to Becker's participation in the cabal was dead. Those who were thought to be alive were outside the country, being protected—or eliminated—by the remaining coconspirators.

But the digital and financial trails would eventually be uncovered, the FBI investigators had assured them. It was just a matter of time, now that they knew what they were looking for. And Max and Renee could testify to what they had seen.

Becker's only hope to avoid a life in jail was to cooperate wholeheartedly. The news media had already begun putting the pieces together, and the cable news channels were featuring wall-to-wall coverage of the senator's international conspiracy.

Each night, the *Washington Post* and the *New York Times* tried to outscoop each other on another major revelation.

Wilkes had gotten about all the information he needed from the senator. It confirmed what Max had hypothesized. Becker was an agent of the ISI, and a coconspirator in Williams's cabal, which had started as a product of the ISI but had morphed into something more. Becker had been feeding Ian Williams and Abdul Syed classified intelligence for years. But now the mole had been caught and the network had self-destructed.

Both were big prizes for Wilkes.

After almost six hours, the senator's debrief was finally wrapping up. The politician's chin was still held high, despite everything that had happened. But there was worry there as well. Having reached the point where he had given up all of his secrets—Becker's only real leverage—his eyes were now searching Wilkes's face for some sign of what would happen next.

Wilkes gave him nothing. He rose from his chair, telling Max, "I need to make a call." Trent entered the room and stood by the wall, arms folded.

Becker vociferously denied having anything to do with his own daughter's death and looked offended at the suggestion. Max didn't believe it.

The conspiracy had been vast, and well planned. Most of the agents inside the US were unwitting. The politicians who had voted with Becker were influenced by their donors, not by foreign spies. But many of their donors were influenced by the cabal. Becker had simply used his inside knowledge to steer the cabal network money to the right politicians. Big Pharma executives around the world were already paying lobbyists and contributing to policies that would help their bottom line. The overt crossover between the legal opioid businesses and illicit industry was almost nil.

But there was coordination.

As Senator Becker admitted, the combined industry growth had been planned and fertilized by Ian Williams and Abdul Syed.

Becker turned to Max. "You don't understand why I did it, do you?"

Max didn't respond.

The senator said, "We won the war on terror thanks to my actions. I was the one of the few people who were willing to do what it took. To get my hands dirty. Come on. You can figure it out. It all comes down to economics. If the poor people in Afghanistan didn't have money and jobs, they would have been just as susceptible to the siren song of the Taliban and others. By keeping their economy going, we made sure that Afghanistan wouldn't transform back into a haven for terrorism. The Pakistanis wanted stability in the region. So did we. I simply made a deal to keep the peace."

"By using heroin as an economic growth tool?"

"It worked. It kept money flowing in. Do you know how much worse Afghanistan would be right now without those jobs? Growing poppy is perfect for Afghanistan. It needs little capital investment, it grows well in their climate, and the profits are enormous. We helped feed and employ the people of Afghanistan by growing those opium plants."

"You made a deal with foreign intelligence operatives and drug cartels."

"You don't make deals with your friends, Max. I did what needed to be done to protect American interests."

"You mean to protect your own interests. Didn't you know that these drugs would be sold in the US? Didn't you think about the consequences?"

"Most Afghan heroin ends up in other countries."

"Is that what you told yourself? Don't be naïve. It's a global market, and Afghanistan makes ninety percent of it. Afghan heroin might not all end up in the US, but it still affects Americans. You also helped facilitate laws that loosened regulations on opioid sales in the US—"

"Regulations kill the economy—"

"Save your political speak. Your actions were calculated. With one hand, you guys opened the valve for heroin coming in. With the other, you made sure that there was a growing customer base. In your own backyard, for God's sake. You made money off narcotics so that you could win elections."

The senator's mask of confidence began to crack. "The people that use that stuff are the scum of the earth. They're leeches on society. So what if they get high? Keep them in the slums. They'll shoot themselves up into oblivion and we'll all be better off for it."

"Decrease the surplus population, eh?"

Becker rolled his eyes. "Spare me. You don't see me out there using drugs on the street. Some people are just weaker."

Max turned to Trent. The veins in his forearm pulsed as he clenched and unclenched his fists. His eyes burned holes into the senator as the muscles in his jaw flexed.

Just then Caleb Wilkes came into the cabin, looking annoyed. "Time to go."

"What's wrong?"

"Nothing. We're done with him."

Max, Trent, and Wilkes departed the home, leaving the senator inside.

When they were alone, Wilkes said, "I just talked to my buddy at the FBI. He says they'll nail him eventually. But he'll spend the next few years in and out of court. Appeals. All that jazz."

Max shook his head in disgust.

"Why did the ISI and Ian Williams go to all this trouble?" Trent asked. "Why clean house with their network? Becker's the only beneficiary."

Wilkes said, "Maybe not. You know that Opioid Epidemic

Bill that Becker was pushing? This ISI-sponsored group of investors stood to earn huge from that. Becker and the remaining members each stood to gain financially."

"How?"

"The Opioid Epidemic Bill would greatly reduce the number of legal opioids in the US. But Ian Williams and Syed's group were planning to capitalize on the black market it would create. Some of my intelligence sources told us that the Sinaloa cartel was going to start buying over three hundred percent more heroin than it ships today. They were going to get it from Afghan suppliers next year to feed the new demand. The cartel would make a fortune. The ISI's investor group was also going to buy a lot of the extra supply from the legitimate international opioid suppliers around the world and make their own unlicensed pills to sell on the black market."

"Who were these investors?"

"Businessmen, criminals. Shady financiers. People the ISI grouped together to help them make money and influence national policy in their favor."

Max nodded. "And Syed and Williams thought they had the perfect American politician in their pocket to provide them cover. One with very strong presidential prospects. They just had to get rid of any remaining connections to him before he got too famous."

"They couldn't really pick someone to become president that far out. Too much uncertainty."

Wilkes said, "The FBI investigators think he's got accounts that they were transferring money into. Sort of a backup payment. Like I said, it'll all come out eventually. Maybe he would get elected president? Maybe he wouldn't. Either way, he was valuable to them."

"Not so valuable anymore, though."

"No, not anymore. He's a wounded animal now."

"But not dead," Trent said. Max exchanged glances with both men.

They walked to the CIA vehicles that remained at the entrance gate. It was dark out. Max and the others watched as the senator, who had been looking at them out his front window, disappeared into the house.

Across the water, they could see floodlights set up in the backyard of the cartel mansion. Yellow tape marking off areas of past violence. A few FBI agents in blue coats scavenging over the yard, looking for clues to assist the forensic investigation.

"Becker's law enforcement detail got called off?" asked Max.

Wilkes said, "Yes. Once it became apparent there was no longer a need. Once they indict him, he'll have another type of police escort."

The men gave a dark chuckle.

Wilkes got into his car, bade them farewell, and departed down the road.

Max and Trent stood alone by their car. A streetlight buzzing above them.

Trent said, "He killed his own daughter and helped encourage a plague of drug addiction around the world, all for his own benefit. Prison is too good a fate for him."

Max got into the driver's seat. "Come on." Trent got in and they drove a half mile down the road, parking behind the same grove of trees near where Max had landed the gyrocopter a few days earlier.

Trent said, "You wait here."

"No. I want to come."

They walked into the woods adjacent to the senator's home, surveilling their prey. The senator had gone out onto his back patio. It was near 11 p.m. He was drinking by himself. Very few lights on in the home. No guests.

"Ready?" Trent whispered.

Max didn't reply. He watched Becker sitting there. A despicable waste of a man.

"I don't think I can."

Trent looked at him.

Max said, "Everything he did. In his mind, he justified it. He tried to say he was helping Afghanistan. Helping fight the war on terror. Everything he did, he had an excuse. A rationalization for why he could make such an immoral choice."

"He killed his own daughter. Or at least knew about it. Didn't stop it. He helped flood our country with opioids. Guy's practically a mass murderer."

"Yes, he did. And he deserves to die for that. But it's not our place to kill him."

"I killed people in Mexico. What's different?"

"Because here he'll face justice. Our country is what's different. The rule of law. We need to let him face justice the right way. Let's not tell ourselves the same thing he did. The ends don't justify the means. We are honorable men, and we should make the less satisfying choice, because it is righteous."

Trent didn't say anything for a long time. Max began to worry that his words hadn't mattered.

Then Trent said, "Can we at least go in and scare the shit out of him? Maybe slap him around a little?"

Max thought about it. He shrugged. "I don't see why not."

A few moments later, they both approached the senator wearing black masks. When Trent's hand came up over Becker's face, he was half-drunk. The old man struggled at first, but he was no match for Trent's brute strength. Max turned the last remaining light out near the rear of the home, and they were engulfed in darkness.

Trent held him nearly upside-down, and Max whispered into Senator Becker's ear.

"You called them weaklings. I knew one of those weaklings.

He was thirty-six years old. An Army veteran. He left behind a wife and a little kid. This guy here? It was his brother."

In the moonlight, Max could see the senator's eyes go wide with fear.

Trent whispered, "You made a deal with the devil, Senator. And he always collects."

Max had placed a zip tie around the senator's wrists, holding his arms behind his body. They placed a gag over his mouth, then carried him towards the water and down a short dock. Trent kneeled down and lowered the senator's head into the water, upside-down, holding him there for a moment, then lifted him up.

Max said, "The next time you speak to investigators, you better tell them everything. Because we know the truth. And we'll come back for you if you don't."

# CHAPTER 33

A WEEK LATER, Max and Renee were back in the Poconos. Max had rented a lake house near the Carpenters' home. He decided that Renee and he could use a vacation—a real one. Max stood on the upper deck, directly above a boat slip. He could hear the sound of water sloshing around below. Waves from the Jet Skis and pontoon boats motoring by.

Renee sat in a lawn chair, wearing a bikini, a towel wrapped around her bottom half. She was sipping a cold beer, a lime wedge tucked in the long neck of the bottle, taking in the carefree scene below. The setting sun cast long shadows over the surrounding mountains. This was the only time of day she partook in sunbathing her fair skin.

Trent had brought Josh Junior to meet them for the afternoon. He and his delighted nephew had spent most of the time jumping off a ten-foot deck into the water. Now they were fishing for sunfish, using mushed-up Wonder Bread as bait.

Renee was reading him an article about the senator's recent confession. "The Justice Department has been very pleased with how cooperative the disgraced former senator has been, however disturbing the details. He has confessed to multiple counts of espionage, bank fraud, and conspiracy to commit murder."

"Nothing else? Any complaints from the senator or anything?"

"What were you expecting?"

"I don't know. Two men. Head dunking. Nothing. Just curious."

Renee frowned. "What will happen now?"

Max used tongs to turn over bratwurst, making sure each one got an even brown. "With what?"

"With the drug ring? All those people, involved in that conspiracy…"

"Many of the ones responsible are already dead. Williams and the ISI saw to that. But there will be countless investigations, I'm sure. Senator Becker was a politician, so Washington will be chewing this up for the next few years. Caleb and his team are already moving on some of the information they uncovered. My understanding is that there are a whole host of punishments waiting to be dished out. The State Department will be announcing sanctions against Pakistan. The Treasury Department is freezing assets of several lobbying firms and Jennifer Upton's political nonprofit."

"Oh, I did read about that. It was Jennifer Upton's nonprofit that much of the foreign political contributions were coming through."

Max nodded. "There are also more than a dozen executives in some overseas pharmaceutical companies that are being brought up on criminal charges."

Max placed the brats on a paper plate, next to a tinfoil-covered plate of roasted peppers and onions.

"Dinner's ready," he called down to Trent, who gave him a thumbs-up.

Renee said, "What about the cartels?"

"Ironically, that may be one of Senator Becker's only lasting policy ideas. There's talk that our military may start deploying larger numbers of special operations personnel into Mexico to crack down on some of the cartels. From what I understand, Becker had proposed it to a few congressmen, and they've begun drumming up serious support after all this mess has come to light."

"That sounds like it'll be even more messy."

"It probably will be. But we've got to do something."

Max grabbed a beer out of the cooler and sat in the lawn chair next to Renee. He leaned over and kissed her, then rested his head back in the chair, enjoying the view over the lake.

Max smiled at Renee. "You know, we really should teach you how to land."

## ABOUT THE AUTHOR

Andrew Watts is the USA TODAY bestselling author of Max Fend thrillers and The War Planners series. He graduated from the US Naval Academy in 2003 and served as a naval officer and helicopter pilot until 2013. During that time, he flew counter-narcotic missions in the Eastern Pacific and counter-piracy missions off the Horn of Africa. He was a flight instructor in Pensacola, FL, and helped to run ship and flight operations while embarked on a nuclear aircraft carrier deployed in the Middle East.

One of the highlights of his Navy career was flying a TH-57 helicopter from Pensacola to Oshkosh to be a static display aircraft for the 100th anniversary of Naval Aviation, in 2011.

Today, he lives with his family in Ohio.

From Andrew:
Thank you so much for reading. Don't miss the next book! I love to hear from my readers. Be sure to sign up for my Reader List today and feel free to drop me a line.

Join the Reader List at andrewwattsauthor.com

## ALSO BY ANDREW WATTS

**The War Planners Series**

THE WAR PLANNERS (Book 1)

THE WAR STAGE (Book 2)

PAWNS OF THE PACIFIC (Book 3)

THE ELEPHANT GAME (Book 4)

**Max Fend Series**

GLIDEPATH

THE OSHKOSH CONNECTION